COLD
THREAT

RYLAND & ST. CLAIR | BOOK 2

COLD THREAT

NANCY MEHL

BETHANYHOUSE

a division of Baker Publishing Group
Minneapolis, Minnesota

© 2024 by Nancy Mehl

Published by Bethany House Publishers
Minneapolis, Minnesota
www.BethanyHouse.com

Bethany House Publishers is a division of
Baker Publishing Group, Grand Rapids, Michigan

Printed in the United States of America

Library of Congress Cataloging-in-Publication Data
Names: Mehl, Nancy, author.
Title: Cold threat / Nancy Mehl.
Description: Minneapolis, Minnesota : Bethany House, a division of Baker Publishing
    Group, 2024. | Series: Ryland & St. Clair ; 2
Identifiers: LCCN 2023033574 | ISBN 9780764240461 (paperback) | ISBN
    9780764242830 (casebound) | ISBN 9781493445240 (ebook)
Subjects: LCGFT: Christian fiction. | Thrillers (Fiction) | Novels.
Classification: LCC PS3613.E4254 C66 2024
LC record available at https://lccn.loc.gov/2023033574

Baker Publishing Group publications use paper produced from sustainable forestry practices and post-consumer waste whenever possible.

24 25 26 27 28 29 30   7 6 5 4 3 2 1

I dedicate this book to Julius and Nancy Darby.

Julius is a respected Vietnam veteran who loves easily and stands strong for his wife, family, and friends. Nancy is a warrior who fights for her husband, her family, and those she loves. I am so honored to call them my dear friends. Thank you for being a part of my life. I treasure you both.

"'For I know the plans I have for you,'
declares the Lord, 'plans for welfare and not
for evil, to give you a future and a hope.'"
JEREMIAH 29:11

PROLOGUE

I watched as fire devoured the house as if it were a living, breathing monster, ravenous for death and destruction. It took effort not to smile as I observed the fire department desperately trying to quench the ferocious flames, the firefighters slipping and sliding on the snow and ice. But winter is no match for me. They would lose this fight. The nightmare has just begun. Inside they will find my Christmas offering. Those whom I'd judged and executed. The beast was at my command and would destroy any evidence that could lead to me.

"It's perfect," she whispered. "I love it."

I smiled at her. "It was a long time coming."

"But you did it. I'm so proud of you."

I had to blink away the sudden tears that filled my eyes.

"Shouldn't we leave?"

I nodded. She was right. At some point, the police would arrive and would most certainly look through the people gathered across the street since many times those who set fires like to watch their creations dance and light up the night. They might even take pictures. This was the only time I felt comfortable hanging around for a few minutes—before anyone had time to scan the crowd. This was important. The first. My debut performance.

I'd just turned to leave when a couple of police cars pulled up, lights flashing, their blue-and-red beams cutting through the night and the falling snow. I walked down the street, hidden behind a curtain of white. I stopped to watch as they exited their vehicles. The sight only added to my excitement. Two officers approached the fire department chief. As they talked, another officer stood on the sidewalk, staring at the structure that was being consumed. Suddenly, he shouted and pointed up toward the second floor. I had to walk back to see why. I stood behind a tree, trying not to look suspicious. That was when I saw it. A face peering through one of the windows.

"Oh no," she said, her voice breaking. "How did you miss her?"

The officer who'd spotted the unthinkable began to run toward the front door, but two firefighters grabbed him and held him back while another one grabbed a ladder and put it up against the house. It was clearly a child staring at them, her eyes wide with fear. They tried to climb toward her, but it was impossible. The flames from the first floor blocked their way. I felt a wave of anger. She had defiled my righteous mission. I fought to push back my rage. I had no desire to hurt a child. She shouldn't have hidden from me. I would have kept her safe. I sighed in frustration. This was her fault. Now all of us would have to watch as she died. There wasn't anything I could do. I felt the urge to leave, but the police were concentrating on her. No one was focused on the crowd, so I risked staying a minute or two longer.

Suddenly I heard a shout and saw the police officer who'd tried to enter earlier suddenly run toward the compromised house and through the front door before anyone could stop him. What a fool. The monster I'd created was too strong. Now there would be two additional lives sacrificed. This wasn't my mission. Only the guilty were supposed to die. I consoled myself with the knowledge that the blame was theirs. Not mine.

"Maybe he'll get her out," she said quietly.

I didn't respond. I knew she was upset. I couldn't find the words to tell her that it was too late for both of them.

Part of the house collapsed on the other side, away from the window where the child still stood. Everyone watched in horror. Two firefighters started to follow the officer into the house, but their chief called them back. It was clear they were frustrated, yet the chief obviously thought it was too dangerous for them to enter. He'd probably already written off the officer and the child.

"It's not your fault."

"I know," I said.

I waited for the rest of the structure to fall, but as we all watched, the unbelievable happened. The police officer ran out of the house, something in his arms wrapped up in a blanket. A firefighter ran over to take the bundle from him as the rest of the building collapsed. The officer fell to the ground. I could see his burns from here. It looked as if the cloth from his shirt had melted to his skin and part of his dark hair had burned away. Now he would always remember this night. I felt no anger toward him. Truthfully, I was relieved that the child had a chance. I'd still accomplished my mission. This was a lesson learned. I had checked out the couple carefully, and I'd watched the house. Hadn't seen any evidence of a child. Still, I'd missed something important. I would never make this mistake again.

She sighed with relief. "I'm so glad she's okay."

A thought suddenly struck me. I hadn't seen the child, but had she seen me? Was she now a liability to my mission? As soon as the thought came, I dismissed it. She'd been hiding. Trying to make sure I couldn't find her. She would have been too afraid to look at me knowing I might see her too. Besides, she was so young no one would take her seriously anyway. Even if she had caught a glimpse of me, soon I would look very different. I breathed a deep sigh of relief. I was safe.

The firefighters began treating the girl and the officer until an ambulance roared up. It was time to leave. I pulled my jacket tighter and let the darkness and the dancing flakes shroud me as I slipped away, but not before I glanced at the snowman ornament hanging on the tree planted near the sidewalk.

As I walked away, I couldn't help but sing softly, "Frosty the snowman . . ."

CHAPTER
ONE

River Ryland stared at her phone, willing it to ring. Unfortunately, it seemed it didn't respond well to mental telepathy. The pastor at the church she'd started attending with Tony had taught on faith yesterday. He'd brought up Mark 11:24 and Philippians 4:6. From what she could understand, faith was something you needed before your prayers were answered. As a child, she'd listened to her father preach, but he'd never mentioned anything like that. His sermons had been about sin and judgment. How to stay pure. Which was laughable since he ran off with the church's secretary and left his daughter, son, and wife behind, humiliated and without any way to survive financially.

As she continued to eye her phone, she wondered if she should start believing that God would bring more clients to Watson Investigations. Was it okay to have faith for something like that? It was clear that faith was important to God, but she didn't want to treat Him like some kind of genie in a lamp who would bring her whatever she asked for. What was His will, and what was selfishness? She sighed quietly. Life with God was proving to be interesting.

She glanced over at her partner, Tony St. Clair, and asked herself the question she'd posed so many times. What was he doing here? She'd had to leave the FBI. Severe PTSD had made it impossible for her to continue working as a behavioral analyst. Tony had been shot by the Salt River Strangler, the serial killer who'd tried to kill her, and was still dealing with some of the aftereffects. Even so, he could have gone back to work. Instead, he talked her into starting this detective agency. They'd only had two cases so far. The results had been positive. One case had to do with teachers at a local high school selling drugs—something they stumbled across. The teachers were arrested, and the drug trade shut down. No paying client with that one. The other case had been pro bono. They'd solved that too. Thankfully, someone connected with the case—not their client—had given them a generous stipend. But how long would that last without some new cases? Was asking herself that question a lack of faith? She really didn't know the answer.

Tony's long legs were crossed, his feet up on his desk. He was leaning back in his chair, writing in a notebook. He reminded her of Benedict Cumberbatch. His curly dark hair was longer than most FBI agents had worn their hair. His long eyelashes sheltered eyes that sometimes looked blue and other times appeared to be gray. Tony was an enigma. A handsome man who never dated. He used to. Before the shooting. There were definitely some women at church who had him in their sights, but he clearly wasn't interested. Of course, she wasn't dating either. Didn't want to. Right now, she just wanted to figure out who God wanted her to be. It was hard to believe He needed a private investigator. She didn't see that among the gifts listed in the Bible.

"Okay, God," River whispered. "I'm asking You to make this agency successful. I thank You for hearing me. And . . ." She gulped. "And I thank You for our new cases." There. She shook her head. Weird, but Pastor Mason would be proud of her. She jumped when Tony's phone rang.

River listened closely. If this was a case . . . Well, Pastor Mason also said something about patience. Surely answers to prayer didn't happen this quickly. If so, she should have started praying this way a long time ago.

"Slow down, Dad," Tony said. "I'm not sure I understand."

River was almost relieved that it was Tony's father. If it actually had been a new case . . . well, it would have freaked her out a little. She began to straighten her desk again, only slightly listening to Tony's conversation. It seemed to be a little one-sided.

Finally, Tony said, "I've got to call you back, Dad. Let me talk to River and see what she thinks. You know her mother is ill." Pause. "All in all, doing pretty good. She has full-time help now." Another pause. "Okay. I'll phone you in a bit."

After he hung up, he pulled his feet off his desk and sat up straight in his chair. His blue sweater was the same color as his eyes . . . when they were blue. Why was she paying attention to his eyes? She gave herself a virtual kick in the pants and realized that Tony looked upset.

"Everything okay?" she asked.

"No, not really."

"Is your dad all right? Your mom?"

"No," he said, cutting her off. "They're fine. And before you ask, my sister's good too." He looked away and cleared his throat. Something he did when he was troubled or thinking. Finally, his eyes met hers. "I told you that when my dad was a rookie police officer, before he was promoted to detective, he was badly burned in a fire?"

She nodded. She remembered the story. It was hard to forget. "He saved a little girl's life."

"Yes. Well, they found two bodies in the house after the fire was put out. The little girl was the granddaughter of the couple. Thank God, Dad got her out in time."

"Yeah. Your father's a hero."

Tony smiled. "Don't say that to him. He won't put up with it. I also told you that they never found the person responsible?"

She nodded again, then waited for him to finish. It was obvious what was coming next. She swallowed. Was this just coincidence? Of course, this was Tony's dad. They couldn't charge him anything for their services. River should have mentioned in her prayer that they needed a *paying* case. She didn't realize God was so literal.

Trust Me.

Although she hadn't heard an audible voice, it was so clear it made her jump.

Trust Me.

She swallowed hard. "Uh, he wants us to help him solve a twenty-year-old crime?" she said. Why was her voice squeaky? "Why now? I mean, I assume he tried to close this case himself. From what you told me, he's an excellent detective."

"He is, but he's retiring."

"And he wants this solved before he leaves?"

Tony nodded. "In a way. You see, there were two other similar murders with the same MOs in Des Moines not long after that one. The police arrested someone. Charged him with all three. Dad was never sure they got the right person."

"You never told me that."

"I never went into details because I thought it was a closed case."

"So, your father wants to make certain the case is truly closed before he leaves? It's still a really cold case. You know how tough they are to solve after so long."

"Well, except he says it's happened again."

"In Des Moines?"

Tony shook his head. "No, up in Burlington, Iowa, where they are now. They moved there years ago because Dad felt it was a better place to live. He was convinced that Des Moines was getting

14

too big. Too dangerous. He wanted a slower-paced life. A safer place for Mom. Truthfully, I think he had a tough time working in Des Moines. He couldn't get anyone he worked with to believe they'd arrested the wrong person for those murders."

"Wait a minute. So, your dad thinks the killer followed him?"

He shrugged. "He doesn't know, although I agree that it seems strange. Look, I know you have questions. I do too. Can you come to Burlington with me so we can write a profile? He wants to see if we can add something to what he has so far."

River hesitated a moment.

"I know you're thinking about your mom. Sorry. Maybe I shouldn't have asked. I can go alone. I shouldn't have put you on the spot."

River shook her head. "You're not. Now that we have Mrs. Weyland, I may be able to come with you."

Hannah, the young woman who had come in to help River's mother during the day, had quit after finding out she was pregnant. She'd recommended her aunt, who had recently lost her husband. Agatha Weyland was sixty-three years old and had nursed her husband through Alzheimer's. When Hannah told her she was pregnant and had to leave her job, Mrs. Weyland had begged her to set up an interview with River. At first, she wasn't sure if it would work since Mrs. Weyland wanted to move in.

"I just can't stay in my house anymore," she'd told River when they talked. "Too many ghosts. Hannah and her husband love the house and they've offered to buy it. I was goin' to move into an apartment, but if you have a spare room . . ." Her hazel eyes had filled with tears, and River had been touched by her. But would she change her mind and quit once she was stronger? She didn't want Rose to get used to someone and then have her leave. River's mother was still dealing with Hannah's quitting. She had loved and trusted the young woman.

"I'm not lookin' for anything temporary," Mrs. Weyland had

said as if reading River's mind. "I intend to take care of your mother until . . . well, until she no longer needs me."

This time it was River's turn for tears.

"Oh, honey," the older woman had said, taking River's hand. "I know what Alzheimer's is like. I know how to take care of your precious mama. My Harold was a happy man until the day he died. I learned how to go with him wherever he was . . . and how to be whoever he needed me to be. We were happy, and your mother will be happy too. You have my word."

River had really wanted to hire Mrs. Weyland, but she was certain Rose wouldn't give up another one of her rooms. She'd gotten upset when River and Tony had moved her original sewing space to another room even though they set it up exactly the same. They'd moved things around so River could be closer to her mother in case she needed help during the night. Now she'd have to give up her sewing room completely, even though she never used it. River was prepared for a meltdown. But after spending a couple of hours getting to know Mrs. Weyland, Rose had said, "Can't we just move the things in the sewing room down to the basement, River? Either Agatha could move in there, or you could move into that room, and Agatha could be right next to me."

Although she was more than surprised by her mother's request, she quickly agreed. River moved into the old sewing room, and Mrs. Weyland set herself up next to Rose.

"Let me talk to Mrs. Weyland," she told Tony. "She's barely had time to get to know my mother. She might feel uncomfortable with me leaving town so soon. How long do you think we'll be gone?"

"Why don't we say the rest of the week?" he said. "I think that's enough time to create a profile. My father's already put together a murder book, although I'm not sure how much information he's been able to get his hands on. Hopefully, we'll at least have some pictures and reports."

"Okay, but if Mrs. Weyland or my mother is uncomfortable . . ."

"I'll go alone and bring everything back with me." He frowned. "I'd really like you to talk to my dad. See if he can convince you the cases are related. I know that's not what we do when we write a profile, so we'll be using our ace deductive skills as well."

River laughed. "I'll call Mom now, but you might as well plan on going alone. My mother will probably have a conniption fit."

"A conniption fit? Where do you get these expressions? I truly think an old lady lives somewhere down deep inside you."

River picked up her phone, stuck her tongue out at Tony, and dialed Mrs. Weyland.

TWO

You're very quiet," Tony said, looking over at River. He was glad she was able to go with him but wondered if taking her away from her mother right now was too stressful. And then there was the concussion she'd suffered last month after a confrontation with a very disturbed killer, although she seemed to have completely recovered.

"I feel like I forgot to pack something."

Tony chuckled. "I've never known anyone as well organized as you. You have the most detailed packing list I've ever seen. When we worked for the Bureau and had to go out of town, you were the only person who never forgot one single thing."

"Maybe . . ." she said slowly.

"It's probably because of your mom. You might feel a little guilty for leaving her, but I truly think Mrs. Weyland is a godsend. Your mom is in good hands."

River turned her head toward him. The morning light shone through the windshield and highlighted her face. The Vietnamese features River had inherited from her mother gave her a rather exotic look. Her brown hair with its golden streaks framed her delicate features as if she were a painting that needed protection.

He gulped and tried to push back a strong and unbidden visceral reaction to her beauty.

"You're probably right," she said. Although she was a brilliant, strong-willed woman, her soft, lilting voice and slight body made her seem vulnerable. She would hate being described that way. Tony would never say it aloud.

"Are you still having headaches?"

River shook her head. "No, all healed. The only headaches I have now are the ones I cause myself."

Tony smiled at her. "Well, stop doing that. There. I solved the problem."

"Well, thank you. Why didn't I just come to you in the first place?"

The touch of sarcasm in River's voice made him laugh. "Seriously, why are you causing yourself headaches?"

She shrugged slightly and turned to look out the window. "That might be a conversation for another time. Right now, I want to know more about the case."

"Are you thinking about. . . ?" Tony didn't even want to finish the question. They were both trying to heal from the Salt River Strangler case. They'd thought it was over. The killer, Joseph Baker, had been caught and was in prison. But now someone else had shown up, claiming to be the Strangler's accomplice. He'd made it very clear that he was targeting River, determined to finish the job the Strangler had begun. As far as they knew, River and Tony were the only people to live after encountering the vicious serial killer. Tony wasn't his objective, though. He'd just been in the way of the Strangler's real goal. Even though he'd been shot four times, Tony wasn't sorry he was with River when the Strangler attempted to add her to his list of victims. Tony and River had discussed at length what they should do to protect themselves. Tony, who was friends with the police chief in St. Louis, had been assured that he and River would be closely watched. They both made certain they were armed at all times, and they were careful to keep their heads on a swivel—and to watch their backs. But they'd decided to not stop living because of someone who may have gone back into the shadows. His threats could be just that. Empty threats he was using as a way to terrorize them. He was obviously a second fiddle to Joseph Baker. River and Tony were trained behavioral analysts. They had been surprised once by the Strangler's protégé, but they wouldn't make that mistake again. They truly believed he wanted attention, but he probably wouldn't do anything to anger his master. Baker's ego wouldn't allow it. If Baker hadn't been able to kill River, and he was infuriated about it, he would never accept someone else acquiring the trophy he let get away. Baker was the kind of killer who wanted all the credit. Still, Tony watched the cars behind them closely. So far, he was certain no one was following them. He'd hoped this trip out of town would give them a break. Help them to refocus. Every mile down the highway made Tony feel more relaxed. It became a little easier to breathe.

The other thing on their minds was the disappearance of the man who'd saved their lives. David Prescott had just happened to see Baker shoot him and throw River into the water that awful night. If he hadn't been there . . . well, it was doubtful he and River would still be alive. But after testifying against Baker in court, Prescott was now missing. His family had no idea where he was or what had happened to him. The FBI was trying to locate him, but the trail had grown cold. Tony and River both feared that Baker had somehow exacted revenge against the man who had thwarted his plans. Maybe he wouldn't let his protégé hurt Tony or River, but perhaps he'd made an exception for the man who'd sent him to prison. Tony prayed David would show up, but as time went on, it became less and less likely.

"You're not going to let this go, are you?" River said suddenly, pulling Tony out of his contemplation.

"You know me so well."

River sighed. "No, I'm not thinking about Baker . . . or his little friend." She turned her head back toward him. "I'm learning so many things in your church that I never heard about in my dad's church. Faith, the Holy Spirit, all kinds of new concepts. Right now, it's a little confusing. I know I'll get there, but I really just want to understand everything now."

Tony laughed. "Well, if you end up understanding *everything*, will you please share it with me?"

She smiled at him. "You know what I mean."

"I do. I really do. But I think the answer is to let the Holy Spirit teach you in the way you can accept for now. You could use my method."

"And what's that?"

"I have this mental shelf," Tony said. "I put some things there and ask God to take them down when He's ready . . . and I'm ready to comprehend them. It works for me. He's always been faithful." He hesitated a moment. "You know, you and I have been trained to understand the psychopathy of criminals. We believe that we can uncover the truth if we work hard enough. But sometimes, I'm not sure our training is helpful when it comes to spiritual things. It takes a level of trust and faith that we're not used to."

River was quiet for a moment as she stared out the car window. When she met his gaze again, there was a frown on her face. "You've got a point. I'm used to trusting in my training . . . my knowledge. This is different. I'm trusting Someone else to give me the answers to questions I didn't even know I'd be asking." She sighed. "It's weird. My dad forced me to read the Bible when I was young, and I didn't get much out of it. I'm now convinced there are new passages written on those pages. Scriptures I never noticed before. It's like the Bible is coming alive. But there are still concepts I'm having a tough time with. Faith is the one I'm having the hardest time understanding."

"I get it. But just remember that I'm here. You can talk to me about anything."

"Thanks. I will, but maybe not yet? I'm thinking. I feel as if I need to keep things between me and God for a while."

River's recent return to her faith was progressing slowly. Not because River wasn't committed to her decision, but because she had such a strong penchant for the truth. She was one of those people who wouldn't accept a theory until she'd examined it three ways to Sunday. It could be frustrating, but when she finally made up her mind and accepted something as true, she'd hang on to it forever. Nothing could shake her from it. That mindset had added some drama to their Behavioral Analysis Unit with the FBI. Their agent in charge had once referred to her as a dog that wouldn't give up a bone when it came to working a profile. It was certainly an accurate description.

Now, River was on her way to meet Tony's mother and father. Would it make her uncomfortable? His parents were very different from hers. Although Tony knew her mother, Rose, he'd never met River's father. Even though it seemed the man was trying to make up for his past actions, River was having a hard time accepting his efforts. Thinking about Rose made him wonder if River was more bothered about leaving her than she'd admitted.

"It's not too late," Tony said, pretty sure she wouldn't accept his offer. "We can turn around."

"I appreciate that, but I really want to do this. Besides, we already said we were coming." River frowned. "Did your dad say anything else about his concerns?"

"Not really. I think he wants us to look at this with fresh eyes. He doesn't want to influence our profile." Tony sighed. "He's obsessed with finding the real killer and seeing him put behind bars. If he hasn't been already."

"Surely he's not the only one who feels that way."

Tony shrugged. "It's been over twenty years. It seems that Des

Moines is convinced their case is solved and they have other crimes to pursue. The chief in Burlington just doesn't see what Dad sees, I guess. We haven't talked about it a lot. I'm not sure exactly what's going on."

River frowned. "What do investigators say about this recent situation?"

"Again, I don't know." He sighed. "I guess we'll find out more when we get there."

"So, we're going in somewhat blind?"

Tony chuckled. "Kind of. Dad knows me well enough to realize I'd probably do some research before hearing him out. I had to promise I wouldn't do that this time. He clearly wants us to look at the case without a preconceived opinion." He pointed at River as she started to take her phone from her pocket. "Put it back. Let's give him what he's asking for. Fresh eyes. Fresh start."

"All right, but just because your dad requested it. I'm curious though."

"About what?"

"About why no one agreed with your father."

"Remember that he was just a rookie officer back then. Didn't have enough pull to influence the case. It was assigned to their detectives. And to be honest, I think a lot of the other officers were upset with Dad. When he brought that child out of that burning house, a local news station was there. They broadcast the video, and before long, he was being touted as the 'hero cop' who saved a little girl from a raging fire. And when they discovered that he ended up in the hospital with severe burns, he was praised even more. Mind you, my dad refused to talk to the media, but that didn't change anything."

"And the little girl?"

Tony shrugged. "I have no idea. My dad wouldn't talk about her. He tried hard not to bring the job home. I look back now and realize that he was frustrated about something, but my sister and I were pretty young. We never really put two and two to-gether. To be honest, he still tries to keep work on the other side of the front door at home. He must have been carrying this case with him all these years. It's been a burden he hasn't wanted to share . . . before now."

"It must have been hard for him." She smiled at Tony. "So even though your father tried to keep his job out of his home life, his son ends up working for the FBI? If he was trying to steer you away from law enforcement, I think he failed."

Tony returned her smile. "Yes, he did. I idolized my dad and wanted to be like him. I hope I inherited something from him."

"Well, if he's incredibly talented, smart, kind, compassionate, and really good-looking . . ."

Tony swallowed hard. Is that what she thought of him? "Shucks, ma'am. I'm touched."

River tapped her forehead. "Yeah, you're touched, all right."

"You're a pill, you know that?"

"That's my goal." River laughed. "So the murders and arson were twenty years ago?"

Tony nodded. "Twenty-four."

"And your dad is sixty?"

"Sixty-two. He was thirty-eight when it happened. My age. He joined the force when he was thirty-four."

"Most people join in their twenties," River said. "Why did your dad wait so long?"

Tony looked over at her. They told each other everything. Well, almost everything. She hadn't heard this story yet. Would his aunt Sarah mind if he told River the real reason his father joined the force? He took a deep breath. "I would appreciate it if you kept this to yourself."

River grinned at him. "Who would I tell? My mother, who won't remember it? Or my mom's cat, who isn't talking?"

Tony smiled.

"Look," River said, "if it's personal, maybe you should ask your dad's permission before sharing it with me."

"It's not my dad's secret," Tony said. "It's my aunt's." He hated telling this story. It made him angry every time he did. "She's my dad's younger sister. She . . . she was brutally raped when she lived in Des Moines. The rapist beat her within an inch of her life and left her for dead." He sighed. "It was awful. We almost lost her. She recovered physically, but the emotional damage took longer. Thankfully, God walked her through it, and she recovered. Today she's married and has two kids." He shook his head. "She still deals with triggers, but many years ago she made the decision to not let that guy steal another moment of her life."

"Please tell me they caught him."

Tony nodded. "It took almost four years. Turned out he'd done the same thing to at least five other women. One of them died. He's in prison and won't ever get out. Sarah's experience is the reason my dad became a police officer. He saw how vital the police are, and he wanted to be one of them. It was a good decision for him. He's a great cop." Tony shrugged. "My dad's commitment to seeing justice done is the reason I joined the Bureau."

"That's awesome," River said slowly.

"What are you thinking?" He knew her well enough to recognize that what he'd said had affected her. But why?

"Your reason for getting into law enforcement is so noble. I just liked *CSI* and *Criminal Minds*." She grinned at him. "My mother didn't want me to go into law enforcement. When I joined the police department and then went on to the FBI, it upset her quite a bit. I guess that was just a side benefit."

Tony couldn't help but laugh. River was nothing if not honest. But her attempt to minimize her commitment to finding justice for people who'd endured suffering at the hands of criminals fell on deaf ears. She'd been one of the most dedicated FBI agents he'd ever met. Her drive to help victims was still fierce. He respected her more than anyone he'd ever met—except maybe his father. Actually, they were a lot alike.

As he approached a stoplight, he touched the brakes because he knew that the color displayed meant he was to come to a complete stop, but for the life of him, he couldn't remember the name of it. Although by the grace of God he'd survived after being shot by the Strangler, he was still saddled with numbness in his arm and his leg—and something called anomic aphasia. Sometimes he would forget things. Names of things. Numbers. Colors. For the most part, he kept the symptoms to himself, but River knew about his condition. She was very kind and compassionate about it—which almost made it worse. Not that he would ever tell her that. It felt like pity—something he hated. It was one of his weaknesses. As they waited for the light to change, the word *red* popped into his mind. That was it. Red.

When the light turned green, he put his foot on the gas pedal and wondered if he and River were too damaged to make a go of the detective agency they'd started because he couldn't think of anything else to do.

Would this venture prove to them that they were no longer useful? That the Strangler had already destroyed them?

Time would tell.

THREE

River and Tony stopped for lunch and then rolled into Burlington a little after two in the afternoon. Tony drove through a neighborhood full of large homes. A couple of them looked new, but most of them were older, Victorian looking, with turrets and large porches. All the houses and yards were beautifully maintained.

Tony's parents lived in a big two-story brick home. White pillars held up the roof of the wraparound porch, which circled all the way to the back. It was English manor house meets Victorian roofline . . . with a plantation-style verandah. The house looked like something straight out of *Sense and Sensibility*. It had recently snowed, which made it appear especially charming. Although the Christmas lights weren't on, River could tell that at night the effect would be beautiful. Magical. For some strange reason, she felt a little awkward. Her childhood house had been an older bungalow—clean but modest. Even after moving out, the places where she'd lived couldn't hold a candle to this . . . mansion. She suddenly felt as if a wedge had just been driven between her and Tony. As if they weren't as similar as she'd believed.

"It's . . . incredible."

"It is now," Tony said. "When my parents bought the house, it was in disrepair. In fact, some of the neighbors wanted it torn down. It was the only house in this neighborhood they could afford. My father spent years fixing it up, adding most of the features you see now. He was determined to make it the kind of home my mother had always wanted. On a cop's wages, it was the only way he could give it to her. Lots of hard work and determination." He smiled at her. "You'll see that my dad is nothing if not determined."

River felt a sense of relief. She knew better than to think Tony would ever be uppity even if his parents were wealthy. She was aware his grandfather had been a very successful businessman and had left Tony a hefty inheritance. That hadn't bothered her. So why had she just compared herself to his mother and father? She sighed inwardly. Something else God needed to work out of her. Good thing God measured time differently than human beings. He was certainly going to be quite busy dealing with all her stupid hang-ups.

They got out of the car and made their way up the sidewalk to the incredible wraparound porch. Now that she was closer, she could see the areas that had been repaired. It had been expertly done. The entire floor of the porch had been reworked with treated wood. It was absolutely beautiful.

Tony opened the large wooden door with stained-glass inserts and they stepped inside. "Hello?" he called out. "Anybody home?"

"Tony!" An older woman came from a room to their left. The kitchen. A quick peek revealed white cabinets and dark blue concrete counters. River wanted to see more of it, but instead she turned her attention to Tony's mother. River could certainly see the resemblance to her son. Her dark hair was streaked with gray. She had warm, dark blue eyes that crinkled at the corners when she smiled. It was evident from her wrinkles that she smiled a lot. River could feel a friendly energy coming from her.

River put her bag down, and Tony's mother grabbed her hands. "In all the years you've worked with my son, I can't believe this is the first time we've met. We kept missing you when Tony was in the hospital. I'm Beth. Ray and I are so happy you're here."

River returned her smile. "Thank you so much for asking us to stay with you, but wouldn't it be easier if I checked into a hotel?"

Beth squeezed her hands. "Don't you dare. I have a room all ready for you."

A man came down the huge staircase to their right. He was shorter than Tony, with light brown hair that he combed back. He had a bushy mustache and very intense eyes. It was obvious from his demeanor that this was a man used to being in charge.

"So, this is River," he said as he reached the bottom of the stairs. "Our son has certainly talked a lot about you. I'm not sure anyone on the planet is as intelligent and intuitive as he thinks you are." He grinned at her. "I'm hoping he's right. He usually is."

Beth had let go of River and was leaning against her son, one arm around his waist. "Of course he's right," she said, winking at her husband. "Smooshy takes after me."

"Mother," Tony said, his face coloring. "Please don't call me that."

Beth laughed lightly at her son's obvious embarrassment.

"Let me take your bags upstairs," Ray said.

"Why don't you both come back down after you settle in?" Beth said. "We can have some coffee and cake before Ray whisks you away to his office."

"We should get into the case as soon as possible," Ray said, frowning.

"Pishposh," Beth said, shaking her head. "There will be plenty of time for that before supper. I want to visit with my son and get to know River." She pointed at her husband. "You intend to take up most of their visit with this case of yours. At least give me a little time with them first."

Ray sighed dramatically. "I know arguing with you will be useless." He winked at River. "My wife has made her famous Italian cream cake. She's aware that the St. Clair men are totally under her control when she brings out that cake. We all might as well just give in."

River laughed. "I love Italian cream cake, but honestly, she had me at *cake.*"

"We'll unpack and be right back," Tony said, nodding at his mother. "You've won this round."

Beth smiled. "Good. I'll put the coffee on." She turned around and headed back toward the kitchen.

"Are the rest of your bags in the car?" Ray asked as he picked up River's satchel.

"We learned to pack light when we worked for the Bureau," River said. "This is it, and I can carry it."

Ray put it down. "Are you sure? I'm offering to be your pack burro here."

"I really appreciate that, but it's not necessary. Believe me, I've carried this thing so many times I feel as if it's a part of me."

"Just lead us upstairs, Dad," Tony said. "I assume you're putting me in my room and River is taking Aimee's room?"

"That's it."

"I didn't think you'd actually lived here," River said.

"I didn't really. Just summers while I was in college," Tony said. "But they've kept my room and Aimee's just the way they were. I think they're hoping we'll move back some day."

Ray laughed. "You've uncovered our evil plan." He smiled at River. "The truth is we use them as guest rooms now, but Tony and Aimee do stay here from time to time."

River frowned. "I guess I misunderstood. I thought Aimee had her own home here in Burlington."

Tony sighed. "She does. Now you see how creepy this really is."

Ray shook his head. "She was sixteen when we moved. Two

years later she started college and only came home on breaks and in the summer. Tony had graduated and had just been offered an internship with the FBI—but we still wanted him to have a room when he came for visits." He smiled. "And no, neither one of them has stayed here much, but at least the rooms are here if they need them."

Tony rolled his eyes, and River grinned at him.

Ray started up the stairs while Tony and River followed behind him. River let Ray get ahead of them a bit before she looked at Tony and whispered, "*Smooshy?*"

Tony shook his head. "Why is it that it only takes a few minutes with my parents before my hip persona is destroyed and I become Smooshy?" He kept his voice low so his father couldn't hear. "Don't ask where the name came from. You'll never think I'm cool again."

"That won't be a problem."

"Really?"

River raised one eyebrow. "Yeah, I never thought you were cool in the first place."

Ray stopped at the top of the stairs and looked back at them. "What are you two whispering about?"

"Nothing important, Dad," Tony said.

He shook his head. "Okay, if you say so. Tony, you know where your room is. I'll show River where she'll be staying."

"You really don't need to, Dad. I can do it."

Ray stood there for a moment and then shrugged. "Whatever you want." He pointed down the hallway. "I've turned our actual guest room into an office. That's where we'll talk after your mother's cake."

"Okay," Tony said. "Thanks, Dad. I'm really glad to be home."

Ray smiled. "We're very happy that you're here. It's been too long. I'll see you downstairs."

As Ray headed down to the kitchen, Tony frowned at River.

"The rest of the time we're here, please refer to me by my given name. I won't respond to anything else."

River tried to look serious. "I understand, I really do. I don't want to make you feel uncomfortable." She swung her hand around, gesturing toward the upstairs rooms. "Now, if you'll just show me to my room . . . Smooshy."

CHAPTER
FOUR

He'd rented an office in her building just to be near to her, and he'd grown a short beard and a mustache. He'd also colored his hair and wore glasses. He was pleased with his transformation. At first, he wasn't certain what kind of business he would tell the landlord he was in. He finally settled on a debt-recovery company. Not a popular concept for most people. He believed most of the building's clients would leave him alone, and if anyone did approach him, he would simply tell them he was too busy to accept new customers. The sign on his door read only TSRS. The building's manager hadn't asked him what the initials stood for, but he was prepared just in case. He was calling himself Thomas Sullivan, so "Thomas Sullivan Recovery Solutions" was a sensible response if he needed one.

Although the initials wouldn't mean anything to River Ryland now, eventually she'd figure it out. Of course, by then it would be too late. He'd killed the punk who'd tried to end her life last month. No one was to have that privilege except him.

He'd stayed late one night after he'd moved in and was able to get into her office after they'd gone home. It didn't take any time at all to install a bug. Although there were some cameras in various places in the building, there weren't any in the area on the second floor where their investigative office was. After installing the bug, he'd listened as they made plans to go to Iowa. He'd thought about following her but then realized that he wanted to end her life here. He'd already formulated a plan and didn't want to change it. The Mississippi River was calling her name, and he intended to respond. They planned to return this weekend. That would give him several days to get everything ready.

Although she didn't realize it, River Ryland's existence was balancing on the edge of a precipice. Soon, he would push her over.

AFTER DRINKING COFFEE and enjoying cake with Beth and Ray, River and Tony headed back upstairs to Ray's office. River was surprised by what she saw. Ray had installed a large dry-erase board on one wall. Next to it was a huge corkboard with pictures and newspaper articles pinned to it. It reminded River of times at the BAU when they'd been working on a profile. It was obvious Tony's father was serious about this case.

River looked around the rest of the room. Ray had a large desk in the corner with papers piled on its top, and next to it were two four-drawer filing cabinets. She glanced over at Tony. He seemed surprised as well by what his father had done. He looked over at her and gave her a quick shrug, confirming that this was beyond what he'd been expecting.

"Hold on a minute," Ray said. "Let me grab a card table and a couple of chairs."

After he left the room, Tony said, "How can this be just one case?" He walked over to the corkboard and began to look through the pictures.

"If it is, he's more than just dedicated to solving it," River said quietly. "He's obsessed."

Tony stepped back from the board and came over to where she stood. "My dad was a decorated detective by the time he left Des Moines. I was surprised by his decision to come here. But being offered the position of head detective was an honor—and he and Mom were looking for a slower life. Dad wasn't home much in Des Moines. I think moving here was like . . . semiretirement. You know what I mean?"

"I do," River said. "Kinda like what we're doing?"

Tony's eyebrows shot up. "That's not what I intended. I still believe we'll get busy. It just takes time."

"And paying clients."

"We got paid for the last case."

River laughed softly. "Not by our client, but yes, we did receive some money. That helped."

Tony started to say something else but just then his dad came back, two folding chairs in hand. Tony went over and took them from him. Then Ray went back out into the hall and brought in a card table, which he put up in the middle of the room. Tony set up the chairs not far from the boards on the wall.

As he and River sat down, Tony said, "Dad, all of this . . ." He waved his hand around, indicating the entire office. "Surely it's not all for the one case you told me about."

Ray frowned at his son. "Yes, it is. I've been working on it for a long time. But the reason I called you is that I'm certain there is a serial killer in Burlington. Unfortunately, I may be the only one who believes that."

"I don't understand, Dad. What about the people you work with? Surely someone else sees the same thing you do."

Ray's face flushed. "They agree with the Des Moines PD. That they caught the killer. They refuse to admit that the murders here are connected to the ones in Des Moines."

"But you disagree?" River asked.

Ray sat down at his desk and sighed. "The man they arrested

in Des Moines was caught near the scene where the last murders occurred. He was clearly responsible. The Des Moines chief of police decided he was responsible for the other killings as well, but they could never prove it. They only indicted the guy for the last one, but he had a heart attack and died before it went to trial."

"And that closed the case for them," River said. "But you don't believe he was behind all three?"

"Right. I couldn't convince them otherwise—especially since I'm in Burlington now."

"So, Dad, you think someone else is responsible for the first two killings in Des Moines and now he's here? But why? Why would he come to Burlington?"

Ray was silent but River knew what he was thinking. "You believe he came here . . . because of you?"

He shrugged. "I don't know, but you have to admit that it's a really strange coincidence. I mean, it's been a long time. Years. Still . . . I've tried to get my chief to listen to me, but I have no hard evidence. I thought maybe you and my son would at least give me a chance to prove I'm not insane."

Tony's eyes narrowed. "Of course we'll try. I wouldn't have come all the way from St. Louis if I didn't trust your instincts."

Ray let out a long sigh. "Thanks, son. My chief has always had a lot of confidence in me—but not in this. I'm basically on my own. There's a cop here who used to work with me in Des Moines, but his hands are pretty much tied. He agrees with me that the murders here are suspicious, but he's not convinced that the killer is still active, not without more proof. The deaths are so similar, though. My friend Bobby sees what I do, but he wonders if we have a copycat."

"Is that possible?" River asked.

Ray shook his head. "I don't accept that for several reasons. The man arrested in Des Moines was so clearly not the same killer.

I really don't want to get into my other reasons now. I'd rather you look at the information I've compiled first. I've put together a murder book. If you'd go over what I have and write a profile that I can give to Chief Munson, maybe I could finally get him to pay attention. If you see it the same way I do, he'd have to take the observations of two trained FBI profilers seriously."

"So, you really believe this same unknown subject has struck twice here?" River asked. "That would be really unusual."

"Yes, I know," Ray said. "Four years ago, and then again two years ago. I have a bad feeling he's getting ready to do it again."

River wasn't certain what to say. Why would a serial killer leave his comfort zone in Des Moines for Burlington? And why the big gap between the killings? Arson was all about rage. There were other ways to make certain no evidence was left behind. This UNSUB chose fire for a reason. That sort of rage wasn't easy to suppress, especially for years. Arsonists tended to set fires more often as time passed, not less often. On top of that, the idea that a serial killer would follow Ray all the way to Burlington just didn't add up. If the UNSUB was angry with Ray, why hadn't he targeted him personally? Something was off.

"What makes you think he might be planning another attack, Dad, other than a feeling?"

River could hear the doubt in Tony's voice. He was seeing the same things she was.

Ray cleared his throat, got up, and walked over to his dry-erase board. "You know about the first case."

"You mean the one that sent you to the hospital?" Tony said. "How could I forget?"

"Tony told me about that," River said. "I know you went into a burning house and rescued a trapped child. You were severely burned." She frowned. "You must have healed well. Your injuries don't show."

Ray lifted his hair on one side and revealed scars on his scalp.

He'd obviously learned how to cover them, but the skin was wrinkled and red. He put his hair back in place and then rolled up his long shirt sleeves. The scarring was evident.

"Is there pain?" River asked.

"Sometimes in my arms because the skin is so tight. When I move them a certain way, it hurts. The worst pain came months after the injuries. The nerves had been damaged but when they began to work again . . . it was terrible. It lasted for a while and then gradually faded. To be honest, I don't think about them much anymore. They're a part of me."

"What you did was very admirable," River said. "Tony told me you were commanded to stand down by your chief, but you went in anyway."

"That's right, and I've never regretted it. That child wouldn't have survived if I hadn't made the decision I did." He shook his head. "To this day I can't understand how others could just stand by and watch her die. Cops and firefighters no less. It was our job to protect civilians—even at the risk of our own lives. Didn't make sense to me then and doesn't make sense to me now."

"That's because not many people are like you, Dad," Tony said. His voice broke a little. It was obvious he was proud of his father. It also helped to explain why he'd put his life on the line that night on the banks of the Salt River. He'd learned his values from his hero father. Tony could have died, but River was incredibly thankful he hadn't. She wasn't sure where she'd be right now if not for Tony. Thinking about the sacrifices both of these men had made in their lives made her determined to do everything she could to help Ray trap the monster he hunted.

If it were possible.

FIVE

I pulled my coat up to cover my neck and part of my face even though I wasn't really afraid of being recognized. No one knew me in this neighborhood. I walked slowly down the block, scouting out my next target. I'd done my research and was certain judgment was deserved. I'd watched her for a couple of days. Found out when she turned her lights off at night. There was no sign of an alarm system. Hunting here was so much easier than it had been in Des Moines. Hardly anyone used security systems in this town. They seemed to trust their neighbors and believed they had no reason to be afraid.

"This one will be easy," she said softly. "But are you sure about her?"

I nodded. "I checked her out. There are a lot of good reasons to punish her."

"But she didn't hurt us."

I took a deep breath. How could I get her to understand? "But she would have if she'd had the chance. What about the others she hurt? Don't they matter?" I turned to look at her. She still looked so young. She never changed.

She gazed deeply into my eyes. It made my heart hurt.

"Okay. I trust you."

"I know."

I could see that this house had a fireplace. Smoke from the chimney turned white in the frigid air. I needed to prepare, and I had to wait for snow. I had no intention of trying to make it look like anything other than an execution. Since the police and the fire department didn't believe in spontaneous combustion, they would recognize that someone had done this—even before they found my victims. They wouldn't believe it was me, though. That was the plan. I only wanted the detective to know the truth. He would soon learn that I had the power to decide who would live and who would die.

The cops in Des Moines were stupid. They'd arrested a guy who'd killed a couple and then set their house on fire. They'd connected him to me. They were too lazy to see that his sloppy job was nothing like mine. That guy killed in the spring, not in the winter. The guilty had to die as the snow fell. It was important.

"When will you let him know who we are?" she asked. "He has to know."

"I'm not sure. But I'll make certain he finds out before he dies."

I had to laugh. He'd never figure it out in time. Ray had a big surprise coming, one that he'd never expect until it was too late. One that would be the final nail in his coffin. Literally.

"THIS WAS THE FIRST INCIDENT," Ray said. "Edward and Vera Wilson. Twenty-four years ago. The one where I was burned." He pointed to several pictures pinned to the top of his corkboard. Then he walked over to his desk and picked up a file, which he handed to Tony. "Copies of the reports from the fire department, the police, and the medical examiner."

Tony perused the pages and then frowned. He passed the file to River.

"It was clearly murder and arson," he said. "The department investigated but had no suspects. There wasn't anyone in the couple's lives or in their pasts that led to a suspect."

"Correct," Ray said. "Besides that, the fire destroyed any evidence that could have helped the investigation."

"You suspect the UNSUB did that on purpose?" River asked.

Ray nodded. "I believe the unknown subject was meticulous in his planning. He knew what we'd look for and made certain we wouldn't find anything that could lead to him. We know he used gasoline to start the fire, but there wasn't any kind of container left behind."

"He wasn't completely meticulous," Tony said. "He didn't realize the couple's granddaughter was there."

"Exactly. The only time he's made a mistake."

"What happened to the girl?" River asked.

"Angie Mayhew," Ray said softly. "She lived with her mother but about six months after the murders, the mother died from a drug overdose. Angie went into foster care. I kept in touch with her for a while. In fact, we never told you this, Tony, but your mother and I thought seriously about becoming foster parents and bringing her home. We even talked to workers in the foster care department, but in the end, we decided it might be too disruptive for you kids. Besides, I was afraid I reminded her of a traumatic event that she needed to move past. We finally bowed out."

"Wow, Dad," Tony said. "Why didn't you ever tell me that?"

Ray shrugged. "Painful subject, I guess. I still wonder if we made a mistake. I think about her sometimes."

"You said you had investigated three murders in Des Moines," River said. "One you believe turned out to be committed by a different person. That means the first two killings and the ones here are what . . . around twenty years apart? That's highly unusual."

Ray nodded. "I realize that. After he killed the first couple and set the fire where I was injured—he waited two years before he struck again. Then the following spring, Arlen Thacker committed murder. Eighteen years later, I believe the same UNSUB who was responsible for the first two killings did the same thing here in Burlington. He followed the same pattern, and two years later, he struck again." He shook his head. "I realize the time frame is odd, but as I'm sure you know, it's not unprecedented. Dennis Rader was quiet for more than ten years, until he was challenged by a police chief and irritated by a book about him. I have no idea why the Snowman waited so long. . . ."

"Hold on," River said. "He's called the Snowman?"

"At first it was just by me and a few people in Des Moines," Ray replied. "Unfortunately, the press got hold of it and started calling him that too. I hate stupid nicknames for serial killers as much as you probably do, but if you'll just hang on, I think you'll see why we called him that." He pointed at the file he'd handed them. "Why don't you both look through the file and all the articles I've posted on the corkboard? While you're doing that, I'll go downstairs and get us some coffee. Dinner won't be ready for a few hours. You don't have to read every single word. Just get a feel for the case." He stood up from his desk. "Tell me if you see what I do. I'll explain later why I'm convinced he's here in Burlington." Before he opened the door to his office, Ray turned back. "Here's a clue to help you. Scan all the pictures . . . carefully. This UNSUB has to know that I'm aware of who he is. It's almost as if he wants me to recognize him. It's weird. I've never encountered any other case like this one." With that, Ray walked out of the room, leaving them behind.

River frowned at Tony. "I'd rather he just tell us exactly why he's so certain there's a serial killer in Burlington."

Tony smiled. "That's not my dad. He's very careful when it comes to crimes. His catchphrase has always been 'Show me the evidence.' He taught me to approach cases the same way."

"Which is smart," River said. "There's no sense in bringing

something before a district attorney that can't be prosecuted because the evidence is shaky."

Tony shrugged. "All we can do is look at whatever he's got and let him know if we agree with him. If we think he's right, then we can start working a profile."

"He realizes we can only offer an opinion, right?" River said. "We're not licensed in Iowa. We can't investigate."

"Yeah, he's aware. He's more interested in the skills we learned in the FBI."

"Okay."

"I'll go through the file," Tony said. "Why don't you study the pictures? You're better at spotting things that don't belong than I am."

"Well, I'm not sure about that."

"I am."

Tony picked up the murder book and took it over to the table, then he pulled his chair up and began studying police and fire reports as well as the results from the ME's office. River got up and walked over to the corkboard where Ray had pinned a variety of pictures. What was it he wanted them to see? The devastation was terrible. The bodies burnt beyond recognition.

"When you get to the ME's reports, I'd like to hear cause of death," she said to Tony.

Tony snorted. "I'm guessing being burned to death would be COD."

"You know smoke inhalation usually kills people before the body is actually burned," River shot back.

"Of course, but there may not be any lungs left, River." Tony stared up at the corkboard. "Those bodies are not much more than charred bones."

"Doesn't this scenario seem weird to you?" she asked. "Why didn't anyone fight back? It's like they just lay there and let themselves be murdered. Weren't most of these people elderly?"

Tony was quiet as he rifled through the file. "Hmmm. You're

right. The first couple was in their sixties. The second death was a woman in her early seventies. I mean, these people aren't what I'd call elderly, but they're all older."

River grinned. "Sorry. The sixties are the new forties, right?"

"We're uncomfortably close to our forties. Does that mean we're actually in our twenties? Because when I get out of bed in the morning, I sure don't feel twenty." He shook his head. "I'm starting to make the old man sound."

"What in the world is the old man sound?" River asked, laughing.

Tony sighed. "When you get out of bed or up from a chair and groan a certain way . . . well, let's just leave it there, okay?"

"I'm thinking being shot four times might be the cause of those noises."

"You're just trying to make me feel better."

River grinned at him. "Yeah, that's it." She went back to looking over the pictures. "You know, there's something else that bothers me."

"What's that?"

"All of these people were lying on their backs." She frowned. "How do you sleep?"

"On my side."

"Me too."

"I'm not sure we can conclude much from that," River said slowly, "but it's rather odd. Especially since bodies tend to contract when being burned."

"Wait a minute," Tony said, turning a page. "Seems their wrists and ankles were bound with wire."

"So, the killer wanted them to be in a supine position," River said slowly. "Were their wrists crossed?"

Tony looked up at her and nodded. "That's significant."

"Yes, it is."

They were both quiet as they concentrated on the case. It was then that River's eye caught something. She picked up a magnifying glass on the top of Ray's desk and held it up to one of the pictures.

"See something?" Tony asked.

"Quiet," she said. As she moved the glass from picture to picture, her heart began to race. Finally, she put the glass down and turned to face Tony.

"Your dad's right," she said. "His serial killer is still at it. And he's in Burlington now."

SIX

Tony got up and walked over to where River stood. What had she noticed that made her so certain his dad was on the right track?

"Show me," he said.

"Okay, we know that the last killing in Des Moines was different. The one where that guy was arrested. But the previous two . . ." She held the magnifying glass up to a photo of the outside of the house where the first fire had been—where his father had been injured.

He looked it over carefully. All he could see was a burned-out house that had collapsed not long after his father had run out with a child in his arms. "Sorry. Nothing looks unusual to me."

"It's not the house. It's the tree outside. And the fact that it's snowing."

"This incident happened in December. Snow isn't unusual for that time of the year."

"Here." River pointed at a large tree in the front yard, its leaves gone.

"I don't . . . Oh, you mean the snowman ornament?" He stood

up straight and stared at her. "Again, almost Christmas. It would be weird if there weren't any Christmas decorations."

"It's the only decoration we can see. True, it's possible there were some on the house that were burned up, but still, who puts one ornament on a tree that far from the house?"

Tony didn't want to offend his partner, but this was hardly evidence. He started to tell her that, but before he could get the words out, she moved the magnifying glass.

"This is the second murder a couple of years later," she said. "What do you see?"

He sighed and bent over again. Another burned-out house. This one in better shape than the other but still a total loss. There were no trees in this yard, but there were several bushes close to the house that were singed but still standing. Again, it was snowing so it made it a little difficult to see much. But then his eye caught something. A familiar feeling made the hair on the back of his neck stand up.

"It's . . . it's the same ornament. Exactly the same."

Behind them, River heard Ray come back into the room, but she was too absorbed in what she was seeing to turn away and break her concentration.

She nodded. "There's no ornament at the third house even though there are two trees in the yard. And of course, it wasn't snowing. The copycat committed his crime in April. The other two murders were in the paper, but there weren't any details. The copycat got some of it right but missed some important facts. For one thing, he didn't realize the significance of the season. The police suspected the first two murders were related, and he knew that, but no one mentioned the ornament. He obviously hoped the police would lump these homicides in with the others." She turned to look at Ray, who had set down a tray with coffee cups on his desk. "It's possible he had some kind of connection to the

47

police or the fire department. Or relatives of the victims of the other homicides, right?"

Ray nodded. "He worked with the nephew of a victim from the second killings. He told him about the way his aunt had died—and he knew the couple in the first attack died the same way. A police officer let the details slip when they talked to the family. That shouldn't have happened, but by the second murders, we knew we could have a serial killer on our hands. When we caught the guy from the third homicides, my chief decided he was responsible for all of them. The suspect, Arlen Thacker, had no alibis for the other murders. I tried to tell Chief Watts that he had it wrong, but neither he nor his detectives would listen to me. Thacker was only charged with those April murders because they couldn't concretely connect him to the first two. To the department, the case was closed." He sighed. "I was so frustrated. I understood that the police were overwhelmed with other cases. The crime rate in Des Moines was beginning to skyrocket. Closing out the Snowman case was the easy way out."

"Wait a minute," Tony said. "So, they called the killer the Snowman, yet the last killing happened in April? That doesn't make sense."

"Exactly. This guy likes to strike in December and only when it's snowing. It's weird. Don't get me wrong, Thacker was responsible for two deaths and deserved to go to prison. But I'm convinced he had nothing to do with the first two attacks." Ray shrugged. "My chief ignored everything we already knew about the Snowman since it was clear Thacker was guilty of the third double-homicide. Seems he knew the couple that died. They went to the same church. The woman had some very expensive jewelry, and the husband didn't believe in banks. Kept a boatload of cash in the house. Unfortunately, they shared this information with Thacker. When the police stopped him a few blocks from the house, the cash and jewelry were found in his car. Pretty open and shut."

"How did they know who they were looking for?" River asked.

"A sharp-eyed neighbor who ran the neighborhood watch called the police. She noticed a strange car in front of the couple's house late at night and saw Thacker go around to the back of the house. She thought it was suspicious. It took the police a while to get there, and by then Thacker had left. But the neighbor had gotten his license number. Thacker's life of crime came to an abrupt end." Ray shook his head. "That poor couple died trying to get out of their bedroom. But they didn't make it. It wasn't like the Snowman's victims. They were always found in their beds."

"Are you absolutely certain the first two killings aren't a coincidence?" Tony said slowly. "I mean, basing a case on two similar Christmas decorations . . ."

"Not similar. Exactly the same. And they look homemade. This is one of the reasons I was so frustrated," Ray said. "We dropped the ball. Completely. I'm sure the lack of any evidence in the first two incidents had something to do with the Snowman getting away with murder."

River moved over to the other side of the board. "Here's a picture of the homicides that happened here two years ago in December," she told him. She handed Tony the magnifying glass.

He took it from her with a feeling of dread. Then he put it in front of the photo of the most recent murders and fire. Through the falling snow he saw it. The prickly feeling on his neck turned into something else. Something colder and much more malevolent.

"The same ornament on the tree," he said. "And the same manner of death. Okay, this isn't a coincidence." He turned toward his father. "It's December. Is this why you're concerned it's getting ready to happen again? Maybe he'll take a breather."

"I just feel it in my bones," Ray said. "I think he's preparing to kill again. It's been two years since the last one. But even if I'm wrong, we still need to find this UNSUB." He picked up two coffee cups and brought them over to Tony and River.

"I understand that," Tony said, "but what I don't get is why your chief doesn't see the connection we do."

Ray stood in front of the board, his eyes scanning the pictures and the reports as Tony and River sipped their coffee. "I wish I could explain it, but I can't. He's friends with the police chief in Des Moines. I'm wondering if Chief Munson feels as though a suggestion from us to reopen the case will put Chief Watts on the defensive. I hate to think that's the reason, but I can't get him to listen. He's made it clear that he's not interested in hearing any more about it. If I go to him again, it has to be with something solid. That's why you're here."

"I've glanced at the reports, but I'd like more time to go through everything," River said. "So far, it certainly seems as if the MO is the same at each crime scene." She paused for a moment before saying, "I'm sure you've looked for any connection the victims have. What they have in common."

"I have," Ray said. "I've spent hours and hours trying to figure it out. But so far there's nothing." He shook his head. "Maybe you can find it, but except for the victims' ages, nothing connects them."

"I doubt the UNSUB is just killing elderly people," Tony said. "There has to be another reason. He's punishing these people for something." He looked at River. "We need to find it."

"If we can," she said. "If you couldn't figure it out, Ray, I'm not sure we'll be able to."

"I'm hoping you'll see something I missed. Something that will make my chief sit up and take notice." He smiled at them. "You both have training that I don't. You're my last hope. Just do your best. That's all anyone can do. I don't want to say anything else right now. I don't want my opinions to influence you."

Tony almost laughed. River Ryland wasn't someone who could be influenced by anyone when it came to her job. She was deliberate, imperturbable, and laser focused. And right now, that's exactly what they needed. He was ready to get to work. He and River would do everything they could to bring another vicious killer to justice. He just hoped it would be in time.

SEVEN

River enjoyed dinner with Tony's parents. They were personable and fun to be around. They made her feel accepted. Ray had taken the rest of the week off work but was still on call. Tony had promised to take her for a tour of Burlington in the morning so she could see the town. From what she'd seen so far, it appeared to be a charming place to live. She looked forward to experiencing more of its allure.

Tony's sister was taking them out to lunch tomorrow. After that, most of their time would be spent working the profile. River had asked if she could take the murder book to bed with her tonight. She wanted to go through it more before tomorrow afternoon. Ray had left the file on her nightstand. As much as she was enjoying dinner, she longed to be alone so she could scour through the reports.

"Did you hear me, River?"

Beth's voice broke River out of her reverie. "I . . . I'm sorry," she said, feeling her face grow hot. "I was thinking about something else."

To her relief, Beth laughed. "Oh, honey. I understand. If I had a nickel for every time these two have tuned me out because they were thinking about work, I'd be richer than Solomon."

River smiled at her. "Guilty, but I didn't mean to let my mind wander."

"I know," Beth said kindly. "I was asking if you liked the baked spaghetti."

River grinned. "Well, I'm on my second helping. That should tell you that I think it's delicious."

"Good. It's one of Tony's favorites. I always make it when he comes home."

"I love everything you cook, Mom," Tony said. He winked at River. "I usually gain weight every time I visit."

River shook her head and looked at Beth. "I don't buy it. He's one of those people who can eat as much as he wants and never gain an ounce."

"You're right," Beth said. "It's one of his most annoying traits."

"And the others?" River asked, smiling.

"How much time do you have?"

"I'm right here, Mother," Tony said, one eyebrow raised.

Everyone laughed.

"I'll save my list for later," Beth said. "When you and I get some time alone, River."

"Sounds good. In the meantime, I'll work on my own list. Hopefully, I have enough paper."

Her comment caused a new round of laughter. After another piece of Italian cream cake and more conversation, River and Tony headed upstairs. River took a shower and then retired to her room, settling into the bedroom that had once belonged to Tony's sister. It was lovely. The four-poster bed was huge. The cream-and-dusky-blue comforter was thick and soft, and the sheets on the bed felt like silk. She wanted to sink down into their softness and drift off, but she was determined to go through the file.

In one corner of the room was an overstuffed chair with a lamp next to it. She got up, then went over and sat down. She'd just settled in and pulled the crocheted blanket over her legs when there was a knock on the door.

"Come in," she said.

The door opened slowly, and Beth came in, a small tray in her hands. "I thought you might like a cup of hot chocolate. I considered bringing tea, but you seemed like more of a hot chocolate girl to me."

River grinned. "I'm assuming it's because I ate two pieces of your wonderful cake? You noticed I have a sweet tooth?"

Beth smiled as she put the small tray down on top of the polished wood table next to the chair. "That was a pretty good clue. I also brought a couple of my snickerdoodle cookies. I make them every Christmas. It's a tradition. I hope you like them." She straightened up and seemed to study River for a moment. "If it was anyone else, I wouldn't bother them this late, but I was pretty sure you'd be up." She gestured toward the file on River's lap.

River realized that some of the graphic photos were showing and quickly closed the folder.

"Don't worry," Beth said with a sigh. "Being married to a police detective has exposed me to a lot of images and details I wish I'd never seen. It comes with the territory."

"It's . . . difficult," River said.

Beth nodded. "I can't say I'm thrilled with the side effects of law enforcement, but I'm proud of Ray and Tony." She shook her head. "When we were in Des Moines, the pastor of our church called us into his office once. Told Ray that he had no business being involved in a world full of crime and violence—even murder. He used the scripture in Philippians that says we should think on things that are pure and lovely."

"What did you say?"

Beth grunted. "I asked him if he truly believed those in law enforcement should all be unbelievers. And then I reminded him that that scripture also mentioned honesty, justice, and virtue. That defending those who have been hurt by evil—bringing justice—is the embodiment of that scripture."

River grinned. "How did he respond to that?"

"He couldn't come up with an answer. Ray and I walked out of his office and found another church. The one we attend now honors those in law enforcement. I believe bringing justice is a high calling. I thank God for people like Ray and Tony. And you."

For some reason, Beth's words impacted River more than she expected, and she felt tears fill her eyes. She tried to blink them away. Sometimes this job took so much from her. Beth's words touched her heart like a soothing balm on a painful wound.

"Oh, honey," Beth said, sitting down on the end of the bed. "Tony's told me some of the things you've been through. I'm so sorry. And I know you're concerned about your mom. I was surprised you were able to come with him."

"If it wasn't for an incredible woman who's moved in with us, I would have had to stay behind. Frankly, I think I needed this. Just a break, you know?"

"I do. Tony told you about his grandfather?"

River nodded.

"Alzheimer's is awful. It was like watching that wonderful man slowly disappear."

"I'm sorry."

"I am too." She sighed. "Tony's battle with aphasia makes him worry, you know. That he'll end up like his grandfather."

"I've wondered about that," River said, "but it's a different situation. And he seems to be handling it pretty well."

Beth smiled. "My son has faith. The kind that can move mountains. But I know him well enough to know that he struggles with his condition." She stood up. "I need to let you get back to it. I didn't mean to stay so long. I'd planned to just drop off the snack and leave."

"I'm glad you didn't."

Beth stared at River for several seconds. Then she said, "I'm glad you're in my son's life." She frowned slightly. "I . . . I just hope you know how important you are to him."

Then she walked out the door, closing it behind her.

River opened the file and pulled out some of the reports, but she couldn't concentrate completely. As she reached for the cup of hot chocolate, she wondered just what Beth had meant by her parting words.

EIGHT

After poring through the file for about an hour, River was left with more questions than answers. What linked these murders together? Why was the killer so angry? She couldn't find a common thread. The victims in Des Moines were older people, as were the first couple killed in Burlington. But the second attack in Burlington involved a couple in their forties. It didn't fit the pattern. Besides that, there weren't any connections between these people that she could see. Different families. Different backgrounds. Different races. She couldn't find one thread of commonality. What was she missing? How could she and Tony write a profile without understanding the killer's trigger?

She finally closed the file and stared at it for a few minutes. All the questions she had filled her mind until she had to force herself to stop thinking about the case. She'd been through this before, and if she didn't push it away, she'd toss and turn all night trying to find the elusive thread that would tie the deaths together.

The only thing she was sure of was that the killer needed snow to act out his rage—and that the ornament was important. Something traumatic had happened to him during a past snowy winter. December seemed to be important, and the ornament was part of it. Not much to go on, but they'd had cases in the past with even fewer clues to go on.

River put the file on the table next to the tray that held her empty cup and plate. Then she got up and walked over to the bed, pausing to gaze around the lovely room. Dusky blue walls with white antique furniture. A bay window with plush pillows that looked like the perfect place to snuggle with a good book. A large wardrobe stood across from the bed. She went over and pulled the top doors open. As she'd suspected, there was a TV inside. She closed the doors. It was then that she noticed a bookcase near the bay window. She went over to it and scanned the titles. She was too tired to read, but she was curious as to what books Aimee read. River smiled when she saw all the inspirational suspense titles. Some people seemed to think that inspirational mystery and suspense books were a step below secular novels. They were wrong. Some of the best books she'd read were by Christian authors. She figured that Aimee would choose romance or something else that was a departure from the life shared by her father and brother. But instead, she'd embraced it. Interesting.

River headed back to bed and slipped between the satiny sheets. She kept the lamp on the nightstand next to the bed turned on. She never slept in the dark anymore—especially in a new place. Although she was getting better, she still dealt with nightmares. Besides, waking up in a place she didn't recognize right away could be very startling.

"Please, God," she whispered, "don't let me cry out tonight. It would embarrass me." She closed her eyes, but the information in the file ran through her mind like a wild river—as if it were pulling her along, the water rushing past her. This time she couldn't vanquish it. What was she missing? Who was the person killing these people, and when would he strike again?

Ray had said that his gut told him it would be soon. Were there people out there who had no idea that this was their last night on earth? Would they die because she and Tony couldn't help Ray stop a killer who was just beyond their reach? She tried to tell herself that worrying because of Ray's intuition was nonsense—that the killer may not strike again for a long time. Yet over the years, she'd grown to respect a gut instinct from those in law enforcement. Especially from Christians. Strangely, she felt something too. As if a voice inside was warning her. Maybe it was her imagination. But what if it wasn't?

River sat up in bed. She really wasn't certain she could sleep. She got up and went over to her bag. She'd put it just inside the closet, but she hadn't unpacked it. She never did. When she was with the Bureau, she had to be ready to go at a moment's notice. It was a habit she couldn't seem to lose.

She reached inside and pulled out her Bible, then she carried it back to the bed. She'd recently discovered that when she couldn't sleep, reading it helped. She opened the cover and flipped through the pages. She loved Psalms. Especially Psalm 91. She found it and began to softly read it out loud.

She took a deep breath and said, "He who dwells in the secret place of the Most High shall abide under the shadow of the Almighty. I will say of the LORD, 'He is my refuge and my fortress; My God, in Him I will trust.'"

The words seemed to sink down deep inside her, soaking up the fear she felt, not only from the possibility of being unable to stop the Snowman before others died—but also fear from the knowledge that the Salt River Strangler's minion might be stalking her. As she read the rest of the psalm, a feeling of calm assurance wrapped itself around her like a cocoon. Especially as she reread the last few verses.

"Because he has set his love upon Me," she read softly, "therefore I will deliver him; I will set him on high, because he has known My name. He shall call upon Me, and I will answer him;

I will be with him in trouble; I will deliver him and honor him. With long life I will satisfy him, and show him My salvation."

God's promise of deliverance gave River comfort. "God," she whispered, "I am calling on You. Thank You for Your promise to answer me. To deliver me. And long life? I'd like that too. For me and for Tony." She paused for a moment, then realized that her cheeks were wet. River was someone who didn't like to cry. What was it about the love of God that moved her so emotionally? It was as if her body reacted to His love without needing her mind to agree.

She closed her Bible and put it on her nightstand. Then she put her head on the pillow and stared up at the ceiling. The apprehension she'd felt earlier dissipated, leaving her mind clear and calm.

"Please show us how to stop this evil man before he takes another life," she prayed. "We need Your help. Your wisdom. You know who he is."

She started to flip over on her side, preparing to sleep, but then she added, "And please take care of my mother. Lord, heal her. Strengthen her. And more than anything, help her to forgive and rededicate her life to You. She needs You so desperately."

River felt herself begin to drift off. Immediately she saw a man and a woman walking in the snow. In his hand, the man held a duplicate of the ornament left behind at each murder he'd committed. The woman was whispering something in his ear, but River couldn't hear her words. It was as if she was speaking so softly, only the man could hear her. Suddenly the man turned and looked River's way. It startled her. His face was hidden, but his eyes burned like fire.

"It's about the children," he said.

Smoke began to fill the air, and the man and woman were hidden behind a curtain of white. River began to cough, as if the smoke was in the room with her. She sat up in bed, trying to catch her breath. But when she opened her eyes, the room was clear.

She started to get up so she could make sure the house wasn't on fire, but when she realized there wasn't even a scent of smoke, she collapsed back down on the bed.

Although she was tired, she lay there for a while, wondering what to do about the dream. Was it real? Was God trying to tell her something? Should she tell Tony? She didn't want him to think she was crazy.

"Show me what to do, God," she prayed. "Did You send this dream?" Although it would have been nice to hear a booming voice respond to her question, there was only silence. River rolled over once more and whispered, "He shall call upon Me, and I will answer him; I will be with him in trouble; I will deliver him and honor him," before she once again felt sleep wash over her.

CHAPTER NINE

River woke up at seven, got dressed, and started to walk downstairs. At the last minute, she turned around and made her way down the hall to Tony's room. The door was open, and the bed was made. Good. She was afraid she'd gotten up too early. She briefly looked around his bedroom. It was large like hers but had a much more manly vibe. The walls were a light gray, and white wainscoting gave it a bright ambiance. White bookshelves lined one side of the wall. River wanted to check out the titles, but she didn't feel right walking into Tony's bedroom. She headed the other way and made her way down the stairs. As she neared the bottom, she heard voices and smelled the aromas of breakfast. She shouldn't be hungry, but her stomach rumbled. She wasn't used to eating much in the morning. A quick bowl of cereal or a muffin from a bakery on the way to the office was the extent of her usual breakfasts.

As she walked into the kitchen, Beth smiled at her. "Here she is. I fought valiantly to protect your waffles and bacon from these two selfish men."

River slid into an empty chair next to Tony. "You have my undying gratitude," she said. "It smells amazing."

"You don't have to humor her," Tony said. "It's really awful. I could take your waffles as an act of mercy if you'd like."

River laughed. "Not a chance. I'm a profiler. I can tell when I'm being lied to."

"Good for you," Beth said. She slipped on an oven mitt and reached into the gleaming silver wall-mounted oven. She took out a plate and carried it to the table, putting it in front of River.

"What time did you all get up?" River asked, noticing that all three of them seemed to have already finished their meal.

"I get up at five every morning," Ray said. "I try to get to work by seven, but I don't like to rush breakfast. It's a habit."

"He even gets up early on his days off," Beth said, pouring River a cup of coffee. "It's annoying."

Ray grabbed her hand as she tried to walk past him. "I always tell her to sleep in, but she never listens. She gets up and makes me breakfast."

"He's ruined me," Beth said, leaning down and kissing her husband on the top of his head. "The last time I slept late was before Tony and Aimee were born."

Tony leaned close to River. She could smell his shaving lotion.

"What Mom isn't telling you is that she's a champion napper," he said.

River looked up into his grayish-blue eyes and gulped. His hair was still a little messy, and he was dressed in sweats. She'd never seen him like this, and it made her feel funny. As if she were seeing something she shouldn't. She tried to swallow past the lump in her throat, but she couldn't. In the end she just nodded.

"I only nap because I get bored," Beth said. "When Ray retires . . ."

Beth sat down in her chair, and River was surprised to see tears in her eyes.

"I'm sorry," she said, picking up her napkin and wiping her

cheeks. "I . . . I just want him home. Safe. So many years of worrying about him." She looked at Tony. "I almost lost him the night of the fire—and then, when Tony was shot . . ." She took a deep, shaky breath and then offered a tremulous smile. "I'm so sorry. I don't usually do this."

Tony reached across the table and took his mother's hand. "We'll be fine, Mom. God is looking out for us. You know that."

Beth nodded. "Yes, I do. But . . . you both need to be careful. Sometimes we can put ourselves in danger if we don't listen to that still, small voice inside us."

"It was my fault," River blurted out, putting her coffee cup down. "I mean, the reason Tony was shot. He was trying to save me. I'm terribly sorry." She met Beth's eyes. "I . . . I've wanted to apologize to you and Ray. I should have realized something was wrong. We shouldn't have gone there. It's just that I thought . . ."

"Hey," Tony said, interrupting her.

The stern tone of his voice brought her up short. She turned to look at him.

"It wasn't your fault at all," he said. "I wasn't forced to go to the river that night. We both thought Jacki had found something we needed to see. There wasn't any reason to think otherwise. If you failed to recognize it was a setup, so did I."

"But there was something in Jacki's tone that . . . I should have realized . . ."

"Stop it." Tony grabbed her hand and looked into her eyes. "Just stop it. Neither one of us felt something was wrong. The fault belongs to one person. Joseph Baker. No one else."

"He's right," Ray said. "Beth and I don't blame you. Or Tony. I probably would have done the same thing. Let's not chastise ourselves for the bad deeds committed by criminals." He looked over at his wife, but Beth was strangely silent. Did she blame River for Tony's shooting? River tried to read her, but she couldn't be certain.

As if noticing his mother's reaction, Tony stared at her for a moment, but when he caught River watching him, he recovered and smiled at her. "No more of that, okay?"

River returned his smile and nodded, but she knew she needed to sit down with Beth and have a talk in private before she went home.

"If you'll excuse us, I promised River a tour of Burlington," Tony said, getting to his feet.

"Let me fix you some coffee to take with you," Beth said. "It's freezing out there." She walked over to a cabinet and opened it. Then she took out two thermal cups with cute Christmas images on the sides. "Pumpkin spice creamer?" she asked.

"Yes, please," River and Tony said at the same time.

Beth laughed. "Glad I bought some. Tony loves it. Seems you two have similar tastes."

"We finish each other's sentences sometimes," Tony said with a smile. "I guess it comes from knowing each other for so long."

"I'm so glad you're both here." Beth's voice cracked and she turned around, hiding her face. River's heart went out to her. She was certain her emotion was directed toward her son, not River, but it was nice to be included in the sentiment.

Tony got up and walked over to his mother, putting his hands on her shoulders. "I'm sorry, Mom. I'll make it home more often."

Beth didn't turn around as she continued preparing the cups, but she reached back and patted Tony's hand. "That would be great," she whispered.

"I . . . I'm going upstairs," River said. "I need to get ready to go."

Tony let go of his mother and turned around. "You look fine." He stared down at his sweats. "I'm the one who needs to change. It won't take me long."

"Okay," River said. "But it won't take me long either. I need to fix my hair and put on some makeup."

"I'll knock on your door when I'm ready," Tony said.

65

"You're welcome to come down here and visit with me while Tony's getting ready," Beth said. "He always takes a lot longer than he says."

River laughed. "I've noticed that too. I'm not certain why it takes him twice as long as it does me. Doesn't make sense."

"Smooshy likes to make sure every hair is in place and his outfits are just right."

"Mother! First of all, quit calling me that. And I don't wear *outfits*. Seriously."

They all laughed at his reaction. He was clearly embarrassed. River found it rather charming, although she would never tell him that.

She followed Tony upstairs but went to her room while he headed toward his. River didn't plan to change clothes. She'd dressed in jeans, boots, and a dark blue sweater. She quickly put on her makeup and brushed her hair. She only wore eyeliner, mascara, and a light blush. Her skin didn't need foundation. In fact, most of them made her face break out.

She used a curling iron in an attempt to give her hair some shape, but it was so thick the curl wouldn't hold for long. Still, she wanted to look her best today since she'd be meeting Tony's sister. When she was ready, she put on her earrings. She only had two sets with her. One for daytime, and then another pair for anything that required her to dress up. They were pretty. Cubic zirconia. She wasn't into diamonds or other expensive stones when something cheaper would do. The earrings sparkled just like diamonds. Why spend money on something else when it wasn't necessary?

After she was ready to go, she slipped out into the hallway and listened. She could hear Tony in his room. Good. She wanted a chance to talk to Beth.

She walked quietly down the hall, hoping Ray wasn't in the kitchen with his wife. When she entered, she found Beth rinsing the dishes and putting them into the dishwasher.

"You shouldn't have to do this," River said. "After that wonderful meal."

"Ray wanted to help, but I made him leave," Beth said with a smile. "I don't like the way he loads the dishwasher. Too haphazard for my liking."

"How about I rinse the dishes and you can put them in the way you like?"

"I'd like that. Thank you."

River gathered up the rest of the dishes on the table and carried them to the big white farmhouse sink. As she rinsed the dishes and handed them to Beth, she tried to find a way to bring up Tony's shooting without offending his mother. Finally, she said, "I wanted to say again how sorry I am about putting Tony in danger that night in Arizona."

Beth had just bent over to put a plate in the bottom rack of the dishwasher. She slid it in and then stayed where she was for a moment. When she straightened up, she turned and met River's gaze.

"I don't blame you," she said. "But I have to admit that I did at first. Tony was supposed to have a safe job. A behavioral analyst for the FBI. Not a field agent. I mean, I knew he had to travel to different locations sometimes, but he wasn't supposed to be in harm's way." She sighed deeply and looked down. "I couldn't figure out why he was out there that night. The Salt River Strangler threw victims into that river. What in the world would possess him to go there? I figured it had to be your fault." She looked up and stared into River's eyes. Then she reached over and put her hand on River's arm. "I forgot that Tony makes his own decisions. Good or bad, no one can force him to do something he doesn't think is right. For whatever reason, he felt he was supposed to be there that night. With you." She smiled slowly. "Besides, I realized something very important after I met you last night."

"And that was?"

"That my son would never have gone there with you if there

had even been a hint of danger. He would have kept both of you away. I believe he cares more about you than he does himself."

Beth let go of River's arm and took the cup from her hand. Not sure what to say to that, River reached for another plate in the sink and ran it under the faucet. Did Beth think she and Tony were a couple? Surely not. River didn't want her to misunderstand.

"Beth, Tony and I are just friends. You understand that, right?"

Beth was silent for a moment before softly saying, "Are you certain about that?"

River was about to repeat her denial of anything beyond friendship, but the words seemed to stick in her throat. Did she have deeper feelings for Tony? Was she trying to suppress them?

"Our partnership is so important," she said finally. "I don't want anything to put that in jeopardy."

"I completely understand," Beth said. "But there's something else to consider. Sometimes if we wait too long to acknowledge what's in our hearts, we may lose something much more valuable than a good working relationship."

River had no idea how to respond to that. She went back to silently rinsing the dishes until Tony strode into the kitchen. "Ready to go?" he asked her, a smile on his face.

He looked so handsome in his black coat and jeans it took River a moment to answer. She felt her face grow warm. "Sure. We're finished here."

She headed for the coat closet in the hallway, Beth's words echoing in her mind. *Sometimes if we wait too long to acknowledge what's in our hearts, we may lose something much more valuable than a working relationship.*

TEN

A fter retrieving the coffee his mother had prepared for them, River and Tony headed outside. Mom was right. The air was so cold it almost took Tony's breath away.

"I should have warmed up the SUV before we came out here," he said. "Sorry."

"It doesn't matter," River said. "It heats up quickly. Besides, we have your mom's coffee to keep us warm."

Tony smiled and took a sip from his cup. He loved Burlington and was excited to share it with River. Maybe someday, when he retired, he'd come back here. It wasn't a tiny town. Around twenty-five thousand people, but it was connected to West Burlington, Middletown, and Gulfport, Illinois, making it seem larger. Situated on the banks of the Mississippi River, Burlington was full of history and charm.

After a couple of minutes, he turned on the heater and the air blew out, filling the car with warmth.

"There we go," he said. He'd just put the car in gear when several flakes of snow drifted down. Although he loved snow, this time it felt a little ominous. Was his father seeing this? Was he worried that the Snowman might strike tonight? Tony had to admit that he felt some concern as well.

He turned on the wipers and the back window defroster. As he pulled out of the driveway, River said, "It's starting to snow."

It was said as a statement of fact, but the seriousness in her tone made it clear she was thinking the same thing he was.

"It doesn't mean anything will happen tonight," he said. "My dad's had this case on his brain for a long time. I'm sure he worries anytime it snows."

"I realize that," River said, "but can't you feel it? Like there's something in the air?"

"Yeah, it's called snow," Tony said dryly. "Look, let's enjoy the tour and lunch with my sister. After that, we'll buckle down and work on the profile for my dad. It's all we can do right now. If this guy is really preparing to kill someone, we have no way to stop him. No way to find him yet."

"So, knowing that, right now, someone may be planning for Christmas, walking around, breathing, but by tonight may be dead . . . that doesn't bother you?"

He looked over at her. "That's not fair. You know me better than that."

River sighed. "I'm sorry. I don't know why I said that. I guess I'm tired of thinking about murderers, rapists, and arsonists. It would be nice to just take a vacation, you know? I mean, what if we could have come here just for fun? No serial killers involved."

"You really do need a break, don't you?"

River grunted. "Don't you?"

Tony hadn't thought about it that way. Life was life. You handled whatever came your way, knowing God was with you. That you'd get through it because He'd make certain you did. But the truth was, he really did feel weary. He was still trying to recover from that night along the riverbank—and now he had to think about death again just because it had started to snow? He could remember being a kid—him and Aimee—bundled up and outside playing in the snow. His mother would make hot chocolate and cookies for them to enjoy when they came inside, their faces red and frozen, yet they were so happy. Did it bother him that some guy who couldn't handle life was trying to take that away from him? That, as River had said, another human being might be smiling out at the snow, not knowing this would be their last day on earth?

"You know what, you're right," he said finally. "Maybe this spring we could go on a vacation. Mrs. Weyland can watch your mom." He gave her a smile. "Where would we go?"

River laughed lightly. "Wow. I don't know. I need to think about that. I've always wanted to take a cruise to Alaska. And I've never been to Hawaii."

"I have. We went with our parents when we were teenagers. It was awesome. Stayed in a hotel on the beach. We left the sliding glass door to the patio open at night. You could hear the waves crashing on the shore. Doves would fly onto the patio to be fed. It was so great."

"Sounds incredible. We used to go camping when I was a kid— before my dad left. But that was it. And after he left, we never went on vacation. My mom had to work—had to support us. After I moved out, I focused on finishing college, joining the police force, and then the FBI. Moving to Virginia was the biggest trip I'd ever taken."

"I'm sorry, River. You deserved more as a kid."

She shrugged. "It is what it is. Hey, I'm in Iowa. Things are looking up!"

Tony laughed. "Another reason for me to show you how cool Burlington is. By the time I'm through, you'll feel like you finally got to experience somewhere really special."

"I'm counting on it."

RIVER WAS IMPRESSED with Burlington. She could see why Tony's father felt this would be a better place for his family rather than Des Moines. She listened as Tony regaled her with the town's qualities. It was situated on bluffs overlooking the Mississippi River. She felt a connection between St. Louis and the much smaller town since the same river ran through both places.

"Burlington has lots of museums and entertainment venues," he was saying. "And although I don't want you to think I'm just trying to impress you, believe it or not, this is the birthplace of the backhoe. In fact, it's the Backhoe Capital of the World."

"Oh my," River said, laughing. "How could any other place compete with that?"

"You're right, of course. But there's something else you definitely need to see."

"And what would that be?"

"It's called Snake Alley. Ripley's Believe It or Not called it 'Unbelievably Crooked.' It's number one on their 'Odd Spots Across America' list."

"Now, that's something I absolutely can't miss."

Tony drove them to the top of a bluff so they could look down at an incredibly curvy road. It really did look like a snake.

"It was built by German immigrants in the 1800s who were trying to replicate vineyard paths in France and Germany. We could drive it, but since it's snowing, I'm concerned it might be slippery. As you can see, there's not much room for error."

As Tony talked about Burlington, River began to realize that he loved the small town too. Is this where he really wanted to be? Was he only in St. Louis because of her? She felt a little sick to her stomach. She didn't want him to sacrifice himself for her. She'd never wanted that. He'd already almost lost his life trying to protect her from the Salt River Strangler.

After sharing a few other things about the town, Tony said, "Just one other thing I want you to see. Then we'll head back to the house."

She was quiet while he drove. Did his parents know he wanted to be here? With them? Did they resent her for keeping him away?

Finally, he pulled into a parking lot. "This is Mosquito Park."

"Yikes."

Tony laughed. "Don't worry. It's too cold for mosquitos today." He pointed toward a viewer next to a railing that surrounded the overlook. "Even though it's freezing outside, if we're lucky, you'll see something wonderful. Are you game?"

River shrugged. "Why not. Let's do it."

They got out of the car and walked over to the railing. The view was breathtaking. Tony pointed out the Great River Bridge that connected Burlington to Gulfport, Illinois. Then he grabbed her arm.

"Look up," he said, a tinge of excitement in his voice.

River cast her eyes toward the sky and gasped. Bald eagles. Four of them swooping across the sky

"Oh, Tony," she said. "They're beautiful."

She watched them for several minutes, but the cold was seeping through her jacket, and she shivered.

"You're freezing," Tony said. He put his arm around her, and she leaned into him before she realized what she was doing. As they stood there, she felt his body stiffen. She looked up and found him staring at her. The look on his face, and the way his eyes bored into hers, filled her with a warmth that belied the icy wind that whipped past them. Although it took almost all the strength she could muster, she gently moved away, embarrassed by his reaction . . . and hers.

"Back to the car?" he said, his voice tight.

She nodded and followed him back to the SUV. Had he reacted without thinking? Was he regretting it now?

Neither one of them spoke for a while. Finally, Tony cleared his throat. "At night, several of the historic buildings in downtown Burlington are illuminated with LED lights. Maybe we can see that while we're here. The Festival of Lights has started, but again, you can't see them during the day. We also have the Christmas tree lighting and the parade, but that will be in a week or so."

"You keep saying 'we,'" she said. "Do you see this as your home, Tony?"

"No. Well . . . I don't know. I'd be lying if I said that I wouldn't like to live here someday. But right now, I want to be in St. Louis."

"Why?"

He turned to look at her. "Don't start thinking I'm only there because of you, River. First of all, it's only a little over three hours from here to St. Louis. Much closer to my parents than Virginia was. Also, we can't grow the kind of agency we want here. For now, I'm exactly where I want to be. You need to believe me. I wouldn't lie to you. You know that, right?"

River immediately felt better. No, as a Christian, he wouldn't lie.

When they got back to his parents' house, Tony pointed at a Jeep parked in the driveway. "Aimee's here. You'll love her. I told you she works in social services, but I don't think I ever got into details. She's a victim advocate at an organization called the Eagle's Nest. They help victims of sexual abuse, domestic abuse, rape, and human trafficking."

"Does her choice to work there have anything to do with what happened to your aunt?"

"It has everything to do with it. It impacted all of us in a big way." He smiled at her. "I hope you enjoyed your tour. No need to tip your tour guide."

"Good to know," she said, returning his smile. The tension between them seemed to have eased, and she was relieved.

As they made their way up the porch stairs, the snow swirled around them. River couldn't help but feel as if each flake was a warning.

ELEVEN

He wished he were there—watching her. But for now, he'd keep his distance. Waiting was hard, but it wasn't time yet. Had they figured it out? Did they know where they'd gone wrong? Would she only realize it at the last minute? That would be so satisfying. But he wasn't going to count on that. Finishing the job would be reward enough.

He'd sent her something to let her know he was still here. Still planning her demise. She would be back soon.

And then he'd finish what he'd started.

FOR SOME REASON, River was a little nervous about meeting Aimee. She wasn't sure why. Maybe it was because of River's rocky relationship with her brother, Dan. A sibling was someone you grew up with. A person who knew you better than you knew yourself. When Dan was upset with her, the hurt was deeply personal. Her parents had clear rules when she and Dan were young. Act like good little pastor's kids. Don't be loud. Don't be obnoxious. And whatever you do, never give away family secrets. Don't tell anyone about the arguments between your parents. Don't let anyone know about what you saw once at church when you opened the door to your father's office and his secretary was with him. Keep your mouth shut, and stay out of the way.

But she and Dan had shared everything. They knew things weren't right. Maybe they had no power to do anything about it, but they were honest with each other. And they protected each other. Where was he now? River knew he had a family—and that had to come first—but she missed her brother. She missed having someone in her life she could say anything to.

Even as the thought came to her mind, she glanced over at Tony. The truth was, she'd told him things she never thought she could share with anyone else. She trusted him completely. She suddenly felt an urge to reach over and put her arm through his, but she stopped herself. There couldn't be a repeat performance of what had happened at the park. It was true that she felt closer to Tony than anyone else in the world, but there was a line. A line that neither one of them seemed willing to cross. She'd felt something when he'd put his arm around her near the river, but he was just trying to keep her warm. It meant nothing . . . or did it? She remembered his face. The way he'd looked at her. She pushed the memory out of her mind. For now, she was happy just to see him at work every day. To know that if she needed anything, he would be there for her. She had no intention of losing that. She couldn't imagine her life without Tony in it.

Maybe that's why she was worried about Aimee. She knew the siblings had a deep, unbreakable bond. What if Aimee didn't like her? Would it drive a wedge between her and Tony?

As he opened the door, she shivered uncontrollably, but this time it wasn't because of the temperature. It was caused by a sliver of fear that snaked down her back.

"Sorry you're so cold," Tony said, obviously seeing her reaction.

"You'll warm up inside. My guess is that Mom will make her famous hot chocolate and give us some of her delicious snickerdoodles."

River laughed. "Your prediction is too late. Your mom brought me hot chocolate and cookies last night when I was getting ready for bed."

Tony grinned. "My mother. So predictable." He closed the door behind them. "She likes you, you know. A lot. I can't wait for my sister to meet you. She'll love you too."

River smiled at him. "I hope so." She pulled off her coat and hung it up in the closet near the door. Then she took a deep breath and followed Tony into the kitchen where they could hear voices.

"Smooshy!" a woman called out as they entered.

Beth was sitting at the large table with an attractive young woman who was clearly related to Tony. She had the same dark curly hair, which was pulled back from her face. She had inquisitive blue eyes framed by dark lashes.

She stood up and came over to River. She had a slight build like Tony, but River sensed that, also like her brother, she could handle herself just fine if she needed to.

She reached out and took River's hand. "It's about time I got to meet you. I've heard about you for years. According to Tony, you're a combination of Wonder Woman, Supergirl, and a female Sherlock Holmes."

River laughed. "I'm not sure anyone could live up to that. I certainly can't."

Aimee's eyes seemed to search hers. What was she seeing?

She let go of River's hand. "I look forward to getting to know you. I'm sure I'll come away impressed."

"I'm afraid your brother hasn't mentioned my many faults. Hopefully, I won't let you down."

"I'm sure you won't. So, are you two ready to go?"

"Where are we headed?" Tony asked.

"Why would you even ask her that?" Beth asked. She looked at River. "We have quite a few lovely restaurants in Burlington, but my children don't know that. They always go to the Drake. It's one of our most popular restaurants."

"Don't listen to her," Aimee said. "The Drake rules, right, Smooshy?"

"Okay," Tony said. "I'll pay for lunch if you'll stop calling me Smooshy."

Aimee clapped her hands together. "You've got a deal." She leaned up next to River. "It works every time," she said in an exaggerated whisper. "Just call him . . . you know . . . and you can get him to do anything you want."

"I'll have to remember that," River said, winking at Tony.

"I'm being persecuted by the women in my life," Tony said dramatically. "It's my cross to bear."

Aimee went over and put her arms around her brother. "And you bear it well. I've missed you, brother."

"I've missed you too," Tony said.

River heard the slight break in his voice. His closeness to his sister was something special. She thought about Dan. Was it too late for them? Was there a way to bridge the gap that had grown between them? Without accepting her father, she wasn't certain it could happen. She knew God wanted her to forgive him for walking out on them, but how could she? Wasn't that asking too much? She hadn't talked much to Dan since he'd told her he'd taken their father in to live with him and his family.

"Hey, are you with us?"

Tony's voice broke her out of her reverie. "Sorry. Did you say something?"

"Yeah," Tony said. "I said, let's go before I change my mind about paying for lunch."

"You all have fun," Beth said. She came over and put her arm around River. "And don't let them talk you into the grilled mac and cheese with brisket. You order whatever you want. I like the fajita salad."

Aimee put her arm through River's. "Don't listen to her. We'll introduce you to the Drake's best dishes. You can trust us. You'll love the raw eel."

"Aimee!" Tony shook his head. "They don't serve raw eel. Just stay close to me, River. I'll keep you safe."

Her children's antics made Beth laugh. River got a lump in her throat. So, this was what a family was supposed to be? She'd never had this. Even before he left, her father had been a judgmental, harsh man. Nothing was ever good enough for him. Their mother hadn't been much better. Quiet and unassuming. Trying hard to please her husband. The woman her father ran away with was just the opposite. Flashy. Loud. Bleached blonde hair. After he left, Rose became not much more than a shadow, there in body, but not in mind or spirit. River and Dan were left to raise themselves.

Tony put his hand on River's back and guided her toward the front door, where she slipped her coat on again.

"We really don't have to go to the Drake if there's someplace else you'd rather go," Aimee said as they went down the stairs toward the car. "You're our guest. You pick."

River smiled at her. "Thanks, but I don't know anything about the restaurants in Burlington. I trust you. The Drake sounds perfect."

"I like this girl," Aimee said to Tony. "You sure know how to pick 'em."

River looked up at Tony and saw his jaw tighten. Did Aimee think they were more than business partners? Friends?

As they got into the car, she expected him to correct his sister, but he stayed silent, which confused her.

Just what had Tony told his family about her?

TWELVE

I parked across the street from the house. I'd already scouted
it out. Knew how to get in. There will only be one victim
this time, but she is certainly deserving of judgment. Beyond
deserving.

Snow is predicted for the rest of the day and into the early
morning hours. Three to four inches. Perfect. It's a clear sign.

I never worry about leaving footprints. The fire department
takes care of that. They never approach a fire like a crime scene
unit does. They think only about rescuing anyone trapped inside
and putting the flames out as quickly as possible. They always
cover up my tracks.

My special knapsack is ready. I am ready.

Tonight, I will once again bring justice.

RIVER WAS IMPRESSED with the Drake from the outside.
The large brick building with the words *The Drake . . . on the
Riverfront* was interesting and inviting. There was an outdoor
area that looked out over the Mississippi River. Although she
could understand how most people would feel that sitting outside

with a view of the river was appealing, memories of being thrown into the Salt River, trussed up inside a large chest, and waiting for death as the water seeped in made her heart beat faster. She'd done fine at the park, but they weren't there long, and she'd been thinking about other things. But sitting for a long time near the massive river's banks? No, thanks. She was glad it was winter and she hadn't been forced to explain why she could only eat inside. She forced herself to focus on the building, ignoring the sparkling river to her right.

"You okay?" Tony asked quietly.

She nodded. "I'm fine. Really. It's been a lovely morning."

"I'm glad," he said. "We probably won't get much more time to be tourists. Sorry."

"It's fine. We came to work."

"What are you two chattering about back there?" Aimee said, turning to look at them.

"We're talking about you behind your back," Tony shot back. "We both think you're a little pushy."

"I did not say that," River said, elbowing Tony. "Your brother can't be trusted."

Aimee laughed. "Believe me, I'm well aware."

They walked up the steps to the entrance of the restaurant. A black awning protected them from the swirling snow. When they entered the door, River was pleasantly surprised. The Drake had a wonderful ambience. Lots of wood and brick. Besides the tables and booths, there was a long bar and lots of kitschy decorations. There was an old-fashioned red phone booth on one wall with two figures of elderly women sitting on a bench next to it. There were also lots of antiques featured in various places and interesting photos on the wall. River loved it immediately.

Once they were seated, a waitress came over to take their drink orders and give them menus. River opened hers but noticed that Tony and Aimee didn't bother to look at theirs.

"I suppose you already know what you want," she said. "Is it the grilled mac and cheese?"

"You've got to try it," Tony said.

Aimee shook her finger at her brother. "Don't let him pressure you. But . . . the mac and cheese really is to die for."

River wasn't willing to die for any food, but if Tony loved it, she probably would too. Their tastes were very similar. "Tony is my partner. Since we work together, if I upset him, he could make life uncomfortable for me. So . . . I think I'll go with the mac and cheese."

Tony and Aimee both laughed.

"I need to go to the little boys' room," Tony said. He pointed at Aimee. "Don't talk about me while I'm gone. No embarrassing stories, okay?"

Aimee struck an expression of feigned innocence. "Would I do something like that to my only brother?"

"In a heartbeat." Tony got to his feet but then leaned over next to River and said, "You can't trust a word she says. Just remember those bullets I took for you."

"You're going to hold that over my head forever, aren't you?" she asked.

Tony shrugged and walked away, a big grin on his face.

River turned back and met Aimee's gaze, but any sign of gaiety was gone from her expression. Was she upset because Tony mentioned the shooting?

"I'm sorry," River said. "Of course, what happened isn't funny. I think we tease each other about it because it helps us to deal with it. I . . . I still have nightmares about that night."

Aimee didn't say anything, just picked up her glass of water and took a drink. An uncomfortable silence followed. River wasn't certain what to do. Finally, she said, "I apologize, Aimee, if what Tony said upset you."

Aimee finally looked at her. "I almost lost my brother that

night," she said, her eyes filling with tears. "He had no business being in that place. From what he told us, he only went there because he didn't want you to go alone. Tony felt something was off and he tried to tell you, but you wouldn't listen. You almost got him killed." She took a deep, shaky breath. "Look, I want to get to know you because you're such a big part of Tony's life, but I'm not sure I'll ever be able to forgive you. I just want to be upfront with you. My parents don't harbor any ill will, but I do." She looked down at the table for a moment, as if trying to regain her composure. When she swung her gaze back to River, she was shocked to see Aimee's eyes narrowed in obvious antagonism. "I think it's good to get things out in the open. I would prefer you keep this to yourself. There's no reason to upset Tony. He's suffered enough, don't you think?"

River was speechless. What was Aimee talking about? Tony had never said he didn't want to meet Jacki that night—that he was suspicious about it. In fact, he'd told her the exact opposite. Had Tony really told his family that he'd only gone to the river that night because he felt he had to protect her? She felt confused and unsure about what to say or do.

"I . . . I don't remember Tony saying anything like that," she said finally, her voice quaking with emotion. "We made the decision to go there together. I . . . I would never do anything I thought might put Tony in danger."

Aimee looked to her left. Tony was walking toward the table. "If you don't mind, I'll believe my brother. And I won't discuss this in front of him." She quickly wiped the tears from her cheeks with her fingers and pasted a smile on her face.

"So did my sister talk about me?" he asked with a grin as he took his seat.

"No, surprisingly you weren't the focus of our attention." River tried to keep her voice steady. She didn't know whether to be angry with Aimee—or with Tony. At that moment, she wished she'd stayed in Mehlville with her mother.

The rest of the lunch Aimee acted as if nothing was wrong, but River had no intention of pretending along with her. She knew Tony could tell something was bothering her, but she refused to look at him. She felt offended . . . and confused. She couldn't believe Tony had told his family that his shooting was her fault. It certainly wasn't what Beth had said. Did Aimee really believe the things she had just accused her of? What should she do? Keep this to herself, or tell Tony what Aimee had said? The last thing she wanted to do was to drive a wedge between him and his sister. But she wasn't sure she could—or should—let this go.

THIRTEEN

After they got back to Tony's parents' house, Aimee said goodbye and left, still acting as if she and River were fast friends. River still wasn't sure what to do, but she was convinced that coming between Tony and Aimee was wrong. He'd suffered enough because of her, and River had no intention of adding more grief to his life.

Beth let them know that Ray was upstairs, waiting for them. But before River was able to head up there, Tony took her arm and led her into the living room.

"What's the matter?" he asked. "And don't say 'nothing' because I know you too well. You're upset about something, and you need to tell me."

River pulled her arm out of his grasp. "For your information, I don't have to tell you everything. Some things are personal."

"River, we don't keep secrets from each other." He put his hands on her shoulders and turned her toward him. As she looked up into his eyes, she could feel her resolve start to melt. But she just couldn't find the words to tell him what was on her mind. Until she knew what to do, she had to keep her conversation with Aimee to herself.

"I told you that it's nothing. I . . . I've been thinking a lot about our profile. I'm sorry I got so distracted. You know how I get when I start working on a case." She forced a smile. "I'm sorry. I really am. I'll be fine once we get this done."

Tony didn't look convinced, but he let her go. "Okay, if you're sure. I guess Dad is waiting on us."

"Great."

River left the living room and hurried up the stairs. She was so conflicted she wasn't certain she could concentrate on the profile the way she should. As she reached the second floor, she shook herself mentally. She was a trained behavioral analyst. She'd had to work under extreme circumstances before, and she needed to give her full attention to the work ahead of them. She'd agreed to do this, so there wasn't any way she could back out now. By the time she walked through the door to Ray's office, she was ready to work; the situation with Aimee was pushed back into the dark recesses of her mind. There were a lot of other things already stored there so adding one more wasn't easy, but she used her iron will to lock it away until another time. It could wait. This couldn't.

She and Tony had just entered the office when Beth called out their names. She walked into the room carrying a tray with a carafe and three cups. "Thought you might like some coffee," she said with a smile.

"Thanks, Mom." Tony took the tray from her. "I tend to get sleepy after lunch. This is just what I need."

"Well, if you're good and your father allows it, I'll bring up some cake in a while."

"As if I would ever turn down your cake," Ray said, winking at his wife. He patted his lean stomach as if trying to say his wife's baking was making him put on weight.

"I'll leave you to it," Beth said.

"You're the best, Mom." Tony went up to his mother and kissed her on the cheek.

Once Beth left, Ray asked them what they were thinking about the case. "I'm not going to bother you while you're working on your profile," he said, "but I know you went through the file last night, River. Any conclusions?"

River was still grappling with the strange dream she'd had and wasn't sure what to say. She decided to save it for Tony. Ray was counting on their profiling skills. Not some strange dream.

She took a deep breath and said, "I believe your UNSUB is a man. He's probably in his forties—maybe in his early fifties. He's angry about something. Setting a fire shows fury. He's smart and could easily commit these murders without leaving evidence. He chooses fire to cover his tracks because of his inner rage." She hesitated. "He's organized. He knows how to get into a house un-detected and has the ability to subdue his victims. They may not have been murdered in their beds. It's possible he's putting them there after he kills them. He binds their hands and feet with wire because he wants them in a certain position." She walked over to the large corkboard with all the pictures. "I didn't see anything in the medical examiner's reports that pointed to trauma to the skull. No broken hyoid bones in the victims' necks. I can't find any trauma that would explain their deaths outside of the fire. Of course, this kind of fire—the intensity—fractures bones. It's almost impossible to find the actual COD." She turned to look at Ray. "He sets his fire around the beds of his victims once they're dead."

"I realize that fire can crack bones," Ray said. "I think you're right about the cause of death. The MEs I talked to couldn't com-mit to anything. Also, the inner organs were destroyed. No way to see if there was smoke in the lungs." He shrugged. "It's a mystery. If only we had a body that wasn't so decimated. All we know is that he soaks the area around them with gasoline and then lights it. By the time the fire department shows up, there's not much left." He frowned. "River, why do you believe these people were dead before the fire was set?"

"Putting them on the bed and crossing their wrists reminds me of the positioning of a corpse in a coffin. The hands are placed this way out of respect for the deceased. It's the *proper* way to display a body. Our UNSUB appears to be giving them this same sign of deference. So, I don't think he would make them suffer more than he had to. Oh, he wants them dead, don't get me wrong. He's angry, exacting some type of judgment, yet his upbringing or his sensibilities have made him sensitive to causing undue pain."

Ray grunted. "If he had real compassion, he would have allowed these poor people to live."

"River's right, Dad. Here's something else to consider. This guy seems to be carrying out vengeance for someone else. The way he kills shows us his distaste for taking a life. Yet the fact that he's doing it—and the way he uses fire—comes from the anger inside of him because he believes he is righting a wrong. It's an odd dichotomy. If you can figure out who he's trying to avenge, you'll find your UNSUB."

Ray sighed. "Like I said, I've been over and over these cases. I can't find one thing any of them have in common. Nothing. Nada. Until I find out why, I can't find out who."

Frankly, even though River had seen a lot of things no human being should ever see when she was with the FBI, this subject was disconcerting. She prayed she and Tony were right—that the victims were dead before the fires were started. If they were alive, his rage really was directed toward the victim. But with the wrists and feet tied together, River was comfortable with her and Tony's assessment. The UNSUB's main motivation was for someone else. Someone he felt these victims had hurt.

Ray went over to the tray Beth had put on his desk. He poured two cups of coffee and carried them over to her and to Tony.

"Thanks," River said. She nodded at Tony. "Do you have any questions for your father?"

He shook his head. "Not right now, but stay near, Dad. We might need to talk to you later."

Ray poured one more cup of coffee and walked toward the door. "I'll be here. Just downstairs. Holler if you need me." He smiled at River. "I hope you had a nice lunch."

River took a quick breath. "Yes, I did. Thank you."

Ray nodded and walked out the door, pulling it shut behind him.

"Let's get to work," River said to Tony. "If your dad's right and this guy is getting ready to take another life, we need to get this profile done as soon as possible."

Tony didn't move, just stood where he was and stared at her.

"Did you hear me?" she asked.

"I'm not doing anything until you tell me what Aimee said to you," Tony said, his voice low and solemn. "If you don't tell me, I'll ask my sister. I mean it."

"Look, can't we work on the profile first? We can talk after . . ."

"No."

Tony's response brought her up short. She knew him well enough to know that there was no way he was going to let this go. What could she do? What should she say?

"Tony, I don't want to cause problems. Can't you just trust me when I tell you that you need to leave this alone?"

"No, River. I can't even begin to think of anything Aimee could say that would upset you so much. I have to know what happened."

"If I tell you, will you promise not to tell Aimee? I can't be the cause of problems between you and your sister. I'm serious. Please."

Tony hesitated a moment before saying, "Okay. If it's the only way I can get you to tell me the truth, I promise. I'll keep it between us."

Although it was against her better judgment, River quickly recounted her conversation with Aimee. As she talked, the color in Tony's face began to flush. She stopped, afraid of his reaction. Had she made a terrible mistake that would cause Tony's family even more pain than they'd already suffered?

FOURTEEN

Tony couldn't believe what he was hearing from River. Why would Aimee say something like that? He'd been so hopeful that River and Aimee would strike up a friendship. They were similar in so many ways. But what Aimee had said made that highly unlikely.

"River, I never told Aimee—or anyone—that I felt something was wrong that night. Because I didn't. Just like you, I truly thought Jacki wanted us to see something important that affected our profile. I didn't suspect anything, and I never told Aimee or my parents otherwise." He shook his head. "I have no idea why she would say something like that."

"Yes, you do," River replied. "We study behavior, Tony. You know exactly why she believes that."

Tony stared at her for a moment, trying to clear his head of the antagonism he felt toward his sister at that moment. "She needs to find someone to blame. And the only way she can do that is to believe I only went to the river that night because you wanted me to."

"Exactly. And I'm sure in her head, she thinks it's true."

Tony understood what River was trying to say—and he agreed with her—but it would take some effort for him to get over what

Aimee had done. River was already dealing with so much. This was just one more hurtful thing, and it was because of her relationship with him. He loved his sister and had to forgive her, yet right now, he was sorry he'd promised not to confront Aimee. It would help if they could talk it out. But for now, he'd have to deal with this on his own.

"Look, we need to work on the profile," River said. "Can you forget about this for a while?"

Could he? He wasn't certain, but he had to try. He nodded at her. "But first I want to apologize for what Aimee said. Maybe it was because of her pain after the shooting, but it was still inappropriate."

"It's okay. Really." River turned and walked over to the corkboard, appearing to study the photos.

"Wait a minute," he said. "You believe me, don't you? You know I'd never tell my family something like that."

River didn't respond for several seconds, but to him it felt like hours. Could she really think he would do something like that? Finally, she turned around.

"Of course I do." She gave him a smile that made his heart hurt because he could see the pain in her eyes. "I have to admit, for just a moment, I wondered. But that was because of my own insecurity. I know you, Tony, and you're the most honest person I've ever met. Besides, I'm pretty sure you don't want God to suddenly strike you with lightning."

It took a moment for her words to sink in, but then he laughed. Her humor helped to diffuse some of the annoyance he felt toward Aimee.

"I'd really rather you not let her know that I told you." River frowned at him. "But I shouldn't have asked you to promise not to talk to your sister. I'm sorry. The truth is, I don't think it will help anything. In fact, it could make it worse."

"Look, I'll have to discuss this with her sometime, but if it helps, I'll wait until I'm not so upset. And don't worry. We're both Christians. We'll work it out."

"She just really loves you."

"I know that. But that's not an excuse for doing something that could have driven a wedge between us."

"Again," River said gently, "she may believe you told her that. You know that the mind plays tricks on us when there's trauma. Getting angry at her for something she believes really happened won't do either one of you any good."

Could anyone really be this forgiving? A lot of people would want to see Aimee called out for what she'd done—but not River. "I hear you. There's one more thing I want to say about this now, though. Please don't keep things from me. Working together the way we do means we need honesty between us."

"I realize that. That's why I told you."

"But you hesitated," Tony said. "Please, don't do that again, okay?"

She nodded, but he thought he noticed an odd expression flick across her face before she turned back toward the wall. What was that about? Maybe it was his imagination. He wouldn't help the situation by becoming paranoid.

"So, let's get started on this profile," River said.

She pulled a chair up next to the table Ray had provided. Tony took two spiral notebooks off his father's desk, handing one to her and taking the other for himself. They liked to make notes before transferring their main points to the dry-erase board. He sat down in the other chair at the table.

"Go ahead and start," Tony said.

"Repeating what I told your dad, our UNSUB is a man. Probably in his forties or early fifties based on the first murders. He's intelligent and organized. Scopes out his victims ahead of time. He knows how to get inside their houses. He must be strong since he's able to control his victims."

"I agree," Tony said. "Restraining an older woman isn't hard, but in the instance with the couples, my guess is he threatens to hurt one of them so that the remaining partner obeys his instructions."

"He may be killing them and then putting them on the bed," River said. "But he doesn't shoot them. I looked through all of the ME reports. No bullets found at any of the crime scenes. He might have stabbed them or hit them, causing either sharp or blunt-force trauma. The fire destroyed any evidence of that since bones crack and splinter at high temperatures. Also, none of the organs remained, so even though we believe the victims were dead before the fire was set, there's no way to confirm that." She shrugged. "If only the lungs had survived. The medical examiner could tell if they'd breathed in smoke."

"If they were dead, the bodies might not contract as much as they would normally while they burned," Tony added. "But we can't be sure about that either since he bound their ankles and their wrists together with wire."

"Why do that?" River asked. "Why was it so important to him for the bodies to be laid out in that manner? As if they were in a coffin? Like I said earlier, it points to the victims being dead before they were burned. I also think it has to do with remorse. He was showing some respect for the victims, which is another reason I believe they were dead before the fire was started."

Tony nodded. "I agree, but again, arson is about anger. So maybe our UNSUB is a little conflicted?"

River was quiet for a moment. "He believes he is delivering justice more than vengeance?"

Tony turned that idea over in his head. "That makes sense," he said finally. "This guy believes he is some kind of judge and jury. Delivering a deserved sentence. But his personality isn't necessarily a violent one. He feels compelled to carry out this justice."

River leaned forward in her chair, a frown on her face.

"What?" He knew her well enough to see that something wasn't sitting right with her.

"Something doesn't fit."

As he waited for her to explain, it hit him.

"Why is he here?" he asked.

"His psychopathy certainly includes egotistical traits," River said, "but I don't see anything that would make me think that one of his main urges is to try to outsmart the authorities."

"And besides, he wouldn't walk away from his number one goal of bringing justice to engage in some kind of contest with my father."

"So why is he in Burlington?" Tony repeated.

"I don't know," River said, "but if we could help find the answer to that question, your father might be able to stop him."

FIFTEEN

River stood at the window, watching the snow fall. It was beginning to pile up. Tony had checked the weather report, which predicted it would snow throughout the rest of the day and into the morning.

She and Tony hadn't said much after asking why the Snowman was in town. What they could profile about him showed nothing to make them think he would have simply followed Ray here because he wanted to go head-to-head with him. The killer was committed to his calling. Playing games with law enforcement didn't line up with his signature. He saw himself as God, and the guilty had to pay. He would never veer from that goal.

"Maybe it's just a coincidence," Tony said suddenly. "We're so used to seeing something in every move someone makes, we've skipped over the most obvious answer. Burlington isn't that far from Des Moines. I'm sure a lot of people have moved here. Crime increased in Des Moines while my father was there. It's even worse now, so a lot of people have moved away. It's happened across the country. It's one of the reasons housing prices shot up in smaller towns like Burlington. Maybe the Snowman's next victim or victims moved here, and he followed them."

River walked back over to her chair. "That's possible. I mean, your parents moved here for that reason." She pointed at him. "And didn't your father say someone else from the police department transferred here? At least your father can narrow down his list of suspects by looking for other people who relocated here a couple of years ago."

"But what about his next victim?" Tony said. "We're assuming they moved here too?"

"Well, he's killed twice here." She frowned. "So, what does that mean? Maybe he's not hunting individuals. Maybe he's looking for people who have all done something he finds reprehensible? Something he believes makes them worthy of execution?"

Tony nodded. "That's got to be it. It's the only thing that makes any sense, but the problem is that my dad couldn't find anything that connected the victims."

"That's a problem we can't deal with right now," River said. "We have to keep working this, hoping we find that link." She turned to look at Tony. "We know that the UNSUB is narcissistic. Could he see your dad as someone challenging his superiority?"

"So maybe this is a two-for-one deal?"

"I'm not saying it is," River said slowly. "But it's possible." She frowned at him. "I mean, his mission still comes first, don't get me wrong. But remember that this guy is organized. How could he not know that the cop who was injured during his first fire is now a detective in Burlington? Is he aware that your dad is determined to catch him? I can't answer that. Unless he's connected to law enforcement, I'm not sure he could access that information."

"At the same time," Tony said, staring at the photos on the corkboard, "he could probably assume it. For the same reason he would be interested that Dad is here—he could also conclude that Dad would be dedicated to catching him."

"Except that someone was arrested," River said. "Maybe he thinks the heat's off of him?"

"Not possible." Tony walked back over to the table and plopped down. "He's already committed murder here. And he left behind the snowman ornament."

River sighed and slipped into the other chair next to Tony. "You're right. Sorry. I'm a little tired. I didn't sleep well last night."

Tony looked at her with concern. "Any particular reason?"

River had been wrestling with her strange dream all day. She'd finally realized that she had to tell Tony about it.

"I had . . . a weird dream." She took a deep breath and let the details of the dream spill out. When she stopped talking, she studied Tony. Did he think she was losing it?

Tony looked down at the floor for a moment, but when he raised his head, River didn't see anything in his expression that made her think he was taking her dream lightly.

"It's about the children?" he repeated softly. "Could you see the woman with him?"

"I . . . I don't think so. She was more like a presence. I *felt* her, but I couldn't see her clearly. Her face was hidden."

"And she spoke in a whisper?"

River nodded. "Hey, are you putting stock in my dream? I mean, it was just a dream."

"God speaks to us in dreams, River. Especially with some people. I've never had a dream from Him, but my mother has. Several times."

"I . . . I don't know. It might just be your mother's cookies talking."

Tony laughed. "Maybe, but there's something about this that feels . . . real. Regular dreams are usually disjointed. Strange. Full of symbolism. But this is pretty specific."

"But just because I *saw* a woman in the dream, that doesn't mean there are two people behind these homicides."

Tony leaned back in his chair. "That's what we thought about the Salt River Strangler. That there was just one UNSUB. But we turned out to be wrong. I think we need to consider that there could be two people committing these crimes. It would explain why the victims were found in their beds—and no one ever escaped."

"One UNSUB subdues them and the other sets the fire."

"Right."

River studied her partner for a moment before saying, "We can't take something from a dream and make it part of our profile. It's not . . . evidence."

Tony laughed lightly. "Writing a profile isn't based entirely on facts, River. You know that. It's also conjecture. True, we use criminal psychology as the basis of our profiles, but many times they come from our experiences as well."

"But they're certainly not based on dreams." She got up and walked over to the window. It was snowing harder. She felt her body tense. Was the killer out there now? Had he picked his next victims?

Tony got up and joined her at the window. "Look at me," he said gently.

River gazed up into his grey-blue eyes. A lock of his curly black hair lay on his forehead. She fought a desire to push it back.

"God speaks to us in dreams. I know you weren't brought up to believe that, but it's true."

"Then why would God pick me to talk to? I'm not special."

Tony put his hands on her shoulders. "That's not true. You're very special. To God, all His children are special. I don't understand how He decides what gifts He gives to us, but I assure you, He knows what He's doing."

He hesitated for a moment. River could feel his hands touching her. It was as if they radiated warmth. It was disconcerting, but she couldn't pull away.

"River, humility isn't thinking you're worthless. True humility is believing you're who God says you are. His beloved child. His chosen. His anointed. Valuable. Gifted."

"But . . ."

"No buts," Tony said firmly. "It's not based on your works or your goodness. It's based on God living in you. Making you into the person He destined you to be. The Bible mentions God speaking to His people in dreams many, many times. If He wants to use you that way, accept it. Take it seriously."

"And if I'm wrong? If it really was the cookies?"

His eyes seemed to gaze into her soul. "River, do you think the dream really was the result of the cookies?" His hands tightened on her shoulders. "Don't tell me what you think you should say. Tell me what you feel down deep inside. Please."

River could hardly believe the words that came out of her mouth, but she couldn't seem to stop them. "No," she whispered. "It wasn't the cookies."

Tony grinned and let go of her. "I believe that too. It's important and we need to pay attention to it."

"Okay, I give in," she said. "But can I ask one question?"

"Sure."

"Why doesn't God just give me the name of the UNSUB? Wouldn't this be a lot easier?"

Tony laughed. "I wish I could answer that. My guess? He sends us what we can accept. What we have the faith to receive." He shrugged. "I'm afraid the answer to your question is above my spiritual pay grade."

"I figured you'd say something like that," River said. She smiled at him. "So what does 'It's about the children' mean?"

"Well, we know that most serial killers were abused children. So maybe God is telling us that the Snowman endured something horrific as a child. And if he has a partner, maybe she was involved in it somehow."

"That makes sense."

"Let's start writing down some of the things we're thinking," Tony said, going over to the dry-erase board. His father had removed all his own notes so that Tony and River could use it. Tony had just begun to list some of their predictions about the Snowman when there was a knock on the door.

"Come in," River called out.

The door opened slowly, and Beth came in holding an envelope in her hand. "I'm so sorry to interrupt, but something was delivered for you, River," she said. "I wasn't sure if it was important so I thought I should bring it to you."

River took the envelope from Beth's hand. "Thank you," she said.

Beth nodded. "Dinner will be at six. I won't bother you again."

"You're not a bother, Mom," Tony said. "You can come in whenever you want."

"I just don't want to interrupt you." She smiled at them. "How about some fresh coffee? Maybe some cookies or cake?"

Tony laughed. "It's a good thing neither one of us is diabetic."

Beth shook her head. "Funny. I like to bake. Shoot me."

Tony walked over and kissed his mother on the cheek. "I really don't think we need to take it that far. I think some hot coffee and a few of your wonderful cookies will give us just the boost we need. Thanks, Mom."

Beth playfully slapped Tony's shoulder. "You're incorrigible. I'll be right back."

She left the room, pulling the door shut.

River stared at the envelope in her hand. She felt cold inside.

"What's wrong?" Tony asked, walking over to where she stood. "Maybe it's a Christmas card from your mother."

River shook her head. "I only gave them this address yesterday before we left. How could a card get here so fast? Besides, this isn't my mother's writing—or Mrs. Weyland's."

"I'm sure it's nothing to worry about," Tony said. "Open it."

River pulled the envelope open and pulled out a Christmas card. The front of the blue-and-white card showed a snowman standing in a snowstorm. The outside read, "Merry Christmas." When she opened the card, she read the inside, which said, "Warm Winter Wishes." Below that someone had written, "I predict a very warm Christmas. Happy hunting!" It was signed, "Your Salt River Friend."

River barely felt the card slip from her hand and fall to the floor.

SIXTEEN

iver!" Tony said, grabbing her as she wobbled. He led her over to her chair and helped her sit down. Then he went back and picked up the card. As he read it, he felt as if his blood had suddenly turned cold. He looked over at River and realized his reaction was important. He couldn't let her know how much this upset him. He pulled the other chair next to her and took her hand in his. "Listen, he's just trying to rattle you. Don't give him the satisfaction."

"Tony, this isn't the time to worry about how I'm handling this. This guy knows about the Snowman. And he knows where your parents live. They're in danger."

Tony looked down at the envelope and the card in his other hand. Then he shook his head. "The envelope was stamped in St. Louis. I don't believe he's here. If he were, he'd want us to know it."

"But how does he know we're staying with your mother and father in Burlington? Tony, he must have followed us. There's no other explanation."

"Yeah, there is. Following us wouldn't have told him anything about the Snowman. I hate to think this, but I have to wonder if he bugged our office."

"But . . ."

"He could have come in when we were out. I'm going to call Arnie and have him check it out. He's got people working for him who know what to look for."

"But even if he did bug the office, he still could have followed us here."

"Don't you think I kept a watch out for that?" he said. "We weren't followed. I'm sure of it."

"But he has this address . . ." River's eyes sought his. "You have to warn your parents. I mean it. They deserve to know."

"Okay. I'll talk to my dad. But I can tell you right now that he won't be worried. He's got a state-of-the-art security system as well as a small arsenal. In his line of work, he's very careful to make sure he and my mother are safe."

"Maybe we should go to a hotel."

Tony put the card on the floor and took her other hand as well. "I really appreciate that you care about my parents, but if I suggest that, my father will have a fit. We're safer here than anywhere else we could be."

River sighed. "Oh, Tony. If anything happened to them because of me . . ."

"It won't. Please, trust me. Everything will be okay."

There was a knock at the door, and Tony stood. "Don't say anything to my mom. I'll talk to my dad after I call Arnie, okay?"

River nodded, but the look on her face hurt him. Her concern for his parents endeared her to him, but he felt strongly that the Strangler's partner had a longer endgame. One he'd already mapped out. Going after them in Burlington wasn't it. He was somewhere in St. Louis, and the attempt to complete what the Strangler had started would happen there. His ego wouldn't allow him to share the stage with the Snowman. The Strangler's protégé wanted all the glory for killing River Ryland to go to his master.

Tony went over and opened the door. His mother stood there with a tray.

"Here you go," she said with a smile.

Tony took the tray from her hands. "Thanks, Mom," he said. "We really appreciate it."

"I'm so happy you're here," she said, her voice breaking a little. She cleared her throat, trying to cover her reaction. "Sorry. Bit of a frog in my throat today. Must be the weather."

It wasn't the weather. He'd already promised to come home more often, and he intended to keep his word. He'd been so focused on River that he'd pushed his mother aside. The idea that he'd caused her pain, even inadvertently, made him feel terrible. She was a wonderful mother and deserved better.

She turned quickly and walked away. He was certain she was trying to hide her tears. He didn't say anything because the last thing River needed right now was to feel guilty because he hadn't visited more often.

He brought the tray in and set it on his dad's desk. Then he picked up River's empty cup and filled it with hot coffee. His mother had added some small paper plates to the tray, so he put a couple of cookies on one, picked up a napkin, and set everything on the table where River sat.

"Thank you," she said. "Your mother is . . . Well, you're very blessed. I hope you know that."

Hearing River voice almost exactly what he'd been thinking should have surprised him, but it didn't. More and more, they seemed to be able to read each other's thoughts. It was comforting, if not a little disconcerting sometimes.

"I want to ask my dad to come in here," Tony said. "We have to tell him about the card. Even though I truly believe we're all safe, you're right. He needs to know."

River nodded and took a sip of her coffee before saying, "I was thinking. The Strangler's protégé is so narcissistic that I don't think he'd want to hurt me here. This is the Snowman's territory. He wouldn't want to share the glory with someone else. He already stopped someone else from killing me. He wants the credit."

Tony stared at her for a moment before saying, "I was just thinking the very same thing. I really wish you'd stop reading my mind. We know it can't be completely trusted."

Even though the situation wasn't funny, River smiled. "I trust your mind." She took another sip of coffee then said, "Have your parents asked about your symptoms?"

"The aphasia?" He shook his head. "No, and I haven't brought it up. It's gotten so much better. I rarely forget things now." He cocked his head to the side. "I'm sorry. What was your name again?"

This time River laughed. "You really are a pill, you know that? You're the only person in the world who could actually make me laugh right now."

Tony sighed loudly. "It's my burden to bear in life. Keeping you entertained." He smiled at her. "Let's finish these cookies, and then I'll ask my dad to step in." He looked up at the clock on the wall. "We only have a couple of hours before supper. Why don't we put a pin in this after we talk to my father and I call Arnie? It will give us time to rest and unwind a bit."

"I'd like that. Tomorrow we can start early." She sighed. "Sure is convenient to have the chief of police in St. Louis as a friend. We've certainly given Arnie a workout lately. I hope he doesn't get impatient with us." She glanced toward the window, and he followed her gaze. The lights from outside the house made the snowflakes sparkle as they waltzed to music only they could hear. It would have been beautiful if it weren't for the concern that the Snowman could strike tonight. Of course, just because it had been two years since the last murders, that didn't mean it would happen again this winter. Maybe he was letting his fear and his father's paranoia get the best of him?

"It will be all right," he said softly. "Don't worry."

"It's hard not to. I usually love snow. But tonight . . ."

"I know."

Tony ate two of the cookies and then took his cell phone out of his pocket. A few minutes later his father knocked on the office door.

This wasn't a conversation he looked forward to having.

SEVENTEEN

I reached under the table and touched my backpack. I'd checked and rechecked it before I left my apartment. I was ready. I turned my head to watch the snow falling past the window. It called to me, like an old friend, urging me to fulfill the thing I'd been called to do. The thing that had to be done. I put my hand in my pocket, and my fingers closed around the ornament.

"Relax. You're prepared."

I nodded at her. "I know. Sometimes I feel a little nervous, though. Everything's got to go just right."

"It will. It always has."

"Except for the first time."

"Let's not talk about that," she said, her voice barely audible above the Christmas music playing in the background.

"Can I get you anything else, sir?"

The waitress's voice startled me. I glanced at the clock. There was still plenty of time.

"How about a piece of apple pie with some ice cream?" I asked.

"Absolutely. Let me get that plate out of your way. I'll be right back."

As she reached for my dish, I noticed her brightly painted fingers. Red. The color of sin. I almost grabbed the plate out of her hand, but I stopped myself. The waitress wasn't my responsibility. If she needed judgment, it wouldn't come from me.

I held my breath as she walked away. For the first time, I noticed her perfume. Cloying. Like rotting flowers. It made me want to gag. My father would have called her a name I don't like. One he'd called my mother many times.

"How could you let her get near you?"

I shook my head. "Not our problem. I've got to concentrate on tonight. Please don't say anything that might sidetrack me."

"Don't get testy," she said. "You know what happens when you get angry. You make mistakes."

"Then don't make me angry."

Her sudden silence made me feel guilty. She was my responsibility. I had to take care of her. The truth was, this was all for her.

"I'm sorry," I said softly, looking around at the other people in the diner. I didn't want to attract attention.

"It's okay. Maybe I should leave."

"Not yet. You inspire me. I don't know if I could do this without you."

She was quiet for a moment, but then she offered me a small smile. "All right. I'll stay."

I sipped my coffee and a few minutes later the waitress brought my pie. I ignored her gaudy, sinful hands and dove into my dessert with gusto. Tonight would bring judgment. And after this punishment, I would finally carry out my most important assignment. Two birds with one stone.

And it would be glorious.

RAY READ THE CARD his son had given him and frowned. "You shouldn't have handled this," he said. "There might be fingerprints."

"Sorry," Tony said. "You're right. I know better. I wasn't thinking."

Ray reached over and took a napkin from his desk. Then he used it to look over the card carefully. "I'll get an evidence bag. Then we'll have our evidence technician, Lyndon Perry, take a look at it."

"You can do that," River said, "but he won't find anything. This guy would never slip up that way."

"We have to try," he said. "Used to be stamps were licked. Even the most careful criminal forgot about them. They know the envelope is handled by lots of people and the police rarely find anything on them. But they forgot about their spit." He shrugged. "Now they all have adhesive. Might be more convenient, but it doesn't help law enforcement at all." He looked up at his son. "I think you need to tell me who this guy is and how long he's been in contact with you." Tony knew his father well enough to recognize the tone in his voice. He was now head detective Ray St. Clair, and he was upset that he was just learning about a threat against his son and his partner. In most ways, his relationship with his father was based more on friendship now that Tony was an adult. But if he was hurt or in danger, that friendship was put on the shelf, and the father came out. This was one of those moments.

"I didn't tell you because . . . well, what could you do?" Tony said. "The police chief in St. Louis knows all about it. He keeps both of us under surveillance and if we need help, he's promised that the police will be dispatched immediately. My place has a security system as does River's house. We're both armed, and I'm very careful." He looked over at River, who was calmer but clearly shaken. "I watched carefully to make sure we weren't followed, Dad. I'm confident that he's in St. Louis. This guy knows about the Snowman, and he won't tread on his territory. He wants River all to himself. He's severely narcissistic."

Ray didn't say anything for a moment. Then he leaned back in his desk chair and stared at the both of them before saying, "If you leave this house, I want you to be extremely careful. Watch your six. I'd like to tell you to stay inside, but I know you won't. Besides, I trust your instincts. I'm going to have to tell your mother that there is a threat, although I don't think I want to mention the Strangler to her. She had nightmares for weeks after you were hurt. I'll just say that someone has threatened me. It's happened before, and we have a good system to make sure we're safe. She's used to it. No one's ever gotten into our house or anywhere near us. My chief might not be certain about the Snowman, but he runs a tight department. We catch almost everyone eventually."

Tony couldn't help but think about the fact that crime in Burlington wasn't anywhere near what St. Louis dealt with, but he still had complete faith in his father. He was the best law enforcement officer he'd ever known.

"Okay, Dad. I'm sorry to bring this here. Even though I'm convinced this guy isn't in town, I realize we have to be careful. I hope this won't affect your Christmas."

Ray laughed, and Tony noticed River looking at him in surprise. Laughter didn't seem to fit the occasion.

"Tony, you know your mother. She had Christmas squared away weeks ago. She bought Christmas gifts in July—and put up the decorations the day after Thanksgiving. Trust me, she wouldn't allow anything to disrupt Christmas. Not even a serial killer."

Tony shook his head and then grinned at River. "He's right," he said.

"I'd barely finished my turkey before she had me up on a ladder, hanging the lights and getting the outside decorations in place," Ray said. He looked at River, concern on his face. "Don't worry. You're safe. We're safe. Everything will be fine. But in the meantime, I'm going to get this card down to the station. See what we can find."

"I'm going with you," Tony said. "If any of us have to leave, we need to go with someone."

"And leave the women here alone?" Ray said. "No. I need you to stay here and keep them safe. I'll be all right."

"I don't like that, Dad."

Ray got up from behind his desk and came over to where Tony sat. He put his hand on his son's shoulder. "I'll ask the station to have officers drive by here frequently. The office is only eight minutes away from here. I'll call you when I get there, and I'll ask a patrol car to follow me home. Okay?"

"I guess."

Ray frowned at him. "You said you don't think this guy is in Burlington. So why are you so worried?"

Tony had to ask himself the same question. "I . . . I guess it's because we missed an accomplice when we wrote the original profile. We believed the Strangler was too egotistical to work with a partner. I still don't quite understand how we overlooked it."

"I . . . I've been thinking about that," River said. "The guy . . . the one who sent the card . . . he's obsessed with making certain I die the way the Strangler intended. What if his obsession isn't with me? What if it's with Joseph Baker? Maybe he's so dedicated to him . . . and to his cause . . . that he feels compelled to carry out his master's intentions."

Tony let the idea roll over in his mind. "He stopped another killer from taking your life, not because he was angry with you for thwarting the Strangler's plan, but so he could please the man who really matters to him?"

"That sounds right to me," Ray said. "I'm not a behavioral analyst like you, but I've seen a lot during my almost three decades in law enforcement, and this kind of obsession? We had a couple in Des Moines who decided they wanted police officers dead. They shot two of us before we took the man down in a shootout. His girlfriend attacked two more patrol officers after her boyfriend was dead. When we caught her, we asked her why she didn't run. Her response was that she had to carry out her

113

dead partner's wishes. It was what she lived for. She wasn't killing officers because of her hate for them, she only wanted to please her boyfriend even though he was gone."

"Did the officers live?" River asked.

Ray shook his head. "We lost two good officers in the first shooting. Thankfully, both officers in the second shooting lived. Unfortunately, one is spending his life in a wheelchair. The other one recovered completely."

"I think we were so surprised to find that the Strangler wasn't working alone," River said so softly that Tony could barely hear her, "we didn't think it through well enough."

"Except that you did bring up the idea of partners when we first started working on the profile," Tony said with a sigh. "I talked you out of it."

River smiled at him. "If I allowed you to change my mind, it was because I decided you were right. You know better than to believe you could send me in a different direction if I was convinced I was right. Sometimes when we wrote profiles, we just threw out anything to see if it would stick. That was the only reason I mentioned the idea."

"You're correct about the first thing you said," Tony said. "You're the most stubborn person I've ever known. I can't get you to change your mind if you're sure you're right. Nobody can."

"It's true, Smooshy."

Tony pointed his finger at his father. "This is all your fault, you know."

Ray laughed and put his hands in the air. "Don't blame me. Your mother let the cat out of the bag."

"But you didn't try to stop her," Tony said.

"Seems like River and your mother have a lot in common. We can't control them, son."

Tony sighed dramatically. "You're right. It's our burden to bear."

Ray laughed and walked over to the door, the card and the

envelope grasped in his hand, the napkin keeping his fingers from touching it. "I'll be back in time for supper."

"Remember to call me," Tony said. He trusted his father, but even though he still believed the Strangler's accomplice was in St. Louis, he couldn't help but worry.

"I will. I'll set the alarm before I leave. There are cameras that cover the first two floors. I'll email you an invitation to tap into them. Download the app onto your phone and you can check them. If there is any movement, inside or outside, the system will alert you."

"Thanks, Dad. I think River and I are going to call it a day. A little rest before supper sounds great."

"Good idea," Ray said.

"And I'll stay here with Mom and River since you asked me to, but if you don't call within thirty minutes after you leave, I'll be in the car and headed to the station. You have my word on that."

"And he says you're the stubborn one," Ray said with a sigh as he left the room.

Tony smiled at River. "Let's go. If you're not too tired, we could put on *It's a Wonderful Life* and watch it until supper's ready. I'll bet Mom could even whip up some of her special hot chocolate."

"Sounds like heaven," River said, getting up from her chair.

Even though he'd done everything he could to reassure River, as they walked out of his dad's office, Tony couldn't stop feeling as if evil were stirring somewhere close by and that it would soon rear its ugly head.

EIGHTEEN

Ray was true to his word and called Tony when he got to the station. He'd told Beth that there had been a vague threat and made it clear that she needed to make certain their security system was activated. She didn't seem overly concerned. Ray appeared to have been right when he said she was used to the kinds of situations that unfortunately plagued many in law enforcement.

Sure enough, she made them hot chocolate and joined them to watch the movie. Tony stayed upstairs for a few minutes after River joined Beth in the living room. She assumed it was because he was calling Arnie. When Tony finally joined them, he suggested asking Aimee to come over, but Beth told them she'd gone out with some friends for dinner. Besides, there were at least a couple of inches of snow on the ground. Although it wasn't very dangerous yet, it could get worse later, and Beth didn't want her driving in it. River was relieved. Knowing how Aimee felt about her still bothered her. She'd tried to put it out of her mind and concentrate on the profile since that was the reason they were here, but it wasn't that easy. She wanted to defend herself, but she couldn't. Aimee was convinced that it was River's fault they were on the riverbank that night. She wasn't angry with Aimee. She understood enough about the human mind to know that people who have experienced trauma can create scenarios they're certain have actually happened. But they're false memories built out of fear. Fear is a powerful emotion. Once someone allows it into their mind, it can create havoc. River was convinced that Aimee needed someone to blame for what happened to Tony. His partner was the only logical one. Aimee couldn't blame her beloved brother.

She and Tony were still both concerned about David Prescott, the man who happened upon Baker's attack on them that night and called the police. His testimony was crucial to Baker's conviction, and now he'd disappeared, just like Jacki. Where was he? Had Baker's accomplice hurt him? Killed him? Or was he so spooked by what happened that he'd gone into hiding? River wasn't convinced of that. He hadn't contacted his family, and they were worried sick about him. Jacki's body had never been found, so if the accomplice had killed Prescott as retribution for helping River and Tony, it was possible they'd never find his body either.

River fought to concentrate on the movie. She loved Jimmy Stewart. *It's a Wonderful Life* was one of her favorite Christmas movies. It would have been really relaxing, sitting in the St. Clairs' family room, a fire crackling in the large fireplace, and watching through windows that almost reached the ceiling as the snow came down—if only the snow hadn't taken on a sinister meaning tonight. River gazed around the beautiful family room. It was tastefully decorated for the holidays, greenery lining the mantel and flickering electric candles woven within the boughs.

The pillows on the large couch were Christmas themed and the hearth held an entire Christmas village with lights shining through the tiny windows. On the floor in front of the hearth, a Christmas train chugged its way along the track with Santa at the wheel and the elves riding along, a bag of toys filling one of the train cars.

The Christmas tree almost reached the ceiling, and the tiny

gold lights highlighted ornaments that had to have been in the family for years. Each one was clearly special.

They had just reached the part in the movie where Uncle Billy realizes he's misplaced the deposit for the bank when Ray returned home.

"How about some hot chocolate, honey?" Beth said when he walked into the living room.

"Sounds great," he said with a smile. "It's getting colder outside. We're supposed to dip below twenty degrees tonight. I'd say we're definitely on our way."

"You all drink your hot chocolate and relax," Beth said. "We'll have dinner after the movie."

"Are you sure, Mom?" Tony asked. "We can take a break from the movie, eat supper, and then come back. We don't want to mess up what you have planned."

Beth smiled at him. "I've got chicken and noodles in the crock pot. I'll just put them on warm. They'll keep just fine." She frowned slightly. "Unless anyone's too hungry to wait."

Tony laughed. "We're so full of cookies and hot chocolate, we can definitely wait a bit."

"I'm sorry," Beth said, her smile slipping. "Have I overdone it?"

Ray walked over and put his arms around his wife. "You're creating a lovely Christmas, sweetheart. Besides, everyone puts on a pound or two during the holidays. It's expected."

His teasing made her laugh. "I'll be right back with your hot chocolate."

"Thanks. Then you sit down and enjoy the movie," Ray said. "And when it's over, I'll warm up the rolls and make the salad, okay? You've done enough."

"And Tony and I will do the dishes," River said. "You really don't need to wait on us, Beth. Let us do our fair share."

Beth blushed, her face turning pink. "Oh, pishposh. I like taking care of my family. I've missed having people in the house."

"Gee, thanks," Ray said with a grin. "Just what am I?"

Beth waved her hand at him. "You know what I mean. Now sit down. I'll be right back."

When she was out of earshot, Ray walked over to the couch and sat down. "I turned the card over to our evidence technician. He's looking for fingerprints and DNA."

"I know I said this already," River said, "but I really don't think you'll find anything."

"You know as well as I do that wearing gloves isn't a guarantee that an UNSUB won't leave behind something we can use to track him with. If he sneezed. If he coughed. If an eyelash fell out. . . . Lots of ways we can find something to track him."

"You're right," River said with a sigh. "Maybe I'm giving this guy too much credit."

"Like we told you, we never profiled this case as involving two UNSUBs," Tony said to his dad. "Once we knew there was someone else out there, we decided he was serving Baker—but was the weaker partner. Someone who would stay in the shadows." He met River's gaze. "We were wrong . . . again. We just can't let down our guard with this guy. Sending that card. . . . Well, he isn't shy. And if he got into our office . . ."

"I have to agree with you," Ray said. "He could be more dangerous than you thought. Of course, maybe harassing you will be the extent of it."

"I hope you're right," River said. She swung her gaze toward Tony. "Did you call Arnie?"

He nodded. "I also called the building manager and told him to let the police into our office. We should hear something back before long." He looked at his father. "Dad, I really think we should tell Mom what's going on," he said, keeping his voice low. "I don't like keeping this from her."

Ray sighed. "I know. Let's finish the movie and have dinner. I'll talk to her after you two turn in, okay?"

"All right," Tony said. "She's a lot stronger than you give her credit for, Dad."

"I know she's tough," Ray replied. "I just hate that she has to deal with this stuff." He took a deep breath and let it out slowly. "It's the main reason I'm retiring. She wants to travel. Spend more time with me. I'd say after everything she's been through because of my job, she deserves to have some years where she can stop worrying about me and really enjoy herself, don't you?"

Tony nodded. "Of course, I do. We'll all feel better when you retire."

"I'm relieved you've left the FBI," Ray said slowly. "When you were shot . . ." He stopped and cleared his throat before going on. "The look on your mother's face when we got the news." He looked at Tony, his eyes shiny with unshed tears. "I never want to see that look again, son. Please be careful."

"We will, Dad. You have my word."

River was moved by the relationship between Tony and his dad. She couldn't help but think about her own father, who had betrayed his family. Now he wanted to be reconciled with his children. Why did she keep thinking about him? She purposely pushed thoughts about her father out of her mind as Beth came back into the room with a cup of hot chocolate for Ray.

They started the movie up again, and River leaned back into the overstuffed chair where she sat. With the fire dancing in the fireplace, snow falling past the windows, and George Bailey finding redemption and love in the midst of bitter circumstances, River finally began to relax. Surely on a night like this, evil would stay hidden in the dark, unable to slither out into a world where people were enjoying the beauty of the Christmas holiday.

Of course, she knew that evil loved beauty because its destruction brought incredible joy.

CHAPTER
NINETEEN

Supper was delicious and once again River ate too much. She enjoyed the easy camaraderie that the St. Clairs shared. Obviously, they'd faced their share of trials—Ray's injuries, Ray's sister's violent rape, Tony's shooting—but through it all they'd bonded. Unlike her family, which had fallen into painful pieces. River was certain that Tony's family's strong faith was the key to their closeness and their ability to weather the storms of life. Instead of the judgmental religious spirit she'd been raised with, the St. Clairs operated in the love and grace River now saw in the Scriptures. Although she wasn't certain she'd ever get married, if she did, this was the kind of family she wanted.

When she and Tony went upstairs to bed, Ray followed them. He called them into his office and shut the door.

"I heard from Lyndon, our evidence tech," he said.

"Did he find anything?" Tony asked.

Ray shook his head. "River was right. There was nothing to work with. I'm sorry."

Although she wasn't surprised, River was still disappointed. This was one time she wished she'd been wrong.

They said good-night, and River headed to her bedroom. She

wanted to take a shower, but she was so tired she decided to do it in the morning. She wasn't sure why she felt so exhausted. It was probably just stress.

Before getting into bed, she called home and talked to Mrs. Weyland.

"We're doin' great," she told River. "I made corned beef and cabbage for supper even though your mother swore she wouldn't eat it."

"Yeah, she's always said she hates it."

"Well, she ate two helpings and made me promise I'd heat some up for lunch tomorrow."

River laughed. "If you can get Rose Ryland to eat corned beef and cabbage, you can do anything."

Mrs. Weyland's sigh came through River's phone. "If I really could do anything, I'd make this terrible disease disappear."

River was surprised to feel tears in her eyes. Her mother's care-giver was right. Alzheimer's was a cruel disease, and she hated it with all her being.

"If you need anything, let me know," River said, trying to swallow the lump in her throat. "And remember to keep the security system armed."

"I will, but don't you worry. We'll be fine. We have some mighty big angels watchin' out for us."

"I know," River said. "Still, I'm sorry you even have to think about this."

"You know, I really don't, honey. My security, and your mother's, comes from God. I gave that to Him when I moved in here. And besides our angels, the police drive by here frequently. I think the neighbors are startin' to wonder why. Maybe they think we're up to somethin' shady." She laughed lightly. "But it's put them on their guard as well. We might be the safest house around for miles and miles."

River smiled. She was upset when Hannah left. She'd certainly understood, but at the time, River couldn't imagine how they'd get by without her. Yet in her place, God had sent an elderly, gray-haired warrior. Just what she and her mother needed right now.

River said goodbye and disconnected the call. She and Tony planned to leave this weekend. That would give River a week before Christmas to decorate the house and finish her shopping. She'd bought her mother several things and had found a beautiful Bible cover for Mrs. Weyland. Her cover was falling apart. She still hadn't purchased anything for Tony. He was so difficult to buy for. He was a typical man. Supposedly, he didn't need anything.

She lay down on the bed, still clothed. Her thoughts went immediately to Aimee. What should she do? It was likely that she would see her again before they went home. Should she call her and try to work things out? Or should she just leave it alone?

As she stared up at the ceiling, thoughts bombarded her mind. Aimee, the Snowman, the Strangler's partner . . . Also, Jacki's face as well as David Prescott's kept coming to her. Jacki was obviously killed by Baker. He'd used her to lure them in. But what about David? If he really was dead, it had to be at the hands of Baker's partner. Was it his idea, or was he getting orders from Baker? Joseph Baker was in prison and was watched closely. Every piece of mail was scrutinized. Every call listened to. Prison officials had been alerted about Baker's partner, but they couldn't find any communication between the two. She and Tony knew it happened all the time, though. Secret codes were given to relatives or messages were sent out through other inmates. Especially those getting out of prison. The last time Arnie checked, though, Baker hadn't made any friends. He stayed isolated from everyone. And there hadn't been any visitors. So, if he was sending instructions to someone, it was being done in some way that had escaped the warden's radar. Unless someone at the prison figured it out, there wasn't much they could do. So far, Baker's partner didn't seem to be following any kind of pattern they'd expected, which made the situation even more difficult.

Knowing that she and Tony had been wrong and that it had almost cost them their lives had shaken them both. Besides the physical and emotional trauma they'd suffered, the loss of faith in their ability to accurately profile Baker had made it easier to leave the FBI.

River sighed loudly. This was getting her nowhere. She needed to sleep. They'd be at it again tomorrow. But this time, there wouldn't be any lunches with Aimee or tours of Burlington. She needed to clear her mind so she could concentrate only on the profile. There were too many voices in her head, competing for space. And then there was the dream. *Look for the children. It's for them.* At least Tony hadn't treated her like she needed psychiatric help.

She forced herself to get up and change into her sweats and T-shirt. Then she climbed back into bed. Maybe tomorrow things would be clearer.

TWENTY

iver was having some strange dream about shopping with her mother in a store that only sold miniature animals when Rose turned to her and began calling her name. River tried to tell her that she was standing right next to her and that she didn't need to keep repeating her name over and over when she realized it wasn't her mother's voice she was hearing. It was Tony's. She opened her eyes and found him standing over the bed. Thankfully, she'd left the lamp on the nightstand on. If she hadn't, his presence might have frightened her.

"River, I need you to wake up," he said, touching her arm.

"What . . . what's wrong?" She sat up and looked over at the bedside clock. Two-twenty in the morning?

Tony sat down on the edge of the bed and ran his hand through his hair. He was wearing sweats just like her but while her T-shirt had a picture of Scooby-Doo, he wore an FBI sweatshirt. He looked upset.

"There's been a fire. Dad got a call about it. They're saying it's arson."

"Is it . . . is it the Snowman?" The fog of sleep was finally beginning to clear a bit.

"Looks like it. But something unusual has happened. Dad thinks it could finally lead us to finding the man responsible."

Now she was wide awake. "What do you mean?"

"I'm not sure. Dad wouldn't tell me. He should be home soon. I'm sure we'll get more details then. If you want to go back to sleep, I can wake you when he gets here. Or maybe you want to wait until the morning. . . ?"

River grinned at him. "You know me better than that." She turned in bed and swung her legs over the other side. Then she got to her feet. "I need to run a brush through my hair. I'll join you . . . in the office?"

"Mom is up and has coffee on in the kitchen. Is that okay?"

River tried to stifle a yawn but failed. "That's perfect. Coffee's exactly what I need right now."

Tony got up and went to the door. "I'll meet you down there."

After he pulled the door shut and left, River checked herself out in the mirror that hung over the chest of drawers. Not too bad. She found her brush and ran it through her hair a few times. Then she slid her feet into her slippers. They were more like shoes than slippers. She took off her T-shirt, put on her bra, and then pulled on her FBI hoodie and zipped it up. If Tony was going to wear his FBI sweatshirt, she had to lose the comic book T-shirt. Then she headed toward the stairs, stopping by the bathroom first.

When she reached the kitchen, she found Beth and Tony sitting at the kitchen table, talking softly. When Beth glanced up and saw River, she smiled.

"Coffee?" she asked.

"If you want me to make any sense at this hour, I think that's a good idea," River said.

Beth laughed and got to her feet. "We need you to have your wits about you. Ray will be home before long. He got called out earlier because of a fire. He seems to think he'll have some good information for you."

Tony pulled out the chair next to him and motioned for River to sit down. She slid into the chair. "Okay, so now that I'm actually conscious, repeat what Ray told you, okay?"

"He said that the Snowman had struck again," Tony said, "but that this time he'd made a mistake. He believes that it's something significant and could help us to finally discover the Snowman's identity."

"How does he know this is really the Snowman?"

Tony took his phone out of his pocket and clicked on something. Then he scrolled down and handed her his phone. River saw a house that had flames shooting through the roof. The fire department was there, trying to put it out.

"Look at the next picture," Tony said.

River did what he said. There, on a tree near the street, was the same kind of snowman ornament that they'd seen at the other crime scenes.

"He has to place them outside the house the same night he strikes," she said. "Otherwise, the homeowner would notice the ornament."

"They might assume someone in the neighborhood put it there," Tony said.

River shook her head. "Too risky. I think this is part of his ritual."

"But isn't he taking a chance of being seen?" Beth asked, frowning. "Aren't most of the ornaments hung on trees near the street?"

"When there's one available," Tony said. "People have outside cameras, but Dad never mentioned catching the Snowman on one. He definitely would have brought it up if it had happened."

"I agree," River said. "But Beth's right. Why hasn't anyone reported seeing him?"

Tony shrugged. "Middle of the night? People are asleep?"

"Take it from someone who has a hard time getting to sleep,"

Beth said. "I think it's a good chance someone saw something. Maybe they just didn't realize what it meant."

"But again, Dad would know that."

"Not necessarily." Beth handed River and Tony their coffee. "Hope you don't mind my two cents, but I've been married to a cop for a lot of years. You pick up things."

"Why do you say he might not know about a possible witness to these murders?" River asked.

Beth sat down at the table. "Ray was just a beat cop when the first killings in Des Moines happened. The police chief didn't share the details of the case with him—or any beat cop. Only with the detectives assigned to the case. Yes, he has copies of the paperwork filed with the case sent by a friend, but that doesn't mean that his friend had access to everything. Especially if the chief or the detectives missed something they shouldn't have. Those things have a history of disappearing. That doesn't mean that's what happened there. I'm not saying that, but still, it's possible. They had no idea they had a serial killer until the second murder. Same modus operandi, and the same ornament outside. They were working hard to investigate when the copycat struck. The chief wanted a big win in his corner. So, he accused Arlen Thacker of all three incidents. They only prosecuted the third one since it meant life in prison, and they had no evidence for the other murders that pointed to Thacker. As I'm sure you know, this happens frequently. The only person who believed the first two fires were set by someone else was your father. Even the friend who sent him the information copied from the files chose to attribute all the murders to Thacker. Still, he respects your father, so he risked his career to get the records to Ray."

"And Ray promised to not tell anyone who sent the files?" River asked.

Beth nodded. "So, anything he learns that might help to connect the killings will have to come through whatever happens here."

"Mom, what do you really think about the Snowman coming here after you and Dad moved?" Tony asked.

"I don't know," Beth said with a sigh. "I know enough about these killers to realize that he can't ignore his obsession and focus on Ray . . . but the coincidence is incredibly strange." She smiled at them. "I think that's one of the reasons Ray asked you both here. He believes, as do I, that you have the training and instinct to answer that question."

River and Tony had already discussed the situation, and they both believed that, as Beth said, the Snowman was incapable of abandoning his self-assigned mission just to go after Ray. But at the same time, River had to wonder if Ray was seen as someone trying to stop him from carrying out his destiny. Could he have added Ray to the group he'd judged and planned to execute? She didn't want to believe that, but maybe ignoring the possibility was a mistake.

"I hope we can give him what he wants," Tony said, "but as we told him, profiling is really just educated guessing. And if Dad really does have a way to find out who the Snowman is, he might not even need us."

"I think you're more valuable to him than you think," Beth said. "There are a lot of evil people in prison because of you. Even if he doesn't need your profile, you can help him in other ways. If he can't get Des Moines to cooperate, he'll need to find a way to connect the murders without using the files he has."

"I hope we can assist him if he needs us," Tony said. "But behavioral analysts really don't put people in prison, Mom. Besides, how would Dad know about our cases? It's not common knowledge who works what case. The FBI doesn't share that information."

Beth laughed lightly. "Your father is a detective, son. Even though you couldn't always tell him about the cases you worked, you're pretty easy to read. He could almost always tie your reactions to crimes around the country to cases that included an

FBI presence. When you were really intense and busy, he knew you were concentrating on something important. Then when you were relaxed, laughed, and were in a good mood, he'd connect it to the capture of someone really bad."

"So, my father is profiling *me*?" Tony shook his head. "Great. And here I thought I was complicated and deep."

His comment made Beth and River both laugh.

"Not even a little," River said.

Tony took a sip of his coffee and then let go a long, dramatic sigh. "A prophet is without honor in his own family."

"So now you're a prophet?" River said, grinning.

"No. I just . . ."

Tony stopped when they all heard a noise from outside. The next sounds were clearly car doors being shut. Then the front door opened, and cold air swept down the hallway. After that, a pause and a series of beeps. It was Ray, coming inside and resetting the alarm. No one talked until he came around the corner and into the kitchen where they all waited. He looked surprised to find them all sitting at the kitchen table. From behind him, another man walked into the room. He was tall, with graying hair and a matching beard.

"I told Tony not to wake everyone up," Ray said to Beth.

"It's not Tony's fault," Beth said. "I'd gone back to sleep after you left, but then I heard his phone ring and figured it was you. Who else would be phoning at two o'clock in the morning? Tony woke River because he was certain she'd want to know what was going on."

Ray shook his head. "I should have known." He pointed to the man next to him. "This is Bobby Truman," he said to Tony and River. "He used to work with me in Des Moines. My son, Tony, and his partner, River Ryland."

"Nice to meet you."

"You too," Tony said.

"Hi, Bobby," Beth said with a smile.

"Hello, Beth. I won't stay long. I just wanted to make sure Ray got home okay. It's slick out there."

"Bobby only lives a few blocks from here," Ray said to Tony and River.

"At least have a cup of coffee with us?" Beth asked Bobby.

"If you're sure it won't be any trouble. Just black, please."

"No trouble at all. Ray?"

"No, thanks, honey. I'm beat. I just need to sleep."

"Not before you tell us what's going on," Tony said.

Ray slumped down into a chair. River could see how tired he was and felt a little guilty about making him talk to them now. But the truth was, she was itching to know what had happened. It was hard to disconnect from a case like this.

Even though he was clearly weary, Ray smiled. "Something went wrong tonight," he said. "The Snowman's plan failed. For the first time, we have a witness."

TWENTY-ONE

What do you mean?" Tony asked. "Someone saw him?"

"Yes, but you might be surprised to know who the witness is."

Ray rubbed his face as if trying to keep himself awake. Then he said, "I can't explain exactly why it went wrong, but a woman named Sandra Cooper was attacked in her home this evening. Someone surprised her while she was in bed. She was injected with something that made her confused and disoriented, but she managed to stay conscious. Thankfully, she had the presence of mind to play dead. After about ten minutes, the person in her bedroom bound her hands and ankles with wire and then poured gasoline on the floor around her bed. Then he struck a match. Thankfully, he left the room before it was fully engulfed. She was able to drop to the floor, roll through and then away from the flames, and struggle to her feet. She grabbed her phone, hopped out of the bedroom and into the living room, where she dialed 911. After that, she called her next-door neighbor who has a key to her house. He came over and got her out before the fire grew out of control. She was transported to the hospital, where she's being treated for burns. The doctors say they don't appear to be life threatening, but at her age and with her health problems, they can't guarantee that she'll survive. At least I was able to take her statement before they started her on a morphine drip. They say it will be at least a day or two before I can talk to her again. If she makes it, they'll have to treat her burns. It will be very painful."

"He injected her with something?" River repeated. She looked over at Tony. "That's why his victims don't fight back. He gives them something that either causes them to become unconscious . . . or dead . . . and then he puts the wire around their wrists and their ankles to keep the body straight before he sets the fire."

"Yeah, it's a lot easier to sneak up on someone and inject them in their sleep than it is to just bind them and set their surroundings on fire," Tony said slowly. "They could fight back, and that could disrupt his plan. That's also why he always strikes at night."

"I don't know why I hadn't thought of that," Ray said. "I assumed it was because he didn't want to be seen. As far as injecting them, by the time we get the corpse there's not enough skin left to find any kind of puncture mark."

"Do the doctors know what was injected?" River asked.

"Not yet."

"So, what does your chief think now?"

Ray offered them a small smile. "Let's just say he's intrigued. This is the third case here in town with the same MO. Even if it was a copycat, which we know it's not, he realizes we're definitely dealing with a serial offender."

"I feel bad about not backing you up before now," Bobby said.

Ray waved his hand at him. "I understood. I appreciated what you said at the station. It's harder for him to ignore two of us."

"He's not unreasonable," Bobby said slowly. "Just . . . cautious, I guess."

"Here, Bobby." Beth put a cup of coffee in front of him.

"Thanks. It's freezing out there. This will help to warm me up."

"You both smell like smoke."

"Sorry, Beth," Bobby said. "We couldn't go inside the house, but the smoke was pretty thick outside. I'm not surprised that we smell."

"So is your chief connecting this incident with the murders in Des Moines?" River asked.

"He's still guarded about that," Ray said. "He's careful about casting aspersions toward Chief Watts."

"The first murders happened over twenty years ago," River said, frowning. "Has Watts been chief that long?"

"Yes and no. I served under Chief Watts, and Chief Watts is the current police chief." He smiled at River's confused look, and Bobby chuckled. "Father and son," Ray continued. "You can see why the current chief would be defensive about the previous chief."

"Yikes," River said. "That could definitely be a problem. A son admitting that his father made a mistake."

"Exactly," Ray said. "For now, I think we need to concentrate on this attempt and the other two here in Burlington."

"I agree," Bobby said.

"So the Snowman murders a couple in Des Moines, waits two years for the next one, and then a little over twenty years later, he starts killing here, each with a two-year gap," River said. "I wonder about the timing." She met Ray's gaze. "I know you feel you should focus on these murders, but I believe the first one is the most important. Why did he kill that couple? I believe it will hold the key to the other murders."

"I think you're right," Tony said. "It's usually the first murder that leads us to the truth."

"I hear you," Ray said with a sigh. "Why don't you two keep working on the profile? We still don't know who we're looking for. Meanwhile, I'll investigate this incident. Hopefully, we'll find a connection."

"Your dad has told me all about your training with the FBI," Bobby said. "It's great that you volunteered to help him."

"Happy to do it," Tony said. "Still not sure we can do anything that will lead to an arrest, but we'll do our best."

"Will you contact Chief Watts?" River asked. "Or should I say Chief Watts Jr.?"

Ray smiled again in spite of his weariness. "Not yet. When I do, I need something solid. Irrefutable."

Bobby stood. "Thanks for the coffee, Beth. I need to head out before the streets get any worse."

"Thank you for following him home, Bobby," Beth said with a smile. "I really appreciate it."

"Not a problem." Bobby smiled at Tony and River. "Nice to meet you both."

"Likewise," Tony said. "Be safe out there."

"I will."

Ray got up and followed Bobby to the door. They could hear him turning off the alarm. Then another burst of cold air, followed by the door closing and the sound of the alarm being reset.

"Ray, do you think we can find the girl from the first murders?" River asked when he came back into the room. "What's her name? Angie something?"

"Angie Mayhew," he said as he sat down again. "Like I said, she went into foster care. It's possible I could locate her. I'll contact the agency that worked her case. As long as some of the same people work there, I think they'll help me. But it will have to be okay with Angie for me to talk to her."

"Good," River said. "I'd really like to pose some questions to her."

"I'm not sure you'll learn anything new," Ray said. "All she told us was that a man dressed in black came into the house and hurt her grandparents. She never saw his face. To say she was traumatized by what happened is an understatement."

"I understand." River caught Tony's eye. She was certain he

realized that talking to Angie could help them with their profile. Maybe the girl didn't see the killer's face, but what did he say? What did he do? Did she smell anything? All these things were really important when it came to creating an accurate profile. She could know something vital. Something she didn't realize she knew. Victims of trauma frequently had buried memories. Asking the right questions could uncover those hidden details. They had no idea what she'd been asked after her grandparents were murdered.

"I didn't see anything in the files about anyone interviewing Angie," River said.

Ray nodded. "I know. I asked my friend in Des Moines about it, but he wasn't able to find anything either. Could be in a different file. One he didn't have access to. Since Chief Watts said Angie didn't have anything helpful to say, maybe it was never entered into the records. I'd guess the latter is probably true."

"We'd like to try," Tony said. "We might know ways to jog her memory. Maybe she repressed things that might help us with our profile."

Ray nodded. "I see your point. I'll see what I can do."

Beth stood up. "I think it's time for everyone to go back to bed. There's nothing more any of you can accomplish tonight. We'll start fresh in the morning. How does that sound?"

River nodded her agreement, but to be honest, her mind was full of thoughts that seemed to be on steroids. It was as if she knew something important, but she wasn't seeing it. Like it was just out of reach.

Even as they all headed back to bed, a voice inside her was nudging her to remember something. But what was it? What was she missing?

She said good-night to Tony, closed the bedroom door, and fell into bed. But instead of going right to sleep, she lay there, trying to grasp whatever it was that stayed just out of her reach.

"God, if there's something I need to see . . . something that will stop the Snowman, please show me. Thanks."

With that she turned over on her side and felt herself drifting away.

ANGER FLOWED THROUGH ME like hot blood. What had gone wrong? I'd followed the same procedure I'd used for my other righteous acts. But the woman obviously hadn't died like the others had. I'd used the same amount of fast-acting insulin.

"You really messed up."

I glared at her as she sat across from me at the table. "I don't need to hear your opinion. Go away."

"You don't have to get mad at me. You're the one who caused this."

The rage inside me felt as if it would boil over. I started to scream something at her that I knew would cause her pain. But then I remembered that it was all for her. What was I thinking? I felt ashamed.

"I did everything the exact same way I always do," I said, trying to keep my voice even. "Why didn't she die?"

She shrugged her thin shoulders. "I don't know, but you have to figure it out." She frowned at me. "She's probably in the hospital. Maybe you can get to her there."

I shook my head. "No, it's too dangerous. There's no reason for me to . . ." I stopped. Was there a way? If I could complete my mission, it would bring me peace. "You know what? Maybe I'll try. I know I can get into the hospital. Getting inside her room is another thing."

"If someone catches you, you could tell them that you made a mistake and were looking for a different patient."

"Maybe," I said slowly. "But I can't put myself on the detective's radar. That could be the end of . . . everything. I need to carry out the last judgment."

She was silent for a moment. "You may be right. I'm sure it will all work out." She smiled at me, dissolving the final, flickering flames of wrath in my gut. "Thank you. I know you do all of this for me. I love you for it."

"And I love you too." I blinked away the tears that suddenly filled my eyes. I couldn't let her down. I'd promised her that even though no one else had been there for her, I always would be. There was no way I could stop until I delivered all the revenge I'd sworn to execute.

TWENTY-TWO

River was inside the chest again—water seeping in. She could feel herself sinking farther and farther down toward the bottom of the river. Suddenly someone began to hit the side of the old trunk.

"Let me in, River! Please, save me!"

It was Jacki's voice. River struggled against the plastic zip ties that bound her wrists and ankles together. She had to help her friend. But how? There wasn't room in the trunk for anyone else. Yet somehow she believed that if Jacki could join her, she would be able to breathe and maybe they would both survive.

As she fought against the ties, she realized that she could see through one side of the old chest. It was made of some kind of hard plastic. Why hadn't she noticed that before? She wiggled around until her face was next to the plastic window.

"Jacki!" she called out. Maybe if she could see her, she could tell her how to get inside. Suddenly, she realized that the solution didn't make any sense. Jacki had to swim up. Up to the surface. Then she could pull the trunk out of the water. This way both of their lives would be saved.

It was then that a face appeared in front of her. There was

someone looking at her. It was Jacki, but her face was white and the skin on her face was peeling away. She stared at River through eyes that were long dead.

River screamed and called out to God. "Please, God. I'm sorry. Save me. And save Jacki. Please, just make this all go away! I promise I'll serve You for the rest of my life. I'll never turn my back on You again!"

Jacki's dead mouth opened, and she began to laugh. "You lied to God, River. You can't go back. He'll never forgive you." Her face twisted into a tortured wail. "You killed me, and now you'll spend eternity in hell!!"

River started to scream again, but suddenly she found herself sitting up in bed. She quickly clamped her hands over her mouth. Another nightmare. She'd been having them ever since that night in the river. Was it true? Was she really lost? She'd convinced herself that God had forgiven her. Was she mistaken?

She listened closely but the house was quiet. Had she yelled out loud? Had anyone heard her? After a few moments of silence, she collapsed back onto the bed. Her screams must have stayed in her dream. She brushed away the tear that rolled down the side of her face.

Would the nightmares ever stop?

TONY WAS STARTLED AWAKE by the sound of someone crying out. He swung his legs over the side of the bed and slid his feet into his slippers. He wondered if his parents had heard it, but their bedroom was quite a distance down the hall. They were probably too far away. His first instinct was to run to River's room to make sure she was okay. He knew about her nightmares. Hannah, her mother's previous caregiver, had told him about them. She'd been concerned about River. He kept waiting for her to bring them up, but she still hadn't. He was certain they were about the night they'd confronted the Strangler.

Of course, he also knew that right now they were facing a real threat, so he couldn't ignore what he'd heard. He looked at the clock. Nine in the morning. Good. They should be up by now anyway. He dressed quickly and ran a comb through his hair, giving River a few minutes to compose herself. He didn't want to embarrass her. Then he headed down the hallway and knocked on River's door. He was relieved to hear her voice.

"Yes?" she called out.

"Sorry. Hope I'm not waking you. It's after nine. Since we planned to start early on the profile, I wanted to see if you were ready to get up."

"Yeah, you're right. Thanks. Go on downstairs. I'll be there in a minute."

"Okay."

He stood there a moment longer, listening for the normal sounds of someone preparing for the day. It was probably insane to think that someone could be in River's room, forcing her to tell him she was okay, but worry for her safety made him feel unsettled. He knew he needed to trust God with her, yet sometimes that was easier to say than it was to do.

He carried some guilt for what happened the night they'd gone to the banks of the Salt River after Jacki called them. Why hadn't he questioned it? Had God tried to warn him? Had he missed it? He'd been tired that night and had wanted to get back to the hotel and rest. He sighed. It was a waste of time thinking about it now. Neither he nor River could have guessed that the Strangler was there, waiting for them. Still, he'd promised himself that he wouldn't rush into another situation like that again without listening for that still, small voice inside him. So, what was he feeling now? Was everything okay? He took a deep breath and tried to make himself relax.

"God, I'm sorry," he whispered. "I know I can trust You. It's just that I don't always trust myself. Or in my ability to hear from You. Can you please give me some kind of sign that it's okay for me to go downstairs?"

He'd no sooner finished praying when he heard River singing "Good, Good Father" to herself. Tony smiled. She loved that song. Said it made her feel peaceful. Hummed it sometimes in the office back in Mehlville whenever she felt stressed. She was okay.

He turned and headed downstairs.

WHEN RIVER WALKED into the kitchen, she found everyone else already eating breakfast.

"Sorry for being late," she said.

"Don't be silly," Beth said. "After having to get up in the middle of the night, we both thought you might sleep even later than this."

She looked over at Tony, who smiled at her. "Sorry. Maybe I shouldn't have knocked on your door."

She shook her head as she sat down. "Not a problem. I was already awake."

River was still worried that she might have yelled out in her sleep, but no one seemed concerned. The scream must have been in her mind. Thank God. She looked around the table at Tony and his family. She wondered if Tony truly realized how blessed he was. She assumed he did. Their work with the FBI had certainly opened their eyes to all the pain and destruction that occurred at the hands of family members. Very few of the disturbed individuals they'd profiled had happy childhoods.

"Did you hear me, River?"

She looked up and realized that Beth was standing over her with a large plate. "I . . . I'm sorry. I guess I am a little tired."

"I just wanted to know if you wanted one waffle or two," Beth said.

River looked at the large waffles on her plate. "I think one should do it," she said. "They smell so good."

"They're delicious," Ray said while Beth stabbed a waffle and put it on River's plate. "But I've got to go. The hospital says Sandra Cooper is conscious. She's doing better than they anticipated. I want to find out what she knows. Sometimes burn patients go south without warning. I've seen it happen before."

"Is there some way we could visit the crime scene?" Tony asked. "I'd like to see how the Snowman got inside."

"Our evidence technician is going over the scene now. He's actually quite competent. You may get what you want by reading his report, but if you still want to check it out yourself, I'll make it happen."

"Thanks, Dad."

"And I'll look for Angie. I'm still not sure she'll be able to help you, especially after all this time, but like you said, you might help her remember something we couldn't." Ray pushed back his chair and stood to his feet. "I'll call you if I find out anything that might be helpful."

"Dad, do you have someone posted outside Sandra Cooper's room?"

"Of course. This isn't my first rodeo, you know."

Tony exchanged a quick glance with River. They knew how important it was to restrict access to the witness. River hoped Ray knew it too.

Beth walked over to the refrigerator and took out a bag, which she handed to Ray. "I put some of those cookies you like in there. Don't share them with everyone else this time."

Ray laughed. "I learned my lesson the hard way. This time I'll keep them for myself."

"Not that I don't trust you but . . ." Beth also removed a plastic tub and handed it to him. "There are enough cookies in there for everyone at the station to have two."

Ray pulled Beth over to him and kissed her on the forehead. "You are the perfect girl for me, you know that?"

"You've been telling me that for over forty-five years," she said, smiling.

"And I'll be saying it for the next forty-five."

Ray said goodbye and left the kitchen. River could hear him getting his coat. Then the alarm disarmed and the door opened and shut. Beth walked out into the foyer and reset the alarm. Then she came back and sat down at the table while Tony and River finished their breakfasts. The silence was filled with casual but comfortable small talk.

When they were finished, Beth refilled their coffee cups, which they carried upstairs to work. As they entered the office, River couldn't help but wonder what Ray might learn from the victim. It could be crucial to their profile. She prayed silently that somehow, since the Snowman had failed in his last attempt, he might slink away and never attack anyone else. Unfortunately, most of these killers reacted quite differently. The truth was, he was probably angry and would see his failure as a challenge to prove his superiority. River had a bad feeling that if he couldn't get to Sandra Cooper, someone else's life might now be hanging in the balance.

CHAPTER
TWENTY-THREE

As they prepared to work, Tony searched for a way to bring up River's nightmares without letting her know that he'd heard her. It would probably embarrass her, and she'd worry that his parents had also overheard her. Of course, the truth was, everyone wanted to help her, but River was proud. If she wanted support, she liked to ask for it. All he could do was pray that God would provide an opening if that was what He wanted. Tony was aware that God didn't actually need his assistance, but at the same time, Tony wanted to be available to Him if He chose to use him.

"I think we need to go over what we have already," River said, sitting at the table and going through the file again. Although it seemed redundant to go through the same information over and over, many times at the BAU, they'd stumbled onto something important that they'd missed before. "I realize what your father tells us may change things."

"Or send us in a better direction," Tony said absentmindedly. He shook his head. "I'm worried about what the Snowman will do next. I mean, since he'll most likely see this morning's failure as an embarrassment."

"I am too. But hopefully, this will be the thing that finally leads to his downfall."

"You mean that he'll feel compelled to strike again so quickly that he'll make a mistake?" Tony said.

"Exactly. What's the weather forecast?"

Tony pulled his phone out of his pocket and quickly looked up the report for Burlington. "It's not supposed to snow again until Saturday."

"We planned to head back on Saturday."

"According to this, the snow will start early Saturday morning and could bring several inches."

River sighed. "Maybe I should rent a car and leave tomorrow. I don't want to take advantage of Mrs. Weyland."

"Shouldn't you call and ask her what she wants you to do?" Tony said. "To be honest, I need your help. And besides, I don't want you driving back alone."

"I thought you said no one followed us here."

Tony nodded. "I don't believe they did, but I don't want to bet your life on it." He hated saying it that way, but it was the truth.

"So, if it snows a lot on Saturday, will we be able to drive back on Sunday?" she asked.

Tony went back to the forecast. After checking ahead, he sighed. "More snow on Sunday. We may be stuck here until at least Monday afternoon."

"Maybe I could fly back."

Tony shrugged. "It's not impossible, but flights are tough to get around Christmas, and the planes out of Burlington are small."

"I should call Mrs. Weyland today."

"Do you want to phone her now?"

River shook her head. "No, let's do some work first. I want to make sure we get this done."

"Okay." Tony sat down at the table across from her and they went over their profile, adding to it and refining it. About two hours into the process, Tony's phone rang. When he picked it up, she saw it was his father. He answered and put it on speakerphone. "Okay, Dad. Go ahead. River can hear you."

"Ms. Cooper wasn't able to talk long. They're keeping her on morphine."

"But you did get to talk to her some?" Tony asked.

"Yeah. She went over what happened again. I still can't believe she had the presence of mind to roll on the floor, which put out the flames, and call 911. Amazing. She did happen to add that she remembered the man actually sitting in a chair near her bed for a few minutes before pouring the gasoline around her. Right after that, she fell asleep again. We're pretty sure we know why she felt dizzy and sick when she woke up and why she didn't wake up when he bound her hands and feet. We found a syringe on the floor. It was tested. Insulin. He gave her an overdose of fast-acting insulin. However, her doctor thinks her A1C was high. That means her body needed the insulin. Her diabetes might have saved her life."

"That's very significant," River said, looking at Tony. "He made two mistakes. Dropping the syringe and picking a diabetic to inject. He's getting sloppy."

"So, she said her attacker was a man," Tony said. "Please tell me she gave a better description than that."

Ray's sigh carried through the phone. "Not much better. She drifted off again. But she did mention that he had red eyes."

"Red eyes?" Tony said. "What does that mean?"

"I have no idea," Ray said. "Like I mentioned, she was heavily medicated."

"Anything else?" River asked. "Since the fire was put out so quickly, maybe there's other evidence that wasn't destroyed."

"The evidence tech hasn't found anything yet, but he took some things back to the lab and is testing them for hair, fibers, anything that can help us."

"How did the Snowman get in, Dad?"

Another sigh came through the phone. "Nothing looks amiss. It's strange. There weren't any keys hidden outside anywhere. Either Ms. Cooper left a door or window unlocked or the Snowman had a key. But that can't be right. He couldn't have keys to all the victims' houses."

"Again, River and I would really like to get a look ourselves," Tony said. "No disrespect to your evidence technician, but through the years, we've heard almost everything. Maybe something we see will click."

"I can take you there either tonight or tomorrow morning."

"The morning might be best," River chimed in. "Better light. Ray, what about footprints? It was snowing."

"Nothing. With the fire department trying to put out the fire, we couldn't find anything that could help us."

"Okay, Dad," Tony said. "We're getting back to work. We'll plan to look over the scene in the morning."

"Sounds good. See you both later."

Tony disconnected the call but stared at his phone for a bit.

"What are you thinking?" River asked.

"First of all, I can't believe he actually left a syringe behind. Why? He's always been so careful."

"Yet he's human," River said. "It was just a matter of time before he messed up." She frowned. "I wonder if he realizes it."

"I have no idea," Tony said. "It depends on how frantic he is now. Someone survived. He might not figure it out right away." He shook his head. "Here's something else that's bothering me. We think we understand why the Snowman sets fires. It's not only as a way to express his anger, but it's also his method to destroy evidence. But the houses aren't his actual target. He isn't trying to obliterate them. Some of them were still standing after he was done. That means he's not afraid that anyone will be able to figure out how he got in. Why?"

River leaned back in her chair and frowned. When she was

quiet like this, he knew she was thinking, so he stayed silent, not wanting to interrupt her. He watched her for a few seconds, but then he finally looked away. Her brown hair with its blonde highlights framed her delicate face while she pursed her full lips and furrowed her forehead as she considered his question. Tony felt his heart thump in his chest and was afraid his expression would give him away. He valued their friendship . . . actually, their partnership. If River ever found out that his feelings for her were more than friendly, would he lose her? He couldn't . . . no, wouldn't . . . take that chance. If she ever walked out of his life, he felt as if his heart would stop beating. He knew it was wrong to think like that. He'd given his life to Christ and had no intention of taking it back. He was aware that almost anything could become an idol . . . even the love you felt for another person. No matter what, he couldn't allow anyone but God to be first in his heart. That would truly destroy him.

"We've assumed that the victims didn't let the Snowman in because they were found in bed," River said finally. "Normally, I'd suggest that we might be jumping to conclusions since he could have forced them back into bed and then injected them. But two things make that seem unlikely. First of all, there were couples killed. I'm wondering why one of them didn't jump to the defense of the other."

"And what about the youngest victims here?" Tony said. "The Craigs. They were in their forties."

"Mr. Craig could have overpowered the Snowman. And you're right. Even when the victims were older, one of them could have called the police while the other dealt with an intruder."

"Right," Tony said.

"So, it seems that he is getting in without alerting the home-owners." River shook her head. "I think we can rule out one of the ways Dennis Rader obtained access to houses. He posed as a telephone repairman to gain his victim's trust and get inside. But that was during the day. Not at night. Somehow, the Snowman gets in very stealthily, without causing any damage to doors or windows."

"We can't rule that out completely since sometimes the house had so much fire damage it was impossible to see any signs of forced entry."

"Yet when doors or windows that survived fire were inspected, entry that way was ruled out."

"You're saying that probability tells us something else is going on," Tony said slowly. "What is it?"

"Remember the next-to-last case we worked before we left the Bureau?" River asked.

Tony tried to remember. The last case was the Salt River Strangler. Was there really life before that?

"It was the serial rapist in California."

Tony thought back, but it was difficult. He was finally able to pull it up in his mind. "The man who got into homes by taking pictures of keys."

"Yes, he followed his victims to bars or restaurants and when they got up to dance or go to the bathroom, he took their purses into the men's room where he took pictures of their keys."

"And then sent the pictures to an online company that makes copies of keys from photos and mails them out." Tony sighed. "Only cost him eight dollars."

"Cost him even less to strip a woman of her dignity and her sense of safety."

Tony frowned at her. "You think this guy is doing the same thing? The first murders happened before this way of getting someone's keys became available."

"That's true," River said, "but I think he's acquiring their keys somehow. It's just a thought. Wouldn't be hard to do now."

"You could be right, but how is he getting in and out of houses without being seen?"

River shook her head. "I don't know. If we could just find some kind of connection between the victims, we might be able to figure this out. But no matter how many times I look through this file, I can't see it. I know it's here somewhere, but I feel like the information we need is either missing or not obvious enough." She slapped the file down with apparent frustration, and it accidentally slid off the table. "Sorry," she said. "I don't mean to get so irritated. I think we're veering off into our jobs as private investigators. We need to focus on the profile. Let your dad and his officers figure out the rest."

Tony bent down to pick up the pictures that had fallen on the floor. "I know you're right, but it's hard not to use every weapon in our arsenal to stop this guy." He straightened up and looked into her eyes. "I really want this guy, River. Not just for my dad and the victims, but also for us. We need this, you know?"

She didn't say anything, but the look on her face told him she understood.

TWENTY-FOUR

I entered the hospital through the front door. No one paid any attention to me. Good. Then I took the elevator up to the intensive care floor. A quick glance revealed that there was another door that led to the unit. Even if I could get past the nurses who guarded those patients, I would never make it to the room I wanted. I could see a police officer sitting in the hallway. He was obviously there to protect my failure. I pretended I'd gotten off the elevator in error and went back downstairs. By the time I reached my car in the parking lot, the anger inside me was back, but it had turned into rage.

"I hope you took care of the problem you caused," she said sharply when I pulled the car door closed.

"I'm tired of you criticizing me constantly," I snapped. "Do you appreciate anything I do for you?"

As soon as the words left my mouth, I was sorry. Why did I keep lashing out at her? She'd fallen silent, which made it worse.

"I'm sorry," I said softly. "I'm just upset because things didn't work out the way I planned them. I'll fix it. Don't be angry with me, okay?"

"I'm not angry," she whispered. "I realize what you're doing is for me. Because of what happened to me." She smiled at me. "I trust you. You'll fix it."

Her encouragement buoyed my spirits. If she thought I could overcome this setback, then maybe there was a real chance. I wasn't sure how to make things right yet, but for now, I'd just move on to the next assignment. It was supposed to be my last mission, but after it was finished, I'd circle back and take care of Sandra Cooper.

"It's supposed to snow on Saturday," I told her. "I'll take care of the next target. Then I'll execute that ridiculous woman as soon as I can get to her."

"That sounds perfect."

She smiled at me again and my heart suddenly felt light. I could do anything as long as she was happy.

AFTER A QUICK LUNCH, Tony and River worked as long as they could on the profile. They'd gone as far as they could without more information.

"Read what we have so far," Tony said.

"Okay." River took a deep breath. "We agree that the Snowman is male, somewhere around forty-four to fifty-five years old. This is based on the first murders which were twenty-four years ago. He has a responsible job, has an above-average IQ. Those who know him would never suspect that he's capable of murder. He's a typical psychopath, organized and capable of almost anything. Whatever drives his anger is personal. We now believe that he kills his targets before he starts the fires. It's done because the actual act of murder is distasteful to him, not because he feels empathy for the victims. He does show some remorse for what he's doing, note the folded hands, the bodies bound not just so he can control them, but also as if he has prepared them for a coffin. A strange sign of respect for their death.

"His victims are targeted. Carefully selected. He painstakingly plans each of his attacks. His MO has been perfected.

"Using fire shows that he is fueled by some kind of extreme inner anger, but it's also a way to destroy evidence. He keeps his true emotions hidden in public. Doesn't share them with anyone. He may have endured a traumatic event connected with fire when he was a child, but not necessarily. However, what drives him was instigated by *something* in his childhood. He grew up in an environment that didn't offer emotional support. Either one or both parents were absent or violent. The snowman ornament he leaves behind is part of that twisted childhood. It's his signature. Also, he feels compelled to kill only when it's snowing. Snow has a special meaning to him.

"He's following the media coverage of his crimes. He has probably shown up to at least one of his crime scenes after the fact."

"But maybe not all of them," Tony said quietly. He looked up at her. "He knows that the police take pictures and interview people watching a fire. He wouldn't risk getting caught. He's too smart."

"So, you think he has some kind of connection to the police?"

Tony nodded. "Maybe. Or the fire department."

River wrote down Tony's hypothesis. He was right. She should have thought of it before. She was having trouble concentrating because of her nightmare. It was as if it was holding her mind with tentacles that wouldn't let go. As they worked on this profile, she was haunted by the knowledge that they'd gotten it so wrong when it came to Joseph Baker. Their mistake had shaken her confidence. Did they have this one wrong as well?

"River?" Tony's voice startled her, and her eyes met his.

"I'm sorry. What did you say?"

Tony frowned at her. "If something's bothering you . . ."

"I was thinking of Joseph Baker again. How we missed a partner." She stopped typing on her laptop and sighed. "The more I think about it, the more I realize that we were so focused on his mental state that we forgot that putting a body in a large chest and tossing it into the river might take two people."

"*Might* being the most important attribute," Tony said. "We profiled him as someone young and strong enough to carry out his crimes on his own. And we were right to see it that way. There was no clear indication that he was working with someone else. He was alone the night he attacked us."

"I know but . . ."

"Look, I know you brought it up when we first started on the profile, and I disagreed. I carried a lot of guilt about that for a while, but I know now that we did the best we could with the information we had. You know profiles aren't one hundred percent accurate. We got it wrong more than once. You remember the female spree killer in Wyoming? We profiled her as a man because she used a certain kind of weapon and killed up close. You didn't take that personally. We learned from it. You've got to let this go."

"But she didn't murder one of our friends and the witness who put our attacker in prison." River stood up and walked over to the corkboard, scanning the pictures again. Photos of horror and death. No wonder she had nightmares. She'd thought they'd left this behind when they walked away from the FBI. Now it was back again. She was tired of feeling responsible for bringing these monsters to justice. Would she ever have a normal life? What did that even look like?

"Maybe coming here was a mistake," Tony said. "I'm sorry. I think it's just too much."

River turned back to look at him. "No. Don't do that. I will not give in to the past. You've taught me that I don't have to. I believe that Jesus has set me free, and I intend to have what He died to give me." She walked over and sat back down in her chair. "I'm the one who's sorry. I need you to promise me something. Promise me you won't allow me to drift back into all of that again.

I really want to be completely free. I want to live my life now. I want the nightmares to go away for good." She forced herself to smile. She meant every word of what she'd just said. She'd hoped God would have delivered her in an instant. Made her instantly okay. But it seemed that many times healing was a process. One that she needed to work her way through.

"Okay, I hear you," Tony said, smiling at her. "But just remember that faith doesn't mean we have to find a way to struggle until we succeed. It actually means giving the struggle to Him and allowing Him to carry us through. Frankly, for some people, surrendering our pain is the most difficult thing we'll ever do. It's actually easier for us to accept the responsibility of our burdens and try to seek our own deliverance. We're used to being strong. But our real strength is found in the acknowledging of our weakness and trusting in His strength."

River could hear the Lord speaking to her through Tony's words. This was who she was. The fighter. The one who struggled until she won. But God didn't want that. He wanted surrender. Would she ever be able to do that? To trust someone labeled *father* when she had no trust in her earthly parent?

"I have a tough time with this," River said haltingly. "Pretending I don't isn't honest, I guess. After my father left, I decided I had to be tough to make it through life. But then the Strangler entered my life. For the first time, our profile became a flesh-and-blood person. One I confronted personally. He didn't live in just our reports. Everything suddenly became real. Too real. Now . . ." She gulped. "I . . . I have nightmares about that night. I had one last night." She looked over at Tony. He didn't seem surprised.

"I hate that you're going through that," he said. He blinked away tears. There was no judgment. No condemnation. Not even a religious saying that made the situation worse. Just compassion. It was like a dam burst inside her.

"Tony, when I was in that chest with the water coming in . . . I

. . . I promised God that I'd follow Him if He saved me. But then I didn't. I turned my back on Him. How could He forgive me? How could He look the other way when I lied to Him? I mean, He's God."

Until she felt something wet drop onto her hand, she wasn't aware she was crying. Since she'd opened herself up to Him, she'd felt as if God was with her. That He answered her prayers. She'd even believed she'd heard His voice. But what if she was fooling herself? Her father's church would have condemned her. Committed her to hell. No one could lie to God. She'd just said she didn't want to live in the past, but her father's voice still whispered in her mind, telling her she wasn't good enough.

Tony pulled his chair up next to hers and took her hands in his. His long fingers completely wrapped around her smaller ones.

"River, what you're saying in effect is that when Jesus went to that cross, even though He knew the horror of what He was going to endure for us, it wasn't sufficient. That His sacrifice wasn't enough to cover your mistakes. Is that what you really think?"

"No. No, I don't believe that. He gave everything for us. For me. More than any of us could ever deserve."

Tony gazed into her eyes. "Then it's time for you to accept His sacrifice. For you. For me."

"And . . ." River cleared her throat. She felt ashamed, but not in a condemning way. Somehow it felt like freedom. "And for my father. Christ gave enough for all of us, didn't He?"

"You know the answer to that." Tony raised her right hand to his mouth and lightly kissed it. "When we are deeply hurt, we may still have scars. And we don't have to feel ashamed of them. We didn't put them there, and we can't heal them by ourselves. He has scars too, you know. No one understands scars more than Jesus. Someday you'll barely notice yours. I promise that God will restore you, but He'll do it in His own time and His own way. And that's okay. Please stop punishing yourself for what someone else did to you. You turned away after getting out of that trunk because of what your father did to you. God understood it. He understands it more than anyone else."

"I've always felt that I had to protect myself from . . . well, from everyone."

"But you don't," Tony said. "Not from Him. Just let Him in. He'll help you let others in too. And He'll give you what you need to respond to your dad. You'll know when you're ready."

"Thank you, Tony. I'm going to try. I really am." She gently slid her hands from his. "I want to call Mrs. Weyland, then we'll finish this profile."

Tony stood up and went back to his chair while River called home. She tried to concentrate on her conversation with Mrs. Weyland, but the spot on her hand where Tony had kissed her seemed to tingle, and she couldn't stop thinking about it.

TWENTY-FIVE

O h, honey, we're doin' just great," Mrs. Weyland said. "Neither one of us wants you to venture out in a snowstorm. You just come home when the roads are clear. We're havin' so much fun workin' on puzzles and watchin' Christmas movies. Tonight is *White Christmas*. It's one of my favorites. Your mother is excited to see it too."

"Thank you so much," River said, thanking God silently for bringing this wonderful woman into their lives. "I'll call you when I know for sure when we're heading back."

"That sounds good. Your mama wants to say hello to you. I'm gonna give her the phone, okay?"

"Sure."

River wasn't used to her mother being happy to talk to her. Or even liking her. Things had begun to change last month after River was almost killed. It was as if her mother suddenly emerged from the darkness of depression and anger and had finally begun to love her daughter. River knew she'd been talking to her brother, Dan, who had taken in her father after he had been dumped by his new wife when he ran out of the money he'd saved up for retirement. Now he wanted to visit Rose . . . and River . . . for what? To ask for forgiveness? River knew she had to give it, because Jesus had forgiven her. But how do you forgive someone when you don't feel like it? Is mental assent enough? Would God accept that? Then something Tony had said echoed in her thoughts.

When we are deeply hurt, we still have scars. And we don't have to feel ashamed of them. We didn't put them there, and you can't heal them by yourself. But God will. He has scars too, you know. No one understands scars more than He does.

Maybe she didn't have to pretend that there wasn't hurt. Maybe just agreeing to see her father was enough. She didn't need to put on a show. She just had to do what she could and let God do the rest.

"River? Is that you, honey?"

River was startled by her mother's sudden voice in her ear. "Hi, Mom. I called Mrs. Weyland to tell her that we probably won't be home on Saturday. There's a snowstorm moving in. It might be better if we wait until it's past us."

"We're doing puzzles. I'm having so much fun. Tonight, we're going to watch *White Christmas*. Do you remember when we used to watch it together?"

Did Rose understand what she'd said? That they weren't coming home right away? It was as if it hadn't registered at all. It seemed as if sometimes Rose could only concentrate on what was happening to her in the moment. It was hard sometimes to know whether the disease was talking or if the thoughts were actually her mother's.

River couldn't remember ever watching Christmas movies with Rose. Her father hadn't allowed them, and after he was gone, Rose ignored Christmas. River was the one who put up the tree, bought gifts for Dan from her and from her mother. One year, she even tried to cook Christmas dinner. That had been a disaster, so she'd ordered something from the Chinese restaurant not far from their house. It was the only restaurant open near them.

After that, it became a tradition. One Christmas, River managed to find a used copy of the movie *The Christmas Story*. Dan loved it, and the idea of eating Chinese food on Christmas suddenly seemed very special. Every Christmas they'd spent together, they ordered Chinese food.

River had seen *White Christmas* but it was on her own. After she moved out. Somehow, Rose had changed her memories in an attempt to make herself feel better. River stuffed down a sudden flare of irritation. Rose couldn't help it. There was never going to be justice for the way Rose had treated her children. There could only be forgiveness. There was no other path to travel. It was the only road in front of her.

"Sure, Mom. I hope you enjoy it tonight. I . . . I miss you."

"Oh, honey. I miss you too. Maybe I can make my famous beef stew for you when you get home."

"That would be great, Mom. I'd better go. I'll see you soon."

"Okay, honey. I love you."

"I . . . I love you too, Mom."

River disconnected the call and stared at her phone. This was hard. How long would Rose be like this? She was slowly becoming the mother she'd always wanted. One that hadn't existed before she became ill. It was true that she'd been a decent mother when her father was with them, but it was as if she were playing a part. There was distance—a kind of disconnect toward her children. Rose had adored her husband. Lived for him. Dan and River were simply the window dressing. A happy family living under the direction of a harsh and vengeful God. Trying to look like the perfect family. It was a ruse but, at least for a while, it worked in a weird way.

"Are you okay?"

River jumped at the sound of Tony's voice. She'd almost forgotten he was there. He'd gotten up and was standing next to the corkboard.

"I don't know. I'm just trying to deal with my mother's illness—adjust to this new reality. It's hard. But what you said earlier helped me. Thank you."

"I'll always be here when you need me, River. You know that, right?"

She looked up at him and saw something in his eyes that made her catch her breath. "I do," she said softly. "You're the best friend I've ever had."

When the words left her mouth, she immediately regretted them. His face tightened, and he looked away from her. She wanted to tell him something different. Express the truth that dwelt deep in her heart. But she wasn't whole yet. She was too vulnerable. Too afraid of commitment. Still, she wanted to find a way to heal the wound she'd just caused. She took a deep, shaky breath.

"Can . . . can that be enough . . . for now? I'm not . . ."

He turned around and met her gaze. "It's okay. I understand. I really do. When . . . or if . . . you're ever ready . . ." He choked up and started to walk away.

"Not if, Tony. Just when."

His slow smile melted something inside her. This was not a man to be afraid of. This was a man she could trust. That she could . . . love someday. As long as he was willing to wait.

Before either one of them could say anything else, Tony's phone rang. He picked it up and looked at it.

"It's Arnie."

It had to be about the possibility of listening devices being hidden in their office. River didn't want to believe it was true. But how else could the Strangler's partner know where they were? Tony was certain they weren't followed, and she trusted him when it came to spotting a tail.

Tony sat down and listened to Arnie. It was definitely a one-way conversation. River realized she was holding her breath and let it out in a rush. She opened her laptop and stared at their profile, but it was as if the words in front of her made no sense. She couldn't do anything but focus on Tony's phone call. When he finally hung up, she still knew nothing. River could feel her heart beating in her chest. If she was certain there wasn't a bug in the office, why was her body reacting like this?

"Arnie had the building manager let his people into our office."

River braced herself for what she knew was coming. What she was afraid to hear.

"They found a bug under your desk, River. It had to be put there by the Strangler's apprentice."

TWENTY-SIX

He's been in our office, River," Tony said, trying to choke back the rage he felt. He didn't want to frighten her, but they had to do something. They couldn't allow this killer—this evil man—to get close to them again. "Maybe we should move."

"That won't stop him," River said. "What would keep him from following us?"

He had no answer for her. He shook his head. "The building manager is installing a camera in the hallway and in our office. Something we should have done before. I'm sorry. It's my fault. We just got so caught up in helping Amy, time got away from me."

He really did feel stupid. He'd been a special agent with the FBI. How could he have been so irresponsible?

"I don't need you to take care of me, Tony," River said firmly. "I knew we needed to beef up security, and I didn't say anything."

"We're also going to install an alarm system. Arnie says we'll have to pay for that ourselves since our landlord won't foot the bill, but that's fine. As soon as we get back, I'll have it put in."

River wrinkled her nose. "I know you're right, but I kind

of hate those things. They always go off when you don't want them to. When we put a system in at my mom's house, she used to set it off regularly. For now, she won't open any doors that lead outside. I worry that she'll forget that as she gets more confused."

"But if that happens, won't it alert Mrs. Weyland that your mom may be trying to leave the house? It could end up being a good thing. My grandfather used to wander off. It was a huge problem."

River smiled at him. "Of course, you're right." She hesitated a moment before saying, "Look, I know this is unsettling, but we're actually safer now. Maybe that's the way to look at it."

Tony was moved by her positive attitude, but he wasn't feeling the least bit optimistic. That creep had been in their office. It felt like a violation. What did he look at? What did he touch? Part of him wanted to burn everything and start over, but that wasn't going to happen.

"Now you're the one who's right," he said, forcing a smile he didn't feel. "I know we've wondered if his plan was just to harass us. To frighten us. But after this, I think we need to accept the possibility that he might be more dangerous than we'd hoped. Frankly, I'm getting tired of feeling like a rat in a trap. We need to find this guy before he tries to carry out his threats. After this profile, we need to finish profiling *him*."

They'd actually started one right before they'd come to Burlington, but it was clear that they needed to keep working on it. It was difficult since he was so entwined with Joseph Baker, and they hadn't profiled Baker as someone who would work with a partner. He was too narcissistic. This accomplice was an anomaly. Yet they had to try. This guy seemed determined to finish what Baker started, and they needed to stay a step ahead of him.

"When we're done here, we'll complete his profile and give

it to Arnie," Tony said. "We need to move out of defense mode and start playing offense. Let's bring him down before he's able to carry out his plans."

"Remember that we're private investigators now," River said. "We can look for him too. We don't have to hide behind the Bureau."

"Fat lot of good that did for us anyway. We still ended up as the targets of a serial killer."

Tony knew he sounded bitter, but it was how he felt. River shouldn't have gone from behind the scenes as a behavioral analyst and ended up in the Salt River, fighting for her life. He made a fist with his left hand. The fingers didn't close all the way, thanks to being involved with Baker. Regardless, he would never be sorry that he was with River that night. He was only sorry that he hadn't been able to take Baker down before he got to her.

"Let's get back to work," River said. "We've got a little polishing to do, but we've almost got this. I want to go over it with your dad tomorrow."

"Tomorrow's Friday," Tony said. "We could head home tomorrow if you want to."

River shook her head. "Your parents need to spend time with you, and I have a reprieve from Mrs. Weyland. Frankly, I needed a break. Let's wait until after the snowstorm."

"You won't get any argument from me." Tony really didn't want to leave tomorrow. He'd planned to have lunch with his sister. He suddenly realized he hadn't said anything to River. "Hey, Aimee and I are going to lunch tomorrow. I'd ask you to come with us, but I think she wants some time with me. Is that okay?"

"Of course. No problem."

Tony caught a brief, odd expression that crossed River's face. She was probably worried that he'd confront his sister about what she'd said to River about the shooting. He couldn't ease her mind because he hadn't decided if he was ready to talk to Aimee about it yet. He probably wouldn't know until he and his sister were together.

"Since we're about done with the profile, I felt like there would be time," Tony said. "I won't be gone long."

River smiled at him. "Don't be silly. I'm happy you get to spend time with Aimee. And as you said, we've got most of this completed. I would like to hear more from Sandra Cooper. I hope your dad is able to get more information from her soon."

"Me too. And I'd still like to talk to Angie Mayhew. The only thing we've heard from her happened when she was a child." He frowned. "I know Dad was reluctant for us to approach her, but I think in all this time she could have remembered something that might help us. Or at least she can verbalize what she saw better as an adult."

"I wonder if your dad found the time to look for her. Things have been pretty crazy."

"Only one way to find out," Tony said. He picked up his phone and called his father. He answered right away.

"Hello, son. What do you need?"

"Dad, were you able to locate Angie Mayhew?"

There was a rather long silence on the other end of the phone.

"Did you hear me, Dad?"

"Yes, I heard you. I . . . I located her. She's here. In Burlington."

Tony was startled to hear this. What was going on? Was everyone in Des Moines moving to Burlington?

"Dad, don't you find that . . . odd? I mean, the Snowman and Angie Mayhew both relocate to Burlington?"

A list of possibilities started clicking through Tony's mind, but none of them made sense. "The Snowman wouldn't have followed Angie here. She wasn't his target. He's never gone after a child. These kinds of killers have very specific victims. It's part of their signature."

"I agree, and before you conclude that a six-year-old child was the Snowman, I can put your mind to rest. Angie was moved to a foster home in Burlington years before we moved here. In fact, that same foster family adopted her. It's less than three hours between Des Moines and Burlington. It's hardly a trek across the country."

"I guess so, Dad, but it still seems a little odd. So can we talk to her?"

"That's up to you. I have her number. She works for a place called Hope House. She helps to train people with disabilities to work in the community."

"That sounds like a really valuable job."

"I think so too," Ray said. "Are you ready for her number?"

Tony said yes and his father slowly gave him a number that Tony added to his phone. "Thanks, Dad," he said. "Have you had a chance to speak to her yourself?"

"No. I feel a little funny calling her. It's been so long. I should have kept in touch. There was a part of me that worried about interfering in her new life. But the other part of me felt guilty for not helping her more than I did."

Tony couldn't keep the incredulity out of his voice. "Not helping her more than you did? You saved her life, Dad."

"I know what you're saying, but she was all alone. We could have added her to our family. Maybe we were being selfish."

"I know you and Mom," Tony said gently. "There's not a selfish bone in either one of you. If you thought God had told you to take Angie in, you would have done it."

"I hope you're right. By the way, I heard from the hospital. The doctor confirmed we were right about Sandra Cooper being alive because she's diabetic."

"People have committed murder with insulin," Tony said. "It's routinely in the blood, and insulin levels tend to normalize by the time toxicology tests are done."

"Exactly. Obviously, the Snowman didn't think to check out his victims for diabetes before injecting them." His dad sighed. Tony could hear weariness in his voice. "Look, son, I love talking to you, but I've got to run. We've got a group of young people in town running into businesses and stealing all they can. We think they saw it on TV and decided to give it a try. They know the business owners can't stop a mob of that size so they're taking advantage of that."

Tony was sad to hear that this shocking practice had made its way to Burlington. More and more cities were trying to protect themselves from young people who'd picked up this destructive behavior.

"Okay, Dad. You'll contact us if you learn anything else from Ms. Cooper?"

"Yes, when I talk to her, you'll be the first to know. She's doing much better by the way."

"I'm glad to hear that. See you tonight?"

"Yeah, I should be able to make it home for dinner. See you then, son."

Tony hung up the phone and looked over at River. He shared what his dad had told him about Sandra Cooper.

"That's what we assumed. Good to know we were right," she said. "Even better for Ms. Cooper. If it wasn't for her diabetes, she'd be dead."

"Also, I have a number for Angie Mayhew. Maybe you should call her. She might feel more comfortable talking to a woman. Be sure to tell her who I am, though. It might help." He looked up at the clock on the wall. "Maybe we could meet her some where? I'd rather talk in person. She works for an organization that works with people who have disabilities. I have no idea what her hours are. We could meet her wherever she wants. Just remember that we're going to Sandra Cooper's house in the morning."

"Okay, give me the number."

Tony read the number off to her and waited to see if Angie would talk to them. As he watched River, he had the strangest feeling that they were on the verge of something significant, but he had no idea what it was.

TWENTY-SEVEN

By the time River hung up her phone, they had an appointment to meet with Angie. After telling his mom that they might be back late for supper, Tony and River got in the car and drove toward the diner where Angie waited. Tony respected the work she did. He wondered if her experiences had made her sensitive to people who needed help. He couldn't imagine how she'd gotten from losing her grandparents, and then later her mother, and living through that terrible fire, to where she was now. He was fairly certain her adoptive parents had a lot to do with it. His father's revelation that he and his mom had seriously considered bringing Angie into their home had left him feeling a little disturbed. If they'd followed through and then adopted her, like the people who'd taken her in, this woman would have been his sister. It was weird.

". . . some kind of emotional damage."

"I'm sorry," Tony said, looking over at River. "Can you run that by me again?"

River frowned at him. "Where are you?"

Tony sighed. "I'm a little freaked out about my parents thinking about fostering Angie."

"I get it. This woman could have been someone you were close to."

He nodded. "Sorry. What were you saying?"

"Just that Angie couldn't have gotten through that awful night and the death of her mother without it affecting her."

"I agree," he said. "I was thinking that maybe she assists people because it helps with her own healing."

"I think you could be right. That's one reason I wanted to work in law enforcement. I guess I had the desire to find some kind of justice."

Tony chuckled. "Did you have a secret desire to arrest your father?"

She laughed. "Not consciously, but it's not a bad idea."

"God kinda messed that up, huh?"

River was silent for a moment. Had he offended her?

"The God I was taught about would have locked him up and thrown away the key," she said softly. She swung her gaze his way. "But then I met you, and you helped me to discover a different view of God. One that loved me completely. Even with all my faults." She sighed deeply. "The downside being that now I know I have to forgive my dad. Not something I ever thought I'd do."

"So, are you going to let him come and see you?"

"Probably, but I might not let him come to the house. I'm not sure how my mother would react."

"And if she says she wants him to come?" he asked.

"You know how quickly she can change. If I could be certain she wouldn't go ballistic, it would be fine. I mean, it's her house, and it should be her decision. But what if she doesn't remember saying he could come? What if she reverts back to the time when he left?" River shook her head. "I can't risk letting her go through that again. It almost destroyed all of us, and it might send her into a tailspin." She took a deep breath. "If he's just looking for a way to make himself feel better, he'll have to deal with it on his own. I can't allow him to do any more damage to my mother."

"The forgiveness conundrum."

River looked at him with raised eyebrows. "Huh? There's a conundrum?"

He laughed. "Kind of. Okay, let's say you're married, and you cheat. You realize how wrong it is and you clean up your act. Do you tell your spouse? I mean, are you trying to make yourself feel better at his expense? Or do you keep it to yourself? If you have a spouse you know loves you and would want to save your marriage?"

"A spouse has the right to know," River said. "I mean, the marriage vows are broken, right? It's like the marriage contract is null and void. The wronged spouse should be able to make an informed decision."

"And carry that pain the rest of their lives?"

River was quiet. Tony could almost hear her mind working. "Well, God would help the betrayed spouse heal, right?"

"Of course."

"We're back to our earlier conversation about scars, aren't we?" River asked.

"Exactly. Do we inflict scars on purpose? Is it selfish?"

"I think each situation is different," she said. "I guess this is where the Holy Spirit comes in. If He tells the cheating spouse to fess up, then they should. If the Holy Spirit tells them to be quiet, they should be quiet."

"I believe that's the best answer," Tony said. "Unfortunately, not everyone is great about hearing the Holy Spirit. A guy I used to go to church with when I was in college cheated on his wife. He decided it was selfish to tell her about it. He repented, he really did. Unfortunately, the girl he cheated with was angry when he told her it was over. She told his wife."

"What happened?" River asked.

"She divorced him," Tony said. "Turns out she was pregnant. She moved to England where her parents lived, had their son, and did everything she could to keep him away from her ex. Bad situation all around."

"If I ever get married, I'll never cheat. That way I won't have to face this."

Tony laughed. "Sounds good."

"I don't think that will ever be a problem anyway. I'm not sure I'll ever marry."

"Ever?"

"I doubt it." She turned to look at him. It was getting dark, and he could just barely make out her face. "I haven't had a great example to follow. You're blessed to have the parents you do. They really love each other."

"Yes, they really do," he said. "They've had their tough times, but they've gotten through them. I think it's because they put each other first. Dad moved here because he wanted my mother to have a better life. He wanted to be home more."

River was silent until Tony pulled into the parking lot of Burgers 'n' Buns. He parked, and they got out. When they walked into the restaurant, he realized he had no idea what Angie looked like. He should have asked. Since it was crowded, he walked up to the counter and asked the young man wearing a paper hat that looked like two hamburger buns holding onto his head if he knew where Angie Jenners was. When he pointed at a woman sitting in a booth in the corner, he realized that if he'd looked around, he would have guessed she was Angie. She looked worried and there was a haunted look in her eyes.

He and River walked over to the booth. "Angie?" he said when they reached her.

She nodded and gestured toward the other side of the booth. Tony waited while River slid in first, then he got in next to her.

"Thanks for seeing us," River said.

"I was shocked when you called. I haven't heard the name Mayhew since I was a child."

"We realize that," River said. "Sorry if it upset you." She gazed around the restaurant. "I understand you help people with disabilities get jobs in the community. Are you working with someone here?"

River was clearly trying to put Angie at ease. If she would relax, it would be easier for her to talk to them. Tony was grateful that River realized this. Angie could be a huge help, but she needed to trust them—and calm down. This was obviously difficult for her.

Angie hesitated a moment as if surprised by River's question. Then she said, "Yes. See the young woman in the back? Behind the counter area?"

Tony and River looked toward the spot Angie indicated. There was a young woman who appeared to be intent on doing something, although they couldn't see what it was.

"That's Megan," Angie said. "She's autistic. She's been working here awhile. She helps to count out the chicken fingers and place them in smaller bags. It may not seem like much, but two years ago, she didn't have a job. Her parents weren't certain she'd ever be able to do anything outside of her home. The management here loves her, and Megan is really proud of herself. It's quite an accomplishment."

Tony could hear the pride in Angie's voice. It bothered him that he and River were going to have to plunge her into a past he was certain she'd rather forget.

"That's incredible, Angie," he said gently. "You've really changed her life for the better."

"Well, it's not just me. It's the program. I'm grateful there's a resource like this for people who need help."

"You sound very fulfilled," River said.

"I am," Angie said. "My life has turned out better than it began." She looked down at the table. "Now you want me to go back to a time I've tried hard to forget." When she looked up, there were tears in her eyes. "I still have nightmares about that night."

"I'm so sorry," River said. "If we didn't need to take you back there, we wouldn't."

Angie hesitated a moment. Then she sighed. "Like I said on the phone, I don't know what I can do to help you. I was only six when my grandparents died. I don't recall much about it."

"We understand," Tony said, "but sometimes children remember things that don't seem important at the time but may make sense later."

"I'm sorry, but why are you concerned about this now?" Angie asked. "Has something happened?"

Tony had been wondering about what to say to her. In the end, he'd decided to tell her the truth. "We believe the man who killed your grandparents is still taking innocent lives. Has been for many years. We also think he's here in Burlington. We're trying to find him before anyone else dies."

Whatever reaction he thought he might get wasn't the one she gave him. Angie Jenners turned completely white and began to cry.

TWENTY-EIGHT

River wasn't surprised by Angie's reaction. She knew what trauma could do. How it could feel like a dark and dangerous animal hiding in your psyche, waiting to pounce. The only way to operate successfully in your daily life was to keep the beast behind bars. She and Tony had just rattled the cage. Although God was with her, helping her to permanently rid herself of the horror trapped in her mind, River wasn't sure Angie had that kind of support. She nudged Tony, who got up and let River out. She went over to Angie's side and slid in next to her. She slowly put her hand on the shaken young lady's arm. Angie jerked when touched, but then took a deep breath, obviously trying to calm herself.

"We're so sorry to make you revisit that night," River said slowly. "Believe it or not, I know how hard it is. The last thing we want to do is upset you. We just want this man stopped before other people are hurt. Do you understand?"

"Yeah," she said shakily. "I do. I really do. It's just . . . well, I've always felt as if what happened that night was my fault."

"I don't understand," Tony said. "You didn't have anything to do with it."

"But I knew someone was in the house. I heard him come inside. I . . . I was downstairs getting into the cookie jar. I was supposed to be in bed. My . . . my mama never made cookies. Sometimes she'd buy them from the store . . . when she remembered to buy food. But my grandmother made the most wonderful peanut butter cookies. She put a chocolate drop right in the middle. I was lying in bed that night, thinking about those cookies. I knew that when I had to go home, I wouldn't get anything like that." She looked back and forth between Tony and River. "I thought that if I took some and hid them, I could take them with me. That way I could have one every day . . . for a while."

"So, you heard someone come in?" River said, trying to get her back to something that might help them. She was deeply moved by Angie's story, but she knew the best thing she could do for her and the Snowman's next victims was to stop him. "How did he get inside? Do you remember?"

Angie nodded. "He used a key. For just a second, I wondered if it was Nana or Papa, but then I remembered that I'd passed their room on the way to the kitchen. They were asleep in their bed." She sighed deeply. "I instinctively knew something was wrong. My grandparents were very careful with their keys. They wouldn't even give one to my mom because when she was using, she would sneak into the house and steal something to support her habit. Of course, I didn't realize that then, but when I got older, I figured out what was going on."

"Why didn't you tell the police what you remembered when they asked you?" River asked. Although she knew the answer, she wanted Angie to say it.

"I . . . I was afraid. Afraid that the man would come back for me if I told them anything. My . . . my mom used to warn me that I had to keep secrets. Especially from the police. That they weren't our friends, and that if I talked to them, they'd take me away and lock me up in jail." She shook her head. "I wish I'd said something." She frowned. "I thought the police in Des Moines caught the guy. How can he still be killing people?"

"The man in Des Moines did set a fire to cover up a murder, but he had nothing to do with the deaths of your grandparents. Or the attacks after that."

A tear slid down Angie's cheek. She started to say something but just then the waitress walked up to the table. River and Tony only ordered coffee. Since they'd be eating at Tony's, River didn't want to ruin Beth's dinner. The waitress didn't seem happy with their choice, but it couldn't be helped.

"I truly regret that I didn't tell the police what I saw," Angie said after the waitress walked away. "But even worse, I didn't do anything to stop that guy. My grandparents taught me how to call 911 if I ever needed help. They worried about me, afraid of the kinds of people my mom let into our apartment. If only I'd called . . ."

"Angie, you were a child," River said. "Children don't always know the right thing to do. You need to quit feeling guilty. I'm sure if you were talking to any other six-year-old who'd been through what you have, you'd tell them the same things I'm saying to you."

Angie picked up her napkin and dabbed at her eyes. "I'm sure that's true, and down through the years, I've told myself the same thing, but for some reason I just can't seem to get past it."

"God is helping me with the trauma I've endured in my life," River said, praying the Holy Spirit would give her the right words to say. "He's healing me." She smiled at the distraught young woman. "I still have a long way to go, but I believe that someday I'll truly be free."

Angie turned her head and stared at her for a moment before saying, "My grandmother used to tell me something similar. That God would get me through." She shrugged and picked up her coffee cup. "So where was He when my grandparents were killed?"

River snuck another quick look at Tony. Was this a question he should tackle? Tony just gave her a small smile. What did that mean? She tried to remember the sermon Pastor Mason had preached about this very thing. It had made sense to her. But at this moment, she couldn't remember his sermon. Why wasn't Tony saying anything? She was certain he could handle this better than she could, but suddenly a response came to her.

"I can't tell you exactly why it happened, Angie, but I do know that it wasn't God's will for your grandparents to die. He wasn't behind it. That's not who He is. There's evil in this world. Evil that God never meant to be here. He's given us weapons against it. But it's like being in a war. Sometimes people are injured. Sometimes they even die. We're not sure how the enemy was able to get to them, but we know that no matter what happens, we can depend on His love. On His healing touch." She took a deep breath. Where was this coming from? "I wish I could explain it all to you, but I can't. I'm just learning to trust Him, and all I know is that, so far, He's never let me down. Every day I get stronger, and I have more peace. He'll do the same for you if you let Him." Tears filled Angie's eyes once again.

"My grandmother used to read me Bible stories and talk to me about God. When she and my grandfather died, I guess I was angry because He didn't save them. I turned my back on Him."

"But now you know that God wasn't responsible for their deaths," Tony said softly. "You've been angry at the wrong person."

Angie nodded. "I get it."

"I understand your mother died not long after you went home," River said. "That must have been devastating."

Angie nodded. "It was. I went into foster care. My mother's family didn't want me, and no one knew where my father was. I'm not sure my mother even knew who he was. It was rough. I went through two pretty bad situations before I landed with my adoptive parents. I . . . I was angry for a while. Angry that no one came for me. But I've put that behind me. I was lucky. Some kids never find people like the Jenners."

The unfriendly waitress walked up to the table and put cups in front of Tony and River. Then she poured coffee into each cup, the edge of the coffee pot touching the rims of their cups. River hated it when servers did this. It was a great way to pick up germs from one cup and spread them to another. In the past, she'd asked for a new cup of coffee after explaining it to the server. But it was clear that this woman wasn't going to take helpful advice well. She exchanged a quick look with Tony. Neither one of them would be drinking their coffee.

"What about your grandfather's family?" Tony asked as the waitress walked away.

"My biological grandfather died when my grandmother was in her forties. She married Edward about seven years later. I never met anyone in his family. He didn't have any contact with them."

River was certain Tony was trying to establish a connection with Angie so that she'd trust them, but they needed to get back to the night of the murders. She didn't want to spook Angie, but they needed to get their questions answered and get back to the house.

"Angie," she said, keeping her voice low and calm. "Did you actually see the man who was in your grandparents' house the night of the fire?"

Angie's body jerked suddenly. It was clear this was very difficult. River felt bad for her, but they needed every piece of information they could get, not only to write an accurate profile, but to help Ray catch the Snowman. She realized in that moment that the behavioral analyst side of her was now working in tandem with the private investigator she'd become. It was a strange combination, but she liked it. When she worked for the FBI, she'd been a little jealous of field agents who actually hunted down criminals and brought them to justice. Now she had the best of both worlds. She might not be able to arrest anyone, but she could still find the bad guys—and gals—and hand them over to the police.

"When I realized someone was breaking into the house, I ran to my grandparents' room. I wanted to wake them up and warn them, but I was afraid the intruder might hear me. I hid in the closet. I could see some through the slats in the door."

"You were right to hide," Tony said. "If you'd tried to call the police, you might have died too."

River wasn't so certain. The Snowman's anger seemed to be directed at adults, most of them elderly. Usually, serial killers stuck to specific victim types, especially if their rage was ignited as a child. If they were hurt as children, they might not feel right about taking the life of a child.

"So, tell us what you saw," River said.

"He . . . he was dressed in black. Black pants, shoes . . . a black hoodie."

"So you didn't see his face at all?" Tony said, disappointment in his voice.

"I didn't say that," Angie said. She took a deep breath. "At one point, he looked toward the closet. My grandparents kept a nightlight on in their bedroom. When he turned toward me, I saw his face clearly. The image is burned into my memory. I can tell you exactly what he looked like."

TWENTY-NINE

I'm not sure we can count on the description Angie gave us," River said as they drove back to the house. "I mean, it's been twenty-four years since she lost her grandparents. We both know what happens to memories over even a year's time. And she was just six years old."

"I know," Tony said. "I feel the same way. But if she was right about the large spot on his face . . ."

"Maybe. Could have been a shadow."

"Or a tattoo."

"Perhaps," River said. "We have no choice but to share her information with your dad. I think we need to warn him that he may have to take it with a grain of salt. You remember the case we had where one of the victims who survived that terrible attack on the girls in a college dorm in Florida was convinced the killer had dyed his hair a shocking orange color?"

"And it turned out that the victim was remembering the killer's cap? The intruder's hair was actually brown?"

River nodded. "This could be the same thing. Of course, if the spot was a tattoo, that could really help."

"It would certainly help to narrow it down."

River frowned. "There was something else Angie said that surprised me."

"What was that?"

"We looked over your dad's files several times because we didn't want to miss anything."

"Yeah, so?"

"Do you remember anything about Angie's grandfather not being related to her biologically?"

Tony hesitated a moment before saying, "No. The police are supposed to investigate anyone connected to the murders. Friends and family. That's an odd omission. Even if he didn't have any living relatives, it should have been mentioned in the report."

"Well, Angie said he had no contact with any family. Maybe he didn't have anyone. But you're right. Detectives should have noted it. I think we need to ask your dad about that. I mean, it may not mean anything, but omissions concern me."

Tony laughed. "Yes, I know. You're a stickler for details."

River wasn't offended. Tony was right. However, in the past, that attention to detail had been a blessing. She'd picked up on things that others had missed. For example, there was the serial killer in Nevada who only killed women who wore red lipstick and had a mole on their cheek. Since most women wore red lipstick when they went out to clubs, his hunting ground, no one else on the team thought of it. But thankfully, River had caught it. And because she had, the FBI was able to catch the killer. In his mind, he was murdering his mother, who wore red lipstick and had the same kind of mole.

"I hope we haven't ruined your mother's supper," River said. "That took longer than I thought it would."

"My mom's lived with my dad long enough to know how to keep food warm without getting upset."

"I'm not sure I could do what she does."

"What do you mean?" Tony asked.

"Live my life dictated by my husband's job. It must be difficult."

"My parents love each other," Tony said. "There's give and take on both sides."

"I think they're very special. We didn't often see marriages at the Bureau last. The pressures of the job were just too much."

"I don't want to spend the rest of my life alone," Tony said, his tone somewhat tense. "My parents have made a go of it. They decided a long time ago that they would accommodate each other. Make allowances so that their marriage would work. And it has."

River reached over and touched his arm. "I'm sorry, Tony. I wasn't talking about them. I . . . I guess I wasn't thinking."

He took a deep breath and let it out slowly. "I'm sorry. I know so many marriages fail among our colleagues in the FBI, but the truth is, I want what my parents have, River. I don't want to give up a family and a chance at love over my job. No matter how much I love it."

"If that's how you feel, then why don't you date? I mean, you used to. But then about a year before we were attacked by the Strangler, it seemed as if you just lost interest."

Another long silence. River wished she'd never started down this road. She had an idea why he'd stopped dating, but she wasn't sure. They'd both touched on their feelings for each other, but she wasn't certain enough of him to assume she was the reason he didn't date anymore.

"Look," Tony said, "I dated. And I enjoyed it. But one day I realized that I needed to put my dating life in God's hands. I really do want to get married and have kids, but I want to marry the person God has for me. I don't want my marriage to fail. I know why some of our fellow agents' marriages didn't make it. But it was heartbreaking. Like Mark and Tanya Rutledge. They were the perfect couple. I would have bet anything they'd make it. But they didn't. And when things fell apart . . . well, it was awful. I'll never forget the look on Tanya's face when she found out Mark was having an affair. She was devastated."

"It really was a shock. Especially since they were Christians. I thought Christians weren't supposed to get divorced."

"Christians are still people, and sometimes we fail." He looked over at her. "She gave him several chances. At one point it looked like they were going to make it, but then Mark cheated again. I couldn't blame her for leaving."

"Mark was involved in that sex-trafficking case. You know, the one with the young girls?" River had tried to put that case out of her mind. Her unit worked with crimes against adults, and Mark was in the unit that handled crimes against children. Although she didn't know everything that was uncovered, she knew the facts were horrendous. Beyond anything most people could even begin to understand. "I think he just broke, you know? I know he loved Tanya. Those other women were just . . . I don't know . . . diversions? Maybe a way to distract him from what he was dealing with?"

"I talked to him," Tony said. "He told me he became so shut down he was just searching for anything that would make him feel something again. It's not an excuse for what he did, but it is a reason. I begged him to get couples counseling, but I guess by then it was too late. Tanya left her job in the administrative offices and moved back home to Indiana with the kids."

"I think we just proved why it's best not to get married when you work in law enforcement."

"But we're not in law enforcement anymore," Tony said slowly. "We're private investigators, and we run a not-very-successful agency. The pressures aren't what they were."

River snorted. "That would be true if it weren't for the serial-killer wannabe following us, promising to finish what his beloved leader started."

Tony laughed. "Now you're just reaching."

She lightly slapped his arm. "Not funny."

As Tony turned toward into the neighborhood where his parents lived, River said, "Well, at least our visit with Angie gave us something new we can share with your dad. Hopefully, he'll have more information from Sandra Cooper. She saw him, Tony. She may have valuable information. After we hear from her, we'll complete our profile."

"Aimee and I are going to have lunch after we go by Ms. Cooper's house. Then we can finish the profile. That means we'll be at my parents' house all weekend. Maybe we can relax some and have a little fun. What do you think?"

"I think that sounds wonderful. I could use some downtime."

"We used to play games a lot as a family," Tony said. "Would you be up for a rousing game of charades?"

River smiled. "It sounds great. But if your mother keeps cooking and baking, you may have to roll me out to the car on Monday."

He laughed again. River loved his laugh. It made her feel better. It was like a soothing salve. Wasn't there a scripture about laughter being like a medicine? It was true.

Tony pulled into the driveway and parked the car. As they headed inside, River couldn't help but look at the house with its Christmas lights and decorations. Snow adorned the trees and bushes, making the house and the yard look like a Christmas card. River loved snow. Always had. As a child she remembered feeling as if snow covered all the ugliness, making the world look beautiful. But knowing the Snowman was out there, and that it was a signal for him to hunt down and kill his victims, the snow seemed less like an ornamentation and more like an omen of death.

THIRTY

I was ready. I'd already cased their home. I had the house key. I'd learned how to follow my victims and get access to their keys. It was easy. Take a picture and then go online. There were locksmiths who didn't care why you needed a key. I always used the same story—I'd lost my keys. I'd taken a picture of my house key because I'd been told I'd be able to get a replacement with a photo if I ever needed to. I knew who to approach, and I'd never had a problem. Getting keys that belonged to my current victims hadn't been too difficult. I'd picked up the wife's purse from the floor next to her chair while she and her daughter had lunch in a local restaurant. I'd gotten the table next to them, then waited until the wife went to the bathroom. I pretended to drop my napkin on the floor and placed it over the purse, which I quickly slid under my jacket. After that, I simply went to the restroom, walked inside a stall where I removed her keys, and took a picture of the house key. It was pretty easy to figure out which key it was, but I photographed two this time, just in case. Then, when no one was in the bathroom, I left the purse on the hook on the back of the stall door. I also removed the cash in her billfold so it would look as if that was the reason the purse had been stolen. Someone would turn it in. I'd actually done it myself before, but the last time, they'd asked me to wait for the police to arrive so I could tell them how I found the purse. I made an excuse and got out of there. That's when I decided it was too risky to be the hero. Better to let someone else do it.

I was aware that my targets had an alarm system, but I knew how to get around it. No one kept their alarms on all the time. I'd wait until I was certain it was off, then I'd enter the house, hide, and wait for my opportunity. Basements were good hiding places. Unless they were finished and there were bedrooms, most people stayed upstairs. Especially in the winter since basements could be cold. This house was perfect. I'd looked through the basement windows. The space was partially finished, but one part was used for storage. There was a room with a pool table, and a small bedroom, but since I'd been watching the house, no one had gone downstairs. It would be a perfect place to wait. I'd get inside tomorrow with my backpack. I was ready. I had my syringes, vials, wire, electrical tape, and gasoline. I'd counted my syringes and was a little worried that one was missing, but in the end, I decided it wasn't important. Either I'd miscounted or I'd dropped one at the woman's house. Even if they knew how I really killed them, it wouldn't make any difference. There wouldn't be any fingerprints—no way to trace it back to me. And there was no way to stop me. Still, it bothered me that I'd been careless. How had that happened? Was I in too big of a hurry? Was I getting too confident? I was also a little upset that I couldn't get the insulin from my regular source. He was afraid someone at the hospital where he worked was on to him, so he'd decided to stop stealing insulin for now. He'd sent me to someone else, but I didn't really like this guy. Still, I had no choice. Regardless, I was ready, and this time there would be no mistakes. I always brought a gun as a backup in case I needed it. I'd only had to use it once, but I'd never had to actually fire it. However, I would if

I had to. This mission would be perfect. No one would get away this time.

I smiled. Tomorrow was their last full day on Earth. Saturday, they would all die.

TONY FELT BADLY that his mother had held dinner for so long, but she wasn't upset at all. Just glad to see them. His father was already home, and Tony could tell he wanted to talk to them. Although he'd mentioned the Snowman in front of his mother, for the most part, Tony's dad tried to keep most of their conversation for the upstairs office.

His mother had made meatloaf and mashed potatoes. It was delicious and everyone cleaned their plate quickly.

"You know, you can talk about what you're working on in front of me," Beth said as they waited for dessert. "You've already shared quite a bit."

"I realize that, hon," Ray said. "I just don't want to take away from the wonderful meal you've made for us. Besides, I don't think it hurts to have some family time without bringing up death and destruction."

Beth laughed. "And I appreciate that, but you always used to tell me about your cases when it was just us."

Ray sighed. "Actually, I didn't tell you about all of them. When you work in law enforcement, there are some things you have to keep to yourself. Things you don't want someone you love to hear about."

Tony knew exactly what his father meant. In his time in the FBI, he'd seen things no human being should see. If you didn't believe in the devil before becoming an FBI agent, you certainly did after a while. There was no way to understand some of the horrific things they saw except to believe that the people who committed the heinous crimes that ended up as reports and pictures given to the BAU to analyze were beyond the scope of human evil. They could only have been empowered by something beyond the comprehension and ability of men. The devil was not only real, but he was corrupted to the point of no return. There was no compassion, remorse, or pity in him.

"You and Tony are both bursting at the seams with information," Beth said. "You've both been fidgeting ever since you sat down."

"Okay," Ray said. "I give in." He smiled at his wife before addressing Tony and River. "Sandra Cooper is conscious and talking. I got more out of her today. She saw her attacker clearly."

"Was she able to give you a good description?" Tony asked.

"Before we go there, she said again that he waited for her to die first before he started the fire. I think we can safely assume that the people he killed were dead before he torched their houses."

"So, he kills them, binds their hands and feet, and then sets the room ablaze," River said.

"I can't believe Ms. Cooper was able to play dead while he bound her," Beth said. "I don't think I could do that."

Ray nodded. "She's a pretty gutsy woman. I don't think our UNSUB checked her very carefully, though. My guess is that he was so certain a large overdose of fast-acting insulin would kill her, he just assumed she was dead."

"At least we know the people he murdered didn't actually suffer horribly," River said. "So, he does have some compassion toward the people he kills. That agrees with our profile." She frowned. "So, we were right. The fires aren't just an expression of anger." She looked over at Tony. "He really is using them to hide evidence. He truly is an organized killer. We were right about that too."

"So did you speak to Angie?" Ray asked.

"Yeah, we did," Tony said. "It was very enlightening."

"Is she okay?" Beth asked.

"I think she's still recovering. But we learned a couple of interesting things." Tony looked at his mother. "Are you sure you don't want us to take this upstairs?"

Beth smiled as she got up to remove the layered pudding desserts from the refrigerator. "I get to spend more time with you this way. Go ahead. Just keep any details about missing heads or cannibals out of the conversation. Oh, and no zombies."

River grinned at Ray. "A lot of decapitations, cannibals, and zombies in Burlington?"

He laughed. "Fortunately not."

"First of all," Tony said, "did you know that Edward Wilson, Angie's grandfather, wasn't related to her biologically?"

Ray frowned at him. "No, that didn't come out during the investigation. It should have. It might have opened up some new possibilities. Maybe the person behind their deaths was related to him somehow. I can't believe that wasn't explored."

"I know things were pretty crazy back then," River said. "Could your chief have just overlooked this?"

"That's something that shouldn't have happened," Ray said slowly. "I can't explain it. I'll check Wilson out tomorrow. Run his social and put him through our facial recognition program."

"The FBI has new investigative tools," Tony said. "If you need help, let me know. I can contact someone with the Bureau."

"The National Crime Information Center should cover any criminal background Wilson had," Ray said. "If I need additional assistance, though, I'll let you know. I appreciate the help."

"Any reason besides being busy that your chief might have ignored this?" River asked.

Ray sighed. "Back then, we were going through cutbacks while crime was rising. Unfortunately, some bureaucrats don't understand what law enforcement needs to make things run smoothly. They just look at the bottom line. Money is everything." He shook his head. "Chief Watts was under a lot of pressure. My guess is that his detectives just didn't pick up on this, and he didn't have the time to follow up. Of course, he shouldn't have had to. I can't blame him for this one."

"If something pops up that might have saved lives, this could have been a huge mistake," Tony said.

"I agree."

Beth set a large dessert glass in front of each of them and then handed everyone a long-handled spoon. The pudding looked delicious, but Tony's stomach was tight. He had a big problem with sloppy police work. He reminded himself that it might not have made a difference. There wasn't any reason to get upset about it yet. Still, the idea that people may have died because someone didn't do their job correctly really aggravated him.

Not wanting to upset his mother, he picked up his spoon. Of course, the layered pudding was incredible. Vanilla and butterscotch pudding layers with whipped cream between them kept him eating until he reached the bottom of the glass. He noticed that his dad only picked at his dessert.

"Unfortunately, I can't take you by Sandra's house in the morning," Ray said suddenly. "The chief won't give me permission. I'm sorry. If you were still with the Bureau or were police officers, he might have approved it."

Tony was disappointed, but for now it was best to concentrate on other things. He knew that law enforcement could be very territorial. This wasn't really a big surprise.

"That's okay, Dad," he said. "We understand."

"I really don't think there's much more you could have seen beyond the photos I brought home. I can go back over there and take more pictures if it would help you."

Tony shook his head and looked at River. "I think we were most interested in how he got in and if he left anything behind. Angie said he had a key for her grandmother's house. After all these years, I'm not sure we can trust her memory. I'm fairly certain he didn't have a key to all his victims' houses. He has to have left something behind. You know, Locard's exchange principle." Dr. Edmond Locard was a pioneer in forensic science. He taught that the perpetrator of a crime will always bring something into a crime scene and leave with something from it. And that both kinds of trace evidence can be effective forensic evidence.

"Well, except for the Christmas ornament, I think the fire may have destroyed anything else he left behind," Ray said. "Hopefully, when we find a suspect, the other part of Locard's theory will help us to nail our killer. We're certain Sandra didn't let him in, but we haven't found any evidence of a break-in. Our crime scene techs are very good. Even if they do work out of Burlington."

River smiled at him. "We've been nothing but impressed by the work done here," she said. "We trust that you're doing everything that needs to be done. Looking over the house wasn't that important to us. We're fine without it."

"Good," Ray said. "I felt as if I was letting you down."

"Not at all, Dad."

"Okay. Well, I'm going back to the office to check out Wilson. If I don't, it's going to bug me all night."

"We're kind of forgetting something important, aren't we?" River asked. "You said Sandra saw her attacker. So did Angie Mayhew. We need to compare notes."

Ray let out an exasperated sigh. "Of course. Sorry. I allowed myself to get upset about the possibility of shoddy police work and telling you about not visiting Sandra's house. I totally spaced it. I'm not certain her fuller description will help us, though. She said the man who tried to kill her was average height. Black jeans, black hoodie, no distinguishing features. She could see part of his hair. Brown. Like I said, not very helpful."

Tony frowned at his father. "What about saying he had red eyes?"

"She's not sure about that now. I think we have to attribute that to the morphine she was on when I talked to her the first time."

"Angie Mayhew said the man who attacked her grandparents had something dark on his cheek. A tattoo or some kind of birthmark," Tony said. "She said it was quite noticeable."

"I don't understand," Ray said, frowning. "Could we be talking about two different killers?"

THIRTY-ONE

River trudged up the stairs to Ray's office, his last words echoing in her mind. Could she and Tony have missed it again? Were there two killers? Her confidence had already been shaken once. Was the same thing happening again?

She walked into the office and sat down. She heard Tony come in behind her and close the door.

"I know what you're thinking," he said, "but don't go there."

"You mean don't wonder if we made the same mistake we made with the Strangler?" she said. "Kind of hard not to."

"Angie was trying to remember something that happened twenty-four years ago. You know how memories change. It could have been a shadow on his face. Besides, she probably imagined it. She was only six years old. I don't think we should pay any attention to her supposed memory."

His words helped to quiet her mind. He told the truth. Memories from years earlier were incredibly unreliable. Why had she reacted so strongly?

"You can't keep second-guessing yourself," Tony said. "Please, let's just concentrate on this case. Can we put the Strangler behind us? At least for now?"

"Hard to do when his minion is out there, waiting to kill me."

"Or just trying to terrorize you."

River's mouth dropped open. "He bugged our office, Tony. He probably killed David Prescott. Todd is certain some of the people we thought Joseph Baker killed were murdered by someone else. It had to have been him. This guy doesn't really sound like someone who doesn't intend to follow through on his threats."

"We're not going to let him get to you, River. We're watching for him. We're armed. Our homes have alarms. Now there are cameras in our office and in the hall outside our office. The police in St. Louis are aware of the situation and are keeping an eye on us, and your mom. I'm telling you, this man is trying to control you by creating fear. I'm not saying you should ignore the threat. I'm just suggesting that you quit allowing him to rent space in your head. Don't let him control you."

Tony had said these same things before, but for some reason, this time, it got through. The man really was controlling her. And it wasn't just his threats against her. It was knowing that he and Joseph Baker had deceived them. It had attacked her confidence, and she was tired of it. Tired of feeling incompetent. Tired of being afraid. Just tired.

"Okay. I get it. Let's get back to our profile," she said. "You're right. This guy could be getting his kicks by trying to get me to think about him all the time. How long does he intend to keep this up? A year? Two? More? I'm done."

"Good girl," Tony said with a smile. "Now, I think we need to make some adjustments to our profile."

"Tell me you didn't just call me a 'good girl,'" River said, glaring at him.

Tony's surprised look made it impossible for her to keep a straight face. "You're easy," she said, laughing. "But seriously, you probably shouldn't call me a good girl again."

Tony grinned at her. "You got it. Now, back to the profile. . . ."

"Okay, although I feel like I'm beginning to wonder how many times we have to go over this."

"We had to redo profiles at the BAU when we got new information," Tony said.

"I know, but this time it's bugging me more."

Tony smiled. "We had a team back then. The weight of helping law enforcement stop a psychopath didn't lie just on our shoulders."

"I think you're right." River sighed. "Okay, here we go. We've learned some things about our UNSUB. He kills his victims first by giving them an overdose of insulin. He doesn't want to cause his victims pain."

"And he uses fire for two reasons. To destroy evidence and to express his anger toward his victims," Tony said. "That's why we decided he kills for someone else. Avenging someone he cares about. If it wasn't for this person, he probably wouldn't be killing."

"He's still a psychopath," River said. "Maybe he doesn't want to kill, but only because it's distasteful to him. Not because he really has compassion for people."

"That makes sense. So, the insulin is a means to an end. It's easier to sneak into a house and quietly inject someone who's sleeping. It's an effective way to kill." He shook his head. "You know, he probably carries a weapon too. A gun. I mean, if people aren't asleep or if one of his victims wakes up, he has to have a way to control them. I don't think he has it in him to stab anyone. He doesn't like to get his hands dirty."

"Yeah, I agree," River said. "Just because no bullets have been retrieved at his crime scenes, it doesn't mean he doesn't bring a gun in case he needs it. And as far as using insulin, we can't completely rule out that he has a modicum of empathy. But as you said, the main reason for his MO is because he's figured out an efficient and less messy way to murder people.

"Why wrap their hands and feet with wire? Do we still think it's out of respect for the victims? I mean, posing them as if they were in a coffin?"

"Maybe," Tony said. "But because he's organized, he must have studied the effects of fire on the human body. The natural reaction is for the muscles to contract and the joints to flex. So why does he care?"

"You know," River said slowly, "we know that burning the body is a great way to destroy evidence. And that's true. But crossing the arms over the chest and securing them—and also keeping the legs in place so that the body stays in place . . ."

"It's not because he's just preparing them for burial, it's also a sacrifice," Tony said. River could hear the excitement in his voice. "Abraham tied his son Isaac to an altar as a sacrifice to God."

"I agree," River said. "Even though the victim is dead, our UNSUB needs to feel that he's making a sacrifice for the person he's trying to avenge. The folded hands are the key."

"It's pretty smart. He kills them humanely, because it's effective, not just because he finds the process distasteful. This way, there's no fighting back or screaming. Neat and simple. Then he binds the body and sets the fire. This is a sacrifice for the wrong caused to the person he's killing for. And, of course, he's destroying evidence." Tony gazed at River silently. "Notice he doesn't set the body on fire. Just the area around the bed. The other idea is too graphic for him. He leaves before the body ignites. That was lucky for Sandra Cooper. If he'd waited around, he probably would have finished her off."

"He's not just smart," she said, restating what Tony had just said, "he's brilliant. He plans his MO down to the last detail."

"Except in Sandra's case. He didn't realize that the insulin might not kill someone who is diabetic."

"Which begs the question," River said, "where is he getting

the insulin? He must not be diabetic, or he would have thought of that."

"Not necessarily. She was in bed. I doubt she was wearing her medical alert bracelet."

"You're right. But if he's diabetic . . ."

"Yeah, he'd know that there could be a problem with his MO."

River frowned at him. "That's a little careless for someone who's so precise. And he dropped a syringe. That never happened before."

"Maybe he's nearing the end of his mission?"

"That's a possibility, but we can't be certain."

"Okay, assuming he's not diabetic, where is he getting the insulin?" Tony asked.

"It's really not difficult. Walmart sells insulin without a prescription. And it can be ordered online from Canada, although I think you'd have to drive to Canada to buy it. If you order it online, you may have to have a prescription.

"Or, he could be working in some kind of medical facility that has insulin. A hospital or a pharmacy." River crossed her arms. "But they're pretty careful to watch their supplies. If he's a doctor or a nurse, he could be fiddling with the files. You know, saying he's giving someone insulin but giving them water instead. It's been done."

Tony stared at her, his eyes wide. It made her laugh.

"Sorry. You weren't working the case we had several years ago. The nurse killing patients in Rhode Island? For a while, the special agents working the case thought she was using insulin as a way to kill patients, but no vials were missing. It sparked my interest, and I did some research on how someone could obtain it without a prescription."

Tony laughed. "You had me worried there for a moment. No matter how much you trust your partner, knowing they could kill you and get away with it can make you a little nervous."

River grinned at him and held up her right hand. "You have my word I won't kill you. Relax."

"Thank you." Tony stared at her for a moment. "Okay, let me ask you this. If you're buying insulin . . . online . . . in Canada . . . or even at Walmart, wouldn't there be a record of it?"

"You'd think so. Of course, the person buying the insulin is probably not using their real name. I'd say our guy isn't. He's too smart for that. It's not hard to come up with a fake driver's license or some other kind of I.D."

"But what he can't do," Tony said, "is to hide from the cameras pharmacies have. If he's buying it, not stealing it, there might be a way to track him."

"My guess is your father is already looking into that. He knows about the insulin."

"You're right," Tony said, "but I'd like to be sure."

He got up, took his phone out of his pocket, and started to make a call. But suddenly, he stopped and put his phone down.

"What's wrong?" River asked.

"My dad left his glasses on his desk," Tony said. "He only wears them when he reads."

River frowned at him. "And that's important why?"

Tony picked up the glasses and turned to look at her. "I think I know why Sandra Cooper said the man who tried to kill her had red eyes."

River shook her head, feeling confused.

Tony put his father's glasses on. "The killer must have been wearing glasses, River. Sandra got a look at him after he set the fire. The flames showed up in the glasses."

It made sense. "I think you're right, but I'm not sure how much that will help us. A lot of people wear glasses."

"I realize that, but every time we learn something new, it puts us just a little bit closer."

"I agree."

Tony picked up his phone again so he could call his dad. While he did that, River walked over to the corkboard and looked at the pictures she'd gone over so many times before. They were getting closer to understanding the UNSUB, but they still couldn't figure out what connected the victims. What was the killer avenging? What did they have in common? Until they knew that, it was entirely possible that more people would die.

THIRTY-TWO

Tony hung up the phone after talking to his father and rejoined River, who was staring at the crime photos again.

"I think we've memorized these pictures," he said. "See anything new?"

She shook her head slowly. "No, but I'm looking at them again anyway. With the new information we have, I'm wondering if the thing that connects our victims is staring us in the face."

"Well, if it is, I'm not seeing it. I asked about checking pharmacies. As I suspected, they're already doing that. As far as the glasses, Dad feels the same way we do. Not sure if it will help much. People can remove their glasses, and Angie didn't mention them." Tony couldn't stifle a yawn.

"Do you want to call it off for tonight?" River asked. "You're tired."

"No, not yet, unless you do. Dad seems to have made some headway with his search on Wilson. I'd like to wait until he gets home and hear what he has to say."

"Should we start revising our profile?"

Tony sighed. "Again?"

"Shouldn't we adjust it to add the possibility of a team?"

Tony shook his head. "I meant what I said about not trusting Angie's memory. I mean, what kind of 'black spot' would someone have on their face? And if our guy really had something like that, why not wear a ski mask to hide it? We've learned that he's smart."

"But if this was his first attempt, maybe he made a mistake. We think he's in his forties or early fifties now. That means he was young when he killed the Wilsons. He could have learned as he progressed."

"I don't know," Tony said. "Explain the twenty-year gap between the Wilsons and the first murders here."

"I can't," River said. She pointed at a picture on the board. "He kills the Wilsons, Angie's grandparents, then he kills Sheila Jackson, an older widow. What's the connection?"

"Maybe he just hates old people."

River looked at him and made a face. "Not helpful."

"Well, it makes as much sense as anything else."

"I know."

Tony took his phone out again. "Checking the weather. I want to know when that next storm hits."

"I thought it was supposed to start on Saturday."

After clicking a few buttons on his phone, Tony felt his stomach tense. "I just want to be sure. Yep. Still predicted for Saturday. Starts early Saturday morning."

"We don't have much time."

"I don't know why we're so worried. He's always waited two years before striking again."

"But he didn't succeed with Sandra Cooper. She lived. The Salt River Strangler didn't take it well when I survived. I'm assuming the Snowman feels the same way." River stepped back from the corkboard. "My instinct tells me if he can't get to Sandra, he may try to execute someone else. That's if he has anyone else lined up. I don't know, he's so organized. Maybe he will wait."

Tony walked over to one of the chairs and sat down. He rubbed the back of his neck, which felt as tense as his stomach did. "I don't know if it's just frustration, or because of Sandra . . . or if the Holy Spirit is warning me that the Snowman has selected a new victim. But I feel like you're right. It's like some kind of loud bell ringing in my ears. He wants to save face."

"I thought wisdom from God is peaceful," River said.

"Yeah, you're right. Unfortunately, our reactions to it aren't always correct." Tony sucked in a deep breath and began to let it out slowly, trying to calm his nerves. "I've got to put this in God's hands. It's just . . ."

"It's just that Burlington is preparing for Christmas," River said softly. "Families are decorating their trees and putting up beloved decorations. Somewhere there's a family that has no idea that this will be the worst Christmas of their lives unless we can stop the Snowman before he strikes again."

Tony gazed at her for a moment, marveling at her intelligence and incredible insight. They'd worked together for so long it was like they were married. His mind suddenly clicked back to that night on the banks of the Salt River. The horror he felt as he watched the Strangler hit her, tie her up, put her into an old trunk, and pull it over to the side of the river. Tony had tried to stop him. Even after being shot four times, he'd crawled toward her, wanting nothing more than to keep her alive. But before he could reach her, he'd passed out. He would have gladly died to protect her. What kind of relationship did they have? He felt closer to River than he did his own sister. What did that mean? Did she ever wonder about him? About how he felt?

He cleared his throat and considered the question she'd just posed. "I'm just not sure we have enough information to really help my father," he said. "We can give him an idea as to what this guy's thinking. We can even tell him why we believe someone else is on his radar, but we can't tell him why he's killing, and we both know that without that information, it's almost impossible to find him."

River pursed her lips and crossed her arms, behaviors she exhibited when she was thinking. "Well, we're pretty sure he's reacting to something in his childhood. Something that happened at Christmas."

"That's true, but how are these people related to him? The police looked carefully at each victim and didn't find anything to explain what's behind these deaths."

"Well, there's still Edward Wilson," River said. "Maybe your dad will find something useful."

"I hope so."

River folded her hands in her lap, then she stared at the far wall, not really looking at anything.

"What?" he asked.

"Let's play *what if.*"

Tony smiled at her. *What if* was a game they used to play when they were stuck with a problematic profile at the BAU. Although most of the time it drifted into some rather ridiculous scenarios that made the analysts laugh and helped to relieve tension, a couple of times they'd actually come up with something helpful.

"Okay, go," he said.

River leaned back in her chair and closed her eyes. "Okay, what if he's a child who was abused in some way by an adult. Let's even say it was Edward and Vera Wilson since they're the first victims. So, they abuse him . . . and someone else . . . let's say there's a sibling, or a mother who is injured in some kind of catastrophic way, and the kid is traumatized."

"Let's say it's a sister, and she dies," Tony said, allowing his imagination to create a story that could match the circumstances in the case.

"All right. A sister who dies. Maybe Edward Wilson had something to do with it."

Tony nodded. "Okay. So, the brother waits until he's an adult and kills the Wilsons as an act of revenge for the death of his sister."

"But why kill Sheila Jackson? What does she have to do with anything?" River asked.

"What if . . ." Tony paused. "She had something to do with his sister's death."

"But there wasn't any connection between the Wilsons and Sheila. Nothing."

Tony looked at her. "Okay, what if Sheila Jackson knew about the abuse and didn't help the killer's sister."

River stared at him for a moment. "Okay, but that's pretty weak."

"I know." Tony sighed loudly. "Even my *what ifs* aren't helpful."

"Don't give up. We believe the Snowman is exacting revenge for someone else," River said. "The victims are sacrifices to this . . . person. Now, we know that most serial killers have some kind of abuse in their past. So, what if the Snowman and his sibling . . . we'll go with sister . . . were abused as children? Since the only person we don't know everything about is Edward Wilson, what if he did it? Sheila Jackson was somehow involved. . . . Wait a minute." She reached for the file on the desk and pulled it closer. After shuffling through the pages for a moment, she said, "Hey, Sheila Jackson used to be a foster parent when she was young. She and her husband took kids in."

"Were Edward and Vera foster parents?"

Again, River shuffled through the pages. "No," she said, disappointment in her voice. "No record of it."

Tony sighed again.

"If you keep that up, you could pass out, and you're bigger than I am. I'm not sure I can pick you up off the floor."

Tony laughed. "I'm sorry. My brain is really tired. I feel like we're close, but it's still a few inches out of our grasp."

"Yeah, me too. Let's put a pin in it and try again tomorrow."

"Now that we're not going to Sandra's house, I'm gonna call my sister to see if we can meet for breakfast instead of lunch. I know she wants some time with me, but I'd like to keep our time tomorrow as uninterrupted as possible. If Aimee and I have breakfast, you and I could hit this again when I get back. We'd have the rest of the day."

"I think that makes sense."

Tony stood to his feet and stretched. He really was tired. Mind and body. Maybe a good night's rest would get him back on track.

River got up too. They were both headed toward the door when it suddenly burst open. Ray stood there with a smile on his face.

"I think I've found something," he said. "Something that could lead us to the Snowman."

THIRTY-THREE

River and Tony quietly waited for Ray to tell them what he'd discovered. Tony hadn't seen his father this excited for a while. Would this new information really lead to the Snowman?

Ray sat down at his desk while Tony and River pulled their chairs closer to him. "First of all, I still can't tell you why he's killing, but I've uncovered something rather interesting. It looks like a dead end, but if we—"

"Dad, you're not really selling this," Tony said with a smile.

"I know." He flipped open the notebook he had with him. "Edward Wilson was married before Vera. His first wife died. He had two children, Michael and Stacy."

"That *is* interesting," River said. "You need to talk to them. Maybe they can . . ."

"That's going to be difficult." Ray sighed and rubbed his eyes.

His dad's excitement was mixed with weariness. Tony worried that this might be too much for him. He'd had a mild heart attack five years ago. He was doing well now, but Tony didn't want him to push himself too hard.

"Why is that?" Tony asked.

"They've disappeared. Seems that, for some reason, Edward

gave them up. Maybe his wife's death was too much for him, I have no idea. I can trace Michael until he's sixteen, but he doesn't show up anywhere after that. Stacy went missing even earlier. No trace anywhere."

River stood up. "Wait a minute," she said, her eyes wide. "Where were they before they disappeared?"

Tony felt his heart rate increase. He knew where this was going. Before his dad had a chance to answer, he said, "Foster care?"

Ray looked surprised. "Yes . . ."

"That's it," River said. She hurried over to the pictures. "Foster care. Sheila Jackson used to have foster children."

Ray grabbed the file on his desk. "Mac and Angela Craig were foster parents, but it was years ago. I have no idea about Sandra Cooper."

"Let's think about this for a minute," River said slowly. "So, Edward Wilson walks away from his kids. They go into foster care. He and his new wife are murdered. Then Sheila Jackson is killed by the Snowman. She used to have foster kids."

"I don't see the connection," Ray said. "Michael went to two different foster families. Sheila Jackson wasn't one of them. Stacy's records are a little confusing. As far as I can tell, she was only with one foster family before she disappeared. And it wasn't Sheila Jackson."

"You need to talk to that foster family," Tony said. "Find out what happened."

"Good idea," Ray said with a smile. "I already did that. The Gordons are very nice people. They tried to help Stacy, but she had some real problems that they weren't equipped to cope with. She tried to hurt some of the other children. The foster care advocate they talked to said they had a better place for her. They tried to check on Stacy after she left, but the advocate left the agency not long after Stacy was moved. No one else seemed to know what happened to her. The Gordons called the agency's administrator, who assured them everything was okay. That was the last thing they heard. I couldn't call the agency because it went out of business several years ago. Tomorrow, I'll do some further checking with the state to see what information they have."

"This sounds a little weird," Tony said. "I've heard of kids lost in the system, but this is the first time I've actually seen it happen."

"We can't assume anything," Ray said. "I may be able to track Stacy tomorrow when the state offices are open."

"Can you visit Sandra Cooper again? Ask her if she was ever a foster parent?"

Ray nodded. "I will."

"I read something once about overloaded foster care agencies dumping children off with people who weren't licensed," River said. "In some cases, the children were abused."

"Could that be what happened here?" Tony said. He met River's eyes. "Follow me here. Let's do another *what if*."

"What if what?" Ray asked.

"It's just a mental exercise, Dad," Tony said. "We try to come up with scenarios that might fit the situation."

Ray laughed. "Detectives do that more than you might guess. Go for it."

"Okay," Tony said. "Edward Wilson's wife dies." He glanced over at his father. "How did she die, Dad?"

"Sadly, she committed suicide. Hung herself."

"Do you know who found her?" River asked.

Ray shook his head. "No idea. All I have is a death certificate."

River took a deep breath. "What if Edward Wilson was an abusive husband and father? His wife commits suicide to get away from him. He dumps his kids into the system, creating two extremely resentful siblings." She frowned at Ray. "How old were they when they went into foster care?"

"Michael was twelve, and Stacy was nine."

River nodded. "Okay, so they're angry. Their mother is dead, and their abusive father has abandoned them. What if they get separated?" She shot a look at Ray, who nodded. "When Michael turns eighteen, he goes looking for Stacy. But he can't find her. She's disappeared."

"So, he turns his anger on his father, kills him, then . . ." Tony stopped. "It's a good theory, but then he kills Sheila Jackson, who has no connection whatsoever to his sister?"

"But we don't know that," River said. "What if she does?"

"But why would he kill her? Because she doesn't know where Stacy is?" Ray asked. "I mean, with the foster care system such a mess, it doesn't mean it was Sheila's fault."

"Unless . . ." Tony didn't really want to say what he was thinking, but when playing *what if*, they took leaps. Even if it was unpleasant. Unfortunately, more than once their worst fears were confirmed later. "Unless Sheila killed her. Maybe Michael found out, and that's why he executed Sheila—because she killed his sister?"

"No, that doesn't work," Ray said. "If she'd died, we would know about it."

"Would you, Dad?" Tony said. "You told me yourself that more people get away with murder than anyone suspects."

"And that's true. So-called *accidents* that aren't investigated. People found dead who have no physical signs of trauma aren't autopsied. It happens every day all around the country."

"So how would someone in foster care get away with that?" River asked. "Sheila Jackson was licensed, right?"

"Yes, but there are several ways a child could go missing. Maybe the social worker in charge of Sheila just didn't follow up. Not only could it occur, it has happened more than once. In some areas, the foster care system is a real mess."

"That's sad," River said. "Children should be our number one concern."

Ray nodded. "I agree, but sadly, it isn't true. To be honest, you can't blame the wonderful foster care workers or families out there. Most of them are incredible. They work hard to protect at-risk children. But when things get out of control and there's not time to check out every family, mistakes happen."

"Do you think Michael Wilson could be the Snowman?" Tony asked River.

"I have no idea. I mean, the childhood trauma fits. Maybe Stacy died in the winter? Perhaps the ornament was something she had when she went missing? It could be true, but we have no way to prove it. And what about the murders here? And Sandra? What possible connection do they have to a child that went missing so long ago?"

Tony let out a deep sigh. His brain was beginning to lock up. "Look, let's call it a day. Besides, we're veering away from writing a profile. Once again, we're trying to do Dad's job."

"You're right," River said. "But I think Michael Wilson fits our profile beautifully . . . if he really is the Snowman. But that's your job to decide, Ray."

Ray stood up. "Look, you've given me a lot to think about. I'm going to follow up on this. Maybe you've hit on something. Maybe you haven't. But at least this gives me some hope."

"Did you find any pictures of Michael Wilson or his sister?" River asked.

Ray shook his head. "Not so far, but we're trying. Checking schools and the state to see what they have. I'm confident we'll find something. Not sure pictures that are almost thirty years old will help us, but we still need to look at them. As soon as we find something, I'll let you know. I doubt they will help your profile, though."

"You'd be surprised," River said. "Even in a headshot, there are clues to personality. Is the subject smiling? Frowning? Are there signs of anger or fear? Photos could actually give us information we can use."

Ray nodded. "Okay, whatever you need. We have to stop this guy. I have a bad feeling. . . ."

Tony and River looked at each other. Ray clearly felt the same thing they did. Three people with experience studying criminals. All of them with the same gut instinct. Tony took it as an omen. One they had to take very seriously.

THIRTY-FOUR

After Ray headed to bed and Tony called Aimee to see if she could meet him for breakfast instead of lunch, River went upstairs and took a shower. Then she went back to Aimee's room. She couldn't shake the feeling that she didn't belong there. River had reminded herself more than once that the room really belonged to Beth and Ray. They were so kind and welcoming, and if they wanted her here, it was okay. River wished she could meet with Beth and Aimee to talk. Beth had dealt with negative feelings after Tony was shot, and she was okay with River now. Maybe Aimee could come around too. She wondered if Tony planned to talk to Aimee about the conversation they'd had the day they met. She hoped not, but it was in Tony's hands now. She had to let it go.

River was trying not to let guilt attach itself to her again. Her talks with Tony had made her determined to walk in freedom. But talking about it and doing it appeared to be two different things. She couldn't stop wondering if she should have heard something in Jacki's voice that horrible night. Something that alerted her. The guilt from her stupidity weighed on her every day. Pastor Mason and Tony had both talked about how carrying guilt was wrong because of what Jesus had done to set her free. It made sense in her head, so why was she struggling with it so much? And why did she still feel so guilty about turning her back on God after He heard her prayer and delivered her that night in the river? She'd apologized to God over and over, but it still felt like a weight in her heart. She knew God was a loving God, but wasn't He also holy? What was the unforgivable sin? Had she committed it?

"Stop it," she whispered to herself. "Just stop it. You're going to drive yourself crazy." She got into bed and closed her eyes. "I'm so sorry," she said quietly. "I don't know what else to say. It seems wrong to just walk away like I didn't lie to You. Like I didn't reject You after You miraculously saved me."

She turned over on her side and felt a tear run down her cheek. She forced the remorseful feelings out of her mind, but it took great effort. She made herself concentrate on the profile they were working on. Several times she'd thought their profile was done . . . or near completion. But things kept changing. Were they trying too hard because this was for Ray? Being close to him made this situation seem so personal. And so threatening. If someone else died, how would she and Tony feel? The last thing she needed was more guilt. As it was, sometimes she felt as if it were crushing her, making it hard to breathe. Wasn't the truth linked to her relationship with her parents? She wasn't able to trust their love, and now she was having trouble believing in God's love for her. She and Tony were supposed to be experts in human behavior. River knew what was happening, so why couldn't she change her thinking? It felt as if she was under a major attack from the enemy.

She gasped and sat up in bed. "God, why is this happening to me now? Please help me. Please deliver me from this." She got up and opened the wardrobe. Then she got back in bed and used the remote to turn on the TV. She needed to focus on something different. Sometimes a light movie or a funny sitcom made her laugh. Hopefully, she could find a show like that. She kept the sound low and added captions. The last thing she wanted to do was to wake anyone up.

As she clicked through the channels, she suddenly found herself watching a scene from a movie that seemed to be about Jesus. Curious, she picked up her phone and entered the title. The director was a famous actor. It was old, released in 2004. She'd had no interest in religious movies back then, which explained why she'd never seen it. She started to change the channel, thinking this might not be what she needed right now, but for some reason, every time she started to initiate a new search, she just couldn't do it. Finally, she gave up and started watching. As the movie progressed, she realized that this movie was about the crucifixion. She didn't want to see anything like that. She needed something that would lift her spirits, and this certainly didn't qualify. But again, she found herself unwilling to switch channels.

Two hours later, she was sobbing into her pillow. Is this really what Jesus went through? And He did it for mankind? For her? Was allowing herself to carry guilt saying He hadn't given enough? His sacrifice wasn't sufficient? This is exactly what Tony had tried to tell her. She'd been so impacted by his words. Had believed she'd been set free. But then she'd fallen back into the same mindset. Tony's words popped into her mind. *It's time for you to accept His sacrifice. For you. For me.* The movie made Tony's admonition come to life in a way she couldn't explain. This wasn't a story. This was real. Real, incredible, all-consuming love.

Then she did something she'd never done before. Something she knew she didn't have to do. God could hear her anywhere she prayed, but she felt the need so strongly, it was as if her body was acting on its own. She got out of the bed and sank down on her knees. She clasped her hands together as she knelt there, leaning on the bed.

"I'm so sorry, Lord," she said, trying to keep her voice low while her tears flowed. "What You did was . . . almost too much to believe. And You did it for me. You took my guilt so I wouldn't have to carry it. How could I act as if it wasn't enough? Tony tried to tell me, but this movie made it so real. Please help me to never question Your forgiveness again. Help me to really walk in freedom this time, not because I deserve it, but because You paid an incredible price so I could have peace. You went through all of that willingly because You love us so much. It's beyond my comprehension, but I intend to live the rest of my life believing that Your sacrifice was more than enough."

The words had just left her mouth when a sensation of warm love seemed to flow from the top of her head and through her entire body. It was so real and unexpected—all she could do was sob. It took about an hour for River to climb back into bed. Her limbs felt like rubber, and her body was so relaxed she wanted to keep the feeling forever.

She prayed for a while but soon felt sleepy. As she drifted off, she realized she was smiling.

WHEN RIVER OPENED HER EYES the next morning, she wondered for a moment if the experience of the night before was a dream. Had it really happened? It took a few seconds for her to accept that it was true. She sat up in the bed, trying to remember what day it was. She felt so good. Calm. Happy. She smiled and swung her legs over the side of the bed. It was Friday. Tony was going to breakfast with Aimee. It was funny, but she was no longer upset about Aimee. River knew enough about people to realize that Aimee had been so traumatized by Tony's shooting that she needed someone to blame. A place to focus her anger. It had nothing to do with River. She'd known that all along, but now it was time for her to accept the truth.

As she thought about Aimee, River considered her own reactions and emotions and realized that guilt had almost become a part of her. Part of her identity. Like a negative friend who followed her around, constantly accusing her. She also realized that guilt was a kind of false humility. She believed if she felt guilty, it meant she was humble.

River found her purse and opened it. Inside she had a small notebook with some of her favorite Bible verses. She found the notebook and opened it. The verse she was looking for was on the third page.

"There is therefore now no condemnation to those who are in Christ Jesus, who do not walk according to the flesh, but according to the Spirit. For the law of the Spirit of life in Christ Jesus has made me free from the law of sin and death."

River had sat in church and heard Pastor Mason read that verse, but for some reason, today it was alive. She understood it now.

She got up and quickly dressed. Then she went downstairs. Beth and Tony were sitting at the kitchen table. She smiled at them.

"Tony's only having coffee since he's having breakfast with Aimee," Beth said, returning her smile. "And Ray left early for the station. I've been keeping some lovely cinnamon rolls warm in the oven. How about a couple?"

"That sounds awesome," River said. "But I'm going to have to start working out when we get back. As it is, I'm afraid to get on a scale."

Beth waved her hand at her. "Oh, please. You're such a little bitty thing. That's not something you'll ever need to worry about."

"I really hope you're right, but I'm not so sure." River picked up an empty coffee cup and filled it, then she sat down at the table. She realized Tony was looking at her oddly.

"Is something wrong?" she asked, patting her hair to make sure it wasn't messed up.

"No. You just . . . look different somehow," he said.

"Oh, son," Beth said. "She looks just as lovely as she did yesterday. What are you talking about?"

Tony sighed dramatically and winked at River. "Never mind, Mother. I wasn't saying she didn't look good. Just a little different. Sheesh."

Beth playfully slapped him on the head. "You think you're funny, but you're not."

Tony stood up and stretched. "That's where you're wrong, dear Mother. I am hysterical. But now, I must leave to meet your daughter for breakfast. I know you'll miss me, but don't worry. I shall soon return to your humble abode."

River laughed at the way they seemed so at ease with each other. It was fun to be around them.

"Tell your sister I said hello," she told him. "Will we get to see her again before we leave?"

Tony shrugged. "Not sure. If that storm moves in today, probably not. We'll all be hunkering down inside."

"You tell Aimee that if she wants to come here and ride it out with us, she's welcome," Beth said. She looked at River. "We have a backup generator. Aimee's apartment building loses electricity every time there's a storm."

"I'll tell her, but she'll want to bring Lulu with her."

"We love Lulu," Beth said. She looked at River. "How do you feel about cats?" she asked.

"My mother has a cat, and we get along very well. I actually adore cats."

Tony frowned at her. "You *adore* cats? I don't think I've ever heard you say you adore anything."

River shrugged. "Maybe I'm changing."

"Maybe." Tony appeared to study her for a moment before saying to his mother, "If Dad needs me, tell him to call. We're hoping he's uncovering something that will help us with the case."

"I'll do that," Beth said. "You and Aimee have fun."

"Thanks, Mom."

Tony walked out of the kitchen, but he was back within seconds. The look on his face caught River's attention.

"What's wrong?" she asked.

Tony didn't answer, just opened the curtain over the sink. He turned around and looked at her and Beth.

All he said was, "It's starting to snow."

THIRTY-FIVE

R iver's heart seemed to beat a little faster at the sight of snow. She quickly grabbed her phone and checked the radar, along with the weather report. She took a deep sigh of relief before she said anything to Tony and Beth.

"Just flurries this morning. The big storm is still predicted for tomorrow. It's okay."

"Do you think the Snowman is going to strike again?" Beth asked. "I thought he always waited a couple of years before his kills. Do you really believe he's going to try to murder someone else?"

Tony walked over to his mother, who was putting cinnamon rolls on a plate for River. He took her hand. "We're not sure, Mom. River and I think it's a possibility. His last victim lived. We've studied enough of these serial killers to suspect that if he can't get to Sandra Cooper, he may feel the urge to murder someone else. He's narcissistic. He could feel the need to show us he's still in control. Of course, this is just conjecture at this point. Nothing to worry about . . . yet."

"I've seen enough during all the years with your father to suspect you may be right." Beth gazed up into her son's eyes. "You all be careful, do you hear me?"

"The Snowman isn't interested in us," Tony said. "We're not on his radar."

"Well, I hope not, but I still want you to be cautious."

Tony raised his mother's hand to his lips and lightly kissed it. "You have my word. We'll watch our backs. We're both armed, and we both know how to protect ourselves."

As Tony tried to comfort his mother, River couldn't help but flash back to the night on the bank of the Salt River. They'd been armed that night too, but it hadn't saved them. She wondered if Tony was thinking the same thing.

Tony said goodbye and left, shooting a look at River before he walked out. She could tell he wanted her to keep an eye on his mother, which of course she would do. Beth put River's plate down in front of her. The scent of warm cinnamon and frosting made River suddenly feel ravenous.

"Thank you," she said to Beth. She bowed her head and prayed silently before stabbing the first roll enthusiastically. She put the first bite in her mouth. It was delicious. River had always thought her mother was a good cook, but Beth was even better.

"You like it?" Beth asked after pouring herself another cup of coffee and sitting down at the table.

"The word *like* isn't strong enough," River said, grinning. "These are phenomenal. I was just thinking that you might be the best cook I've ever known."

Beth laughed. "I appreciate that, but my mother outshone me in every way. Almost all the recipes I use came from her."

"Is she still alive?"

Beth's smile faded. "No, she's not. She died a few years ago. I miss her every day."

River wondered if she'd feel that way when her mother passed away. She couldn't be sure, but she doubted it. Although Rose had been sweeter lately, the years of disapproval and harsh judgments had taken their toll. Suddenly, an image from the movie last night flashed in her mind. Christ had also taken her mother's sins upon Himself. Could River place her mother's failures on that cross? Could she forgive and grant her mother a fresh start? Somehow, she had to find a way.

"You okay?" Beth asked.

"Yeah, I'm fine. I . . . I watched a movie last night that really impacted me."

"Which movie?" Beth asked.

When River mentioned the title, Beth nodded. "I saw it once many years ago. In fact, I saw it in a theater. It was . . . well, it changed my thinking. I'd never been in a theater where people sobbed so openly. After it was over, we were actually hugging each other. It . . . it was something I'll never forget."

"Have you seen it again since then?"

Beth shook her head. "No, one time was enough for me. Besides seeing what our Lord suffered for us, it also made me think about Mary. What she went through seeing her son treated like that. Watching him die an excruciating death." Tears filled her eyes. "I used to say that I couldn't imagine it, but when Tony was shot . . . well, I actually thought about that movie. I mean, Tony wasn't dying for the sins of the whole world, but he came near death because he was trying to help people. Attempting to bring an evil man to justice."

As well as trying to save my life. The familiar rush of guilt began to fill her, but this time she shoved it away. *Not this time.*

"I understand," she said. "You know, I think Tony is the best man I've ever known. You and Ray did an incredible job in raising him. You should feel proud."

Beth reached over and put her hand on River's. "Thank you. We are proud of him. We really are. I have to say, though, I do worry about him."

"Are you talking about the aphasia? He's really improved lately."

Beth hesitated for a moment before saying, "No, that's not it, although I'm certainly happy to hear that he's doing better." She cleared her throat, moved her hand, and met River's gaze. "Is he dating anyone? I mean, I know his job is important to him, but in the last year, he hasn't mentioned any women. I don't want him to allow his job to push out everything else."

River was taken aback by Beth's question. "I . . . I don't think so. We don't talk much about who we're dating. Of course, now that we've moved to Missouri, he hasn't had much of a chance to meet anyone."

"Not even at church?"

What should she say? She didn't want to be dishonest. She tried to choose her words carefully. "The truth is, I'm not sure. I mean, we're close friends, but I don't know everything he does. You really need to ask him."

"Okay," Beth said slowly, after taking a sip of coffee. "What about you? Are you dating anyone?"

River had just taken another bite of her cinnamon roll and almost choked at Beth's newest question. She coughed a couple of times and then swallowed the piece of food in her throat.

"Are you okay?"

River nodded, still having a hard time speaking. "Yes, I'm fine," she finally got out, her voice raspy. "I'm not dating anyone right now. I haven't met anyone . . . yet."

"I know you told me that you and Tony are only friends and partners," Beth said, "but maybe you should consider something more. I mean, have you ever wondered if it could happen?"

Had she wondered about it? *How about a thousand times?* She certainly couldn't say that. "Look, Beth, I understand why you're asking these questions. You're concerned about Tony. But I really feel uncomfortable talking about this. Like I said, you really need to talk to Tony yourself."

Beth sighed. "Believe me, I've tried. He just clams up. It's like he's some kind of castle, and when I ask about his romantic life, he pulls up the drawbridge and barricades the door."

River had to laugh. "I've seen him do the same thing. Not about dating, but about anything he doesn't want to talk about."

"Ray is the same way. That's where Tony gets it."

"Look," River said gently, "you just need to trust Tony. He's the smartest man I've ever known. He'll find someone . . . when the time is right. Now he's concentrating on getting stronger after the shooting and making sure our agency grows. He'll fall in love someday. I'm sure of it."

"And what about you?"

Once again River was surprised by the directness of the question, but thankfully, this time she didn't choke. "I guess I'd give you the same answer. If God has someone for me, He'll let me know. I have to trust His timing."

"And I need to do the same." Beth's words were said with conviction. "I know I worry about my kids too much, but unfortunately, it's something mothers do too easily." She smiled at River. "Thank you for reminding me that God's got this. I only have one more question for you."

River braced herself. Now what?

"Did Aimee tell you that she blames you for Tony's injuries?"

THIRTY-SIX

'm ready. I'm going there tomorrow at dusk. It gets dark early now, so it will be easy to slip into their backyard unseen. They turn off the alarm a lot during the day. I've watched them carefully. There's a back door that leads directly to the basement. I've already tried the door, and know I have the right key. As soon as I'm certain the alarm is off, I'll slip in, go downstairs, and wait until the right moment. I can wait as long as I need to. I even have one of those plastic things some men buy for long trips in case they have to go to the bathroom and don't want to stop. I keep it in my backpack. It's come in handy many times. I can't flush a toilet. That could alert someone that there's an intruder in the house. My plan's perfect. Everything has always worked like clockwork . . . except when it came to Sandra Cooper. I felt a quick burst of anger, but I pushed it down. No time for that now. I'll take care of her later. She'd been judged and found guilty. She'll get what she deserves.

I made sure my travel mug was clean and waiting on the counter. Tomorrow, I'll fill it and take it with me, although the anticipation is enough to keep me awake. The coffee's more of a distraction.

"What time do we do this thing?" she asked, startling me.

"*We* aren't doing anything. You're staying here."

"No. I have to come with you. You need me."

I sighed. I love her, but sometimes she gets on my nerves. "Of course I need you, but this one is different. More complicated. I can't allow you to make me nervous. Please understand. I absolutely can't get distracted."

She glared at me. "This is personal to me too, you know. We're righting a wrong. Not just for me but for everyone who has suffered at the hands of evil people. People who hurt innocents."

"I know that." I sighed. "All right, but you have to be quiet."

She laughed at this. "Don't be silly. I won't be the one who blows it. That's not possible. If anything goes wrong, it will be all your fault."

"That's exactly the kind of thing I don't need to hear."

"All right, all right. I'm sorry. I'll be quiet, but I *will* be there."

There wasn't any point in arguing with her. I wouldn't win. "Okay. Just do what I tell you and everything will be okay."

She made a gesture as if zipping her lips. It made me laugh and helped to remind me again that she was the reason I had to see this through.

"You stay here until I'm ready tomorrow, then we'll go. Deal?"

She smiled at me. "Deal."

Tomorrow, as the snow fell, the guilty would be punished and the innocent, whose voices had been stilled by death or by trauma, would finally have a say.

RIVER JUST STARED AT BETH. How should she respond? Aimee was Beth's daughter. River couldn't very well tell her what she really thought of her.

"I . . . I don't know what to say," she said finally. "Yes, Aimee

228

told me her feelings about the shooting, and I understand why she thinks that way. You told me you saw things the same way at first—until you realized I would never purposely put Tony in danger. Hopefully, Aimee will come to that same conclusion."

Beth took a sip of her coffee and then set her mug down. Her hesitation meant that what was coming next was hard for her to say.

"I'm not so sure, River. Aimee has always been very protective of her older brother. Of course, he's the same way with her. In fact, when they were teenagers, Aimee's commitment to him got a little aggravating. Tony told her over and over that he didn't need a little mother hen trying to watch out for him all the time. Aimee never listened. When Tony decided to study criminal justice in college and then announced that he was applying to the academy . . . Well, let's just say that tears were shed. In fact, Aimee pleaded with Tony not to go. But obviously, that didn't work. Then when he got shot . . ."

"She blamed me," River said. "She truly believes Tony went to the river that night because I wanted him to."

"Yes." Beth sighed. "Look, I understand that you thought your friend was going to meet you. That she had some kind of new evidence. But you're not field agents. Why didn't you send someone else? Someone trained to handle situations like that?"

"We've been over this, Beth. I really don't want to . . ."

Beth waved her hand at River. "You're right. I'm sorry. I'm sounding like Aimee." She took a sip of coffee before saying, "Aimee has talked about you . . . no, complained about you so many times, it's gotten inside my head."

"Look, I've gone over that night more times than I can count. I've asked myself why I didn't hear a tone in my friend's voice that should have warned me that something was wrong. I've berated myself so much that I began to believe everything that happened was my fault. It's . . . it's been weighing me down. Unfortunately, I can't go back in time, Beth. I can't change things. Maybe I did miss something, but it wasn't on purpose. Tony and I both thought Jacki had found something she wanted us to see." River took a deep breath. "I've finally realized that if I made a mistake, all I can do is accept God's forgiveness. Jesus paid an incomparable price so that I can do that." River stood up. "I'm sorry, but I'm done hating myself. I'm not trying to be cavalier about what happened. It was terrible. For both of us. But I'm not carrying it around with me anymore. Not for Aimee. And not for you. I hope you can understand. If not, I'm sorry."

Her hands shaking, River picked up her coffee cup, went over to the coffeemaker, poured another cup, and headed up the stairs. She listened for Beth, hoping to hear something. Anything. Encouragement to come back. Maybe even an apology. But there wasn't a sound. Giving up, River opened the door to Ray's office and went inside.

Although she was glad she'd stood up for herself, she was also nervous. Had she blown it with Tony's family? She didn't want that. She loved being around them. They had something she'd never experienced, and she really enjoyed it. She was learning that being part of a family could be a great thing. A healing thing. But no matter what, she was determined she wasn't going back to the deep well of despair that she'd just climbed out of. Never again.

"Thank You for forgiving me," she whispered as she pulled a chair over and parked it in front of the corkboard. "Thank You that now there is therefore no condemnation . . ." She stopped quoting the Bible verse that meant so much to her when she heard something behind her. River turned around to find Beth staring at her. Was she angry? Was she going to ask her to leave?

Instead, she stepped into the room and pulled the door closed behind her. Her eyes were shiny with tears.

"I'm so sorry," she said. "I truly don't feel that way anymore.

I was just trying to explain Aimee's reaction to you. Please don't think I blame you for what happened. I don't."

She walked over to River, who stood up to face her. Beth suddenly threw her arms around River, hugging her tightly. "What you said is absolutely right. Jesus did pay a high price for us. I'm so thankful. We need it every day. You do, I do, and so does Aimee." She let go of River and slumped down into the other chair. "I've tried to talk to Aimee about her attitude toward you, but I haven't gotten very far. She's so stubborn. Kind of like her brother. That pigheadedness has made her resent you, and it's not right." Beth wiped her eyes with the back of her hand. "Please, know that I think you're incredible. If it was my job to pick someone for my son, it would be you. Unfortunately, it's not my right or my business." She gave River a tremulous smile. "I intend to keep my nose where it belongs from now on. Maybe you can breathe a deep sigh of relief?"

River couldn't help but smile. She sucked in a deep breath and let it out slowly, causing Beth to giggle. "I can only guess how hard this has been on you and your family," she said. "But please believe me when I say that I'd lay my life down to protect Tony. I'll always do everything I can to keep him safe."

Beth was quiet and looked away. At first River was surprised by her reaction, but suddenly, she understood.

"How did you find out?" she asked.

"I know when Ray is keeping something from me," she said. "I knew there was something wrong with the Christmas card that arrived here for you. I made him tell me what it really meant."

"I worry that being here is putting Tony in danger," River said. "Maybe I should leave."

Beth reached over and took her hands. "No. You're safer here. Besides, no one's going anywhere once that storm hits."

"I can get a taxi to a hotel in town. Tony doesn't have to know where I am. I . . . I really think I need to keep my distance. Just in case."

"You may think I'm telling you this only because it's the right thing to say," Beth said, "but after being around you two, I honestly believe you're wrong. And so was I. Somehow, you're stronger when you're together. Walking away from my son would make him weaker. More vulnerable. I can't explain it, but I know it's true." Her eyes bored into River's. "Listen to your heart. What I'm saying is true, isn't it?"

Now it was River's turn for tears. Finally, she nodded. "I never thought of it quite that way before, but yes. In my heart, I believe you're right." She gently let go of Beth's hands. "Okay, I won't leave. For now. But if I ever believe that being near him will put him at risk, I'll go. You have my word."

"I hope that day never comes. I think if you left his life, it would break my son's heart."

Although she didn't say it, River knew it would break hers as well.

CHAPTER
THIRTY-SEVEN

iver was going over their profile again. No matter what they did or how well she felt they understood the Snowman, she had a nagging feeling they were missing something. She just couldn't put her finger on it.

A little after ten o'clock, the door to the office opened and Ray walked in. "Tony's still with Aimee?" he asked.

"Yes. He should be back soon."

Ray nodded. "Good. I have some new information."

"Do you want to wait for him?"

"I can't," Ray said. "Burlington doesn't have a lot of crime, but unfortunately, around Christmas it seems to get worse. We've got some burglaries to investigate. Nothing major, but the people who were robbed deserve our full attention. We've got some suspects, but we need to round them up and see if we can at least let the victims know we've recovered some of their items. My visit with Sandra Cooper will have to wait. I'm sorry."

"I understand."

"I sent you some photos before I left the station. Have you seen them yet?"

River shook her head. "Haven't checked. I'll do it now." River clicked over to her email. Seconds later she was opening pictures of a young boy and an even younger girl.

Ray walked up behind her. "The boy is Michael Wilson. These are some of his early school photos. I couldn't find all of them."

Michael Wilson was an attractive boy with blue eyes and blond hair. Although he was attempting to smile, there wasn't any joy in it. Or in his intense eyes. In all three pictures, he was leaning his cheek on his hand, a classic school pose that wasn't used much anymore.

"This is it?" River asked. "No other photos?"

"No. He was enrolled for three more years in the same school, but I guess he didn't show up for picture day."

"What about a driver's license photo?" River asked.

"Nothing. He has a Social Security number, but it's never been used."

"You said he had a decent foster family?"

Ray nodded. "Seems like it. Until the father died, that is. Then Michael disappeared."

"Can you talk to the foster mother?" River asked.

"I tried to contact her, but she recently passed away too. Cancer."

River couldn't help but wonder what had happened to Michael. Where was he now? Was he even alive? Had they been wrong to suspect him of being the Snowman?

She turned her attention to Stacy. Only two school photos. One in first grade and another in second. The look in her eyes made River's stomach turn over. This little girl was afraid.

"Anything from her school that might help?"

Ray shook his head. "Like I said earlier, they were both dumped into the foster system. I can't find anything about Stacy. No idea of what happened to her or where she went. I called Tony and told him about it. I have a contact with a foster care group downtown.

I called him to see if he could meet you and Tony after lunch. Maybe he can shed some light on what happened to the Wilson kids. He has access to records I don't have."

"Okay," River said. "Anything new about the people who died?"

"Yes, but it's sketchy. Hard to find information about people who are dead. The Greers, the first couple killed here, were definitely foster parents, but only for a short time over twenty years ago. The interesting thing about them? They used to live in Des Moines." He shrugged. "Again, we're realizing that a lot of people leave Des Moines and move to smaller cities. So, I'm not sure we can assume much about that. That's all I know. Again, my contact should be able to help you. You can ask him about Sandra Cooper."

"Does Tony have your contact's information?" River asked.

"Yes, but I'll give it to you too. His name is Donnie Schweizer. He works for Able House Family Services. He's worked with us several times when we needed him. If anyone can fill in the blanks, it's Donnie. But to be completely honest, I don't know how much he'll be able to help us. He's seen children disappear into the system too. It really frustrates him as well as the other hardworking foster care workers who really try to help children in crisis. You'll like him." He smiled. "You both fight evil."

"Okay. We'll let you know what we find out."

"Thanks. By the way, it seems that the storm will be here early in the morning and snow will continue throughout the day."

"And you still feel the Snowman plans to kill someone else?"

"Your profile makes me suspect it. I hope we're all wrong, but you said something about him being angry because Sandra lived? If he really does feel he's on some kind of righteous crusade, I think you're right about his compulsion to deliver his so-called justice now that he's been thwarted. I also have to wonder if he still has Sandra in his sights. We're guarding her carefully for now,

235

but we won't always be able to do that. Let's pray we catch him soon so that she won't have this death sentence hanging over her head."

"I agree," River said. "From what I understand about him so far, I would say he will definitely try to finish the job he started."

As she said the words, she was aware that they also applied to the Strangler's apprentice. She shivered, not because she was cold, but because the reality of knowing there was someone out there who could be completely committed to taking her life frightened her.

TONY SPEARED THE LAST PIECE of his pancakes with his fork and mopped his plate with it so he could soak up the last bit of maple syrup. Benny's Grill made the best pancakes he'd ever tasted. He'd missed them. And he'd missed Aimee. They'd had a great time together talking about things they'd done as kids. Aimee had a way of snorting when she laughed. When they were younger, Tony had made fun of her. Even though he thought it was humorous then, he felt a little bad about it now.

After talking and laughing since they'd first met for breakfast, Aimee had suddenly grown strangely silent.

Tony put his fork down. "You okay?" he asked. "When you get quiet, I worry. When we were kids, that's how I knew you were planning something. It usually involved me, and it was never good."

Aimee gave him a small, strained smile. "I know you're heading back to St. Louis on Monday. I . . . I guess I worry about you. After what happened . . ."

"Hey, I worked for the FBI for a long time. Only got shot once. All in all, I'd say I'm doing pretty good."

Aimee pointed her fork at him. "You're not funny. We could have lost you."

"But you didn't." Tony smiled at her. "Look, sis, pray for me and trust God. It's the only thing any of us can do. We don't know what we're going to face, but we know who has us in His hands. What I went through was awful. I shouldn't have lived. But I did. God took care of me."

Aimee hesitated a moment before saying, "I believe God protects us, but I also believe that He expects us to make wise decisions. Not to put ourselves in harm's way on purpose."

"Trust me, I didn't purposely try to get shot. You know my job with the FBI was in the BAU. Usually, I was completely safe. I wasn't a field agent."

Aimee's eyes turned shiny with tears. "But you almost died. You went with . . . with River even though it was dangerous. She should have known better. She talked to that woman—Jacki, was it? If River's a trained behavioral analyst, how could she not have realized that something was wrong?"

Tony studied her for a moment. "Aimee, I know what you said to River. I also know she doesn't want me to bring it up, but I think I have to. What happened wasn't her fault. It was the fault of a very evil man who tried to kill River too."

Aimee looked away and then picked up her napkin and dabbed at her eyes. Then she stared at him. "I know what you're saying, but I do blame River. Before you let her into your life, you were safe. No one shot at you. Since working with her, you almost died, you've walked away from your career, and now you're . . . what? Magnum P.I.?"

Tony loved his sister and realized that her anger toward River was because of the fear she experienced when he was hurt. His mother had voiced similar feelings right after it happened, but after Tony talked to her, she mellowed. She'd finally realized that it wasn't River's fault. Still, he was frustrated with Aimee and felt defensive of River.

He took a deep breath before saying, "Aimee, for your information, becoming private investigators was my idea. Not River's. After what happened to her, she was dealing with severe PTSD. She couldn't work with the FBI anymore. Some of the things we hear . . . the cases we work. . . . Well, let's just say there are things that happen in the world that I wouldn't want you to ever know about. The stuff of nightmares. And what River went through that night . . ." He stopped talking and shook his head. "You think being shot was traumatic? River's trauma was much worse than mine. Thankfully, she's let God back in her life after many years of not trusting Him. As a Christian, you should be supporting her. Not blaming her for things that weren't her fault. Your accusations really hurt her."

"You didn't want to go there that night. She made you go. It's all her fault. All of it."

Tony shook his head. "River told me that you'd said that, but it's not true. Not a word of it. We both made the decision to go. River certainly didn't try to talk me into it."

"That's . . . that's what happened."

Tony was quiet for a moment before saying, "Aimee, you've constructed something in your mind that's fantasy. We do that sometimes when we need to believe something so badly we create incidents that aren't real. I've never said anything like that. Mom and Dad know it's not true. I understand why you did it, but I'm telling you, River didn't ask me to go. Nor did she try to talk me into going." He studied her for a moment. "Do you believe me?"

Tony waited for his sister to respond, but after several seconds of silence he realized he hadn't changed her mind. He got to his feet.

"I love you, Aimee. You're my sister, but I'm going back to

the house now. River and I are trying to help Dad stop a very bad man from hurting someone. I need to focus on that. Mom wanted me to tell you that if you want to wait out the storm at their place instead of in your apartment, you should gather your stuff together, get Lulu, and come home before it hits."

With that, he put cash on the table to pay for their breakfast and walked out of the restaurant.

THIRTY-EIGHT

As soon as Tony opened the door to the office and stepped inside, River could tell he was upset. She had a pretty good idea what had happened. She wondered if she should say something, but she was afraid to bring it up. If he and Aimee had talked about what had happened between them, it was best if he told her when he was ready. They really needed to talk about it, but she was willing to wait on him to do it. For now, she shifted her thoughts back to the case. Worrying about Tony and Aimee was a distraction they couldn't afford right now.

"Anything new?" he asked as he approached her.

"Your dad found several interesting things."

She showed him the pictures and filled him in on the information Ray had uncovered. "He wants us to meet with his contact at a local foster care agency. Ray thinks this guy may be able to either give us more specific news about the Wilson children, or at least help us to understand how these children could have disappeared."

"Sounds good. When are we supposed to be there?"

"After lunch. I think we should probably try to get there around one."

Tony sighed. "You eat. I think I'm good for a while. Pancakes, eggs, bacon, biscuits . . . well, you get the idea."

River laughed. "Kind of overdid it, huh?"

"Kind of."

"Okay. I don't want your mother making lunch just for me. Maybe we could pick up a cheeseburger on the way home from our meeting?"

Tony's raised eyebrow said it all.

"I take it that if your mother found out I was buying a cheeseburger, she'd be offended?"

"She'd be mortified. She loves having company. My dad isn't around that much. She enjoys having family to cook for. It makes her happy. Just go with it."

"But I'm not family."

Tony shrugged. "In her mind you are."

River felt her face grow hot. What did Tony mean? Did he see her that way too? "Maybe we should go over the questions we have for this guy." She looked down at her notebook, thankful for the chance to hide her face. "His name is Donnie Sch weizer. Your dad's used him on several cases. Says he's been very helpful."

Tony pulled the other fold-up chair next to River. He gestured toward her notebook. "Do you want to write down our questions or do you want me to?"

"I will."

"Okay." Tony said the word slowly, dragging it out. "I guess the first thing we need to know is whether or not he can tell us more about Michael and Stacy Wilson. What happened to them? We're not certain they had anything to do with their father's death, but we need to follow up on them."

"I'm beginning to wonder if the police actually did try to investigate the kids but reached an impasse just like we did."

"Well, it's not in the report Dad was able to get from Des

Moines, but it's not impossible. If they checked them out, all we can do is hope we have better luck than they did."

"We also need to follow up on the people who have died. Were they all foster parents? Were there problems?"

Tony nodded. "Anything else?"

"Those are the biggest questions. I guess if this Donnie guy can give us answers, we'll know a lot more than we do now."

"Okay. If we think of anything else, we can add it to our list on the way to meet with him." He looked at the clock. "Frankly, I'm tired of thinking about this. As for our profile, I'm beginning to dream about it. If you don't mind, I think I'll chill out for a while. Why don't you go downstairs and try to make a sandwich?"

"*Try* to make a sandwich," River said with a grin. "You know I'm capable of putting cheese between two slices of bread, right?"

"Yes, I'm aware, but I predict you won't get the refrigerator door open before my mother pops up and offers to make you something."

River laughed. "I'm not going to take that bet."

"Smart lady. I'll meet you downstairs by twelve thirty, then we'll head to the agency."

"Sounds good."

Tony left, probably headed to his room. River was still concerned about him. Had she read him wrong, or was he really just tired? It was possible, but she wouldn't bet on it. She knew when he was upset, and something was definitely bothering him. He wouldn't look at her directly, and he kept working his jaw. Two signs that he was trying to keep something from her. She hated the feeling that he wasn't being honest—and that she wasn't either. Tony was the only person in her life she could completely trust. But if she was being truthful, she'd have to admit that they both kept things from each other from time to time. Tony looked out for her, and she did the same for him. That's why she hadn't told him about the nightmares at first. She didn't want him to worry.

But sharing the truth had turned out okay. He'd helped her. He probably wasn't telling her about Aimee because he didn't want to upset her. She thought about Beth and how she'd confronted River about Aimee. She was glad Beth had been honest. They were closer now—the air cleared between them. She and Tony needed to do the same. She decided to talk to him, but it would have to wait until after they got back from talking to Ray's friend.

River closed her notebook, went to her room to get her purse, and headed downstairs. When she reached the kitchen, she slung her purse over the back of a chair. Sure enough, before she could open the refrigerator door, Beth came in from the living room.

"Ready for some lunch?" she asked with a smile.

"I was just going to make a sandwich. You really don't need to bother."

"Don't be silly. I enjoy having people at home. Someone to take care of. It's lonely with Ray gone so much." She sighed. "He took the week off, and he still has to go into the station."

River was surprised to see her blink away tears.

"Things will change when Ray retires," River said.

"I know. It will be wonderful. I worry, though." Beth gestured for River to sit down at the table.

"You worry about what?"

As River sat down, Beth opened the door to the refrigerator. "What will he do with his time? He's not the kind of person who can sit around and do nothing."

"You two can travel. Do the things you don't have time to do now."

"Maybe." Beth grabbed some plates and carried them over to the table. "Ham or turkey?" she asked. "I have Swiss, cheddar, American, pepper jack, and provolone cheeses. Oh, and some Gouda."

"How about ham and cheddar with mustard?"

"Okay, and what kind of bread? I have . . ."

"Sourdough is fine," River said since she knew Beth had some.

Beth quickly put together a sandwich. Then, after putting everything away, she took out some potato salad, along with some macaroni salad. River would have been happy with chips, but she had no intention of saying anything. Was this how women without careers ended up? Worrying about what everyone wanted to eat? Using their extra time to clean the house and bake rich desserts? River was pretty sure she'd be miserable if this was all she had to do.

"Did you ever have a job outside your home?" River asked after Beth put her lunch plate in front of her. "Tony's never mentioned anything."

"I did." Beth sat down next to her. "I was a schoolteacher. Sixth grade. I loved it. But then Tony and Aimee came along, and I wanted to stay home with them. I thought about going back once they were in school, but Ray and I worried about them. What if they were sick? Most of the time Ray couldn't come home and stay with them if they needed someone. We didn't want them to be latchkey kids. I saw too many problems with children who had too much free time before their parents got home. Of course, that was in Des Moines. By the time we moved here, Tony was gone, and Aimee was in high school. Just for two years. Then she went to college. I wanted to be here when she had breaks." Beth sighed and stared wistfully at a place somewhere to River's left. That meant she was probably remembering. Seeing something from the past.

"In all these years you never thought about going back?" River asked after swallowing a bite of her sandwich.

"I did. But . . . I don't know . . . schools are different now. Children don't act the same. I did some substitute teaching for a while, but even in a town like Burlington, it wasn't enjoyable. I got tired of having kids swear at me and challenge my authority." She waved her hand at River. "Don't get me wrong. Most of them were great. Wanted to learn. I still hear from a few of them, believe it or not. It's just not for me now." She was silent for a moment and then smiled at River. "You must think I'm rather silly."

River put down her sandwich. "I don't think that at all. Tony adores you. Look at the kind of man he is. And Aimee. They're both good Christian people. You should be proud."

Beth's small, forced smile turned genuine. "I am. I really am. You know, I realize some people do incredible things. Become Bible teachers, evangelists, missionaries. Lead thousands of people to Christ. I'm sure God will reward them greatly when we stand before Him. Maybe all I can show for my life is my children, but they've impacted lives. Someday their children will do the same." She cleared her throat, obviously moved. "I think good mothers quietly change the world. They may not receive any fanfare, but God sees them. He knows. And that's what really matters, isn't it?"

River found her own eyes filling with tears. Boy, ever since she'd regained the ability to cry, it was as if she couldn't stop.

"Oh, honey, I didn't mean to make you weepy. Tell me what you're feeling."

River cleared her throat. "I . . . I want children, I've just never found the time. I guess I'm afraid I've waited too long. Made my job too important." She laughed lightly. "Don't tell Tony I said that. He wouldn't believe it. I told him I didn't think marriage was for me."

River had never told anyone about her desire to have children. She'd been so proud of her job with the FBI that it had become her identity. The idea of doing something so unimportant . . . so pedestrian . . . had been almost forgotten. Beth's words had struck something deep inside her.

Beth got up, came over, and put her arms around River. Although the gesture embarrassed her, she felt comforted and safe in Beth's arms. She was wiping away tears from her cheeks when Tony walked into the room. He looked at them both in surprise.

"Gee whiz, Mom. What did you do to River?"

His startled expression made them both laugh. River shook her head.

"This ham sandwich is just so good," she said, sputtering between giggles. That made them both laugh harder. This time River's tears weren't from sadness. She finally stopped laughing and smiled at Beth. She mouthed *thank you*, and Beth nodded.

Tony got a glass from the cabinet and then filled his glass with iced tea from the fridge.

"I swear, I never know what's going on in this house," he mumbled.

"It's really not that strange," Beth said, trying to sound innocent. "We were talking about you, and it made us both cry."

"With happiness, I hope," he said, sitting down at the table.

Beth nodded. "Of course, dear," she said. "If that's what you need to hear."

He shook his head. "I give up. Are you about ready to go?" he asked River.

"Just about."

While Tony and Beth talked about the latest weather report, River finished her sandwich. But the whole time, her eyes kept drifting toward Tony, although she couldn't really understand why.

THIRTY-NINE

The receptionist at Able House led Tony and River to an office down a short hallway. The agency wasn't very large, but Tony was pretty sure they handled a lot of cases. How could they possibly keep up with everything? The Salvation Army also did some foster care work in the area, but they were probably spread thin too.

The receptionist stopped and knocked on the door to one of the offices. A sign on the door read *Donnie Schweizer—Foster Care Social Worker.*

"Come in," a voice called out.

She opened the door and smiled at the dark-haired man sitting behind a desk, two piles of files stacked on top. He smiled, stood up, and extended his hand, first to Tony, then to River.

"Donnie Schweizer," he said.

"I'm Tony St. Clair, and this is River Ryland."

He had a strong, firm handshake, a sign of confidence. He gestured toward the chairs in front of his desk. "Please sit down."

"We appreciate you seeing us," River said, "especially since we're not with the police."

"Not a problem, although I'm sure you know I can't discuss

anything confidential with you," Donnie said. His dark brown eyes fastened on Tony. "You're Ray's son?"

Tony nodded.

"I've worked with him several times. Unfortunately, sometimes the children that pass through the system end up in trouble." He sighed. "The system isn't perfect. There are simply too many problems for all of us to handle. And not just with the children. Sometimes it's the foster parents." He frowned at them. "Ray told me you're private investigators?"

"Yes, but we're not licensed in Iowa," Tony said. "We work out of Missouri."

"Ray also said you used to work for the FBI and you're help-ing him with a case. I understand you're looking for a couple of children who were in foster care but seem to have disappeared?"

"Yes," River said. "Michael and Stacy Wilson. Their biologi-cal father died almost twenty-four years ago. We think Michael may have had something to do with it, but we can't find him or his sister. Ray tracked a few years of their whereabouts, but he couldn't locate either one of them now."

"Let me see what I can do." Donnie pulled two files off one of the stacks and put them in front of him. "I can tell you that Michael was in a good foster home for a while, but when the husband died and the wife couldn't keep him any longer, he was transferred to another home. I can't find any records that prove he actually showed up there. I know he went somewhere, I just don't know where." He closed the file. "It sounds terrible, but there are quite a few children who went missing once they were put into foster care. Sometimes foster parents actually give the kids to someone else and split the money they were paid to take care of them. Things have improved quite a bit during the last several years, but we still have more cases than we can handle the way we'd like to."

"And what about Stacy?" Tony asked.

Donnie pulled another file off the pile on his desk. "This one is even stranger. After being surrendered, she was placed in a different foster home than her brother. I believe in keeping siblings together if at all possible. Maybe the case worker wasn't able to do that. I'd ask him but he retired ten years ago, moved to Florida, and then died not long after that."

"We keep losing leads because of people who have passed away," River said. "It's frustrating. Foster parents dead. Now this guy."

"I certainly understand your frustration." His dark eyes narrowed. "I looked up the names Ray gave me of some foster parents. There's Sheila Jackson. She is deceased, I understand?"

"Yes, she passed away in a fire two years after Edward Wilson, Michael and Stacy's father, died," Tony said.

Donnie frowned. "A fire? Isn't that the way Mr. Wilson and his wife died?"

Not being able to go into specifics, Tony just nodded. Although he wanted to tell Donnie everything, at this point in the investigation, it was best to keep things close to the vest. Obviously, he didn't know that the victims were murdered before the fire.

"That seems odd." Donnie studied them for a moment, but then shrugged and went back to the file in front of him. "I can tell you that Sheila Jackson is the name of the woman who took Stacy Wilson in after the Gordons."

Tony felt as if someone had hit him in the stomach. They'd suspected that Sheila was connected to Michael and Stacy somehow, but this confirmation was still surprising. He looked at River, who seemed just as startled as he was.

"And after Sheila?"

"That's where we lose her. Sheila told the case worker that Stacy had been put in another home, but we can't find anything that proves that."

"Donnie, do you have any record of foster parents named Greer? Terrance and Vanessa?"

It was Donnie's turn to look surprised. "How do you know those names?"

"They lived here in Burlington. They died about four years ago."

"Goodness, the bodies are piling up, aren't they?"

It was clear that Donnie was suspicious, but Tony kept his mouth shut.

"So, you know about them?" River asked.

"Yes. They're the people Sheila claimed took Stacy in. But when the foster care worker checked with them, they said they didn't know anything about her. After that, the trail goes completely cold."

"What about Mac and Angela Craig?" Tony asked.

Donnie frowned. "They were great foster parents who died tragically a couple of years ago. Some people suspect it was a murder/suicide."

"Why?" Tony asked.

"There was a child who died in their care. It wasn't their fault. The girl climbed a tree in their backyard and stepped on a branch that broke. I did the same thing when I was a kid." He touched a scar on his cheek that Tony wouldn't have noticed if he hadn't pointed it out. "Thankfully, I just got cut and scraped. The girl in their care broke her neck. I tried to talk to them. Let them know that it had happened to me, and that I had perfect parents, but it didn't help. They were devastated and stopped fostering." He sighed. "You see, they couldn't have their own children. Fostering was their way to have the family they wanted so badly. We all tried to help them, but they just couldn't accept what happened, I guess."

Tony was surprised by his statement. Obviously, the police hadn't informed Donnie of the circumstances behind the Craigs' deaths. There was no way they'd committed suicide. No one binds their hands and feet, kills themselves, and then sets their house on fire. The police were keeping the details quiet. Maybe they weren't certain the Snowman had returned, but they knew the Craigs were murdered.

"I'm afraid there's nothing more I can tell you," Donnie said.

"Let us toss one more name at you," River said. "Do you know Sandra Cooper?"

"Yes. She was one of our foster parents."

Tony and River looked at each other. They definitely had their connection.

"You said *was*?" Tony said.

"I'm not her worker," Donnie said. "That's Martin, and he's on vacation. Not in the state, I'm afraid. He went on a ski vacation with his family. All I know about Sandra was that there were some complaints lodged against her, but that an investigation didn't turn up any corroboration. I think she quit, though, because what happened really hurt her. You really need to talk to Martin." He paused a moment. "I would appreciate it if you'd keep everything I've told you to yourself. I'm walking a pretty thin line here, especially since you're not actually law enforcement."

"We won't repeat anything you've said," Tony said, "except to my father. I'm sure he understands how important it is to protect you."

"Yes, he does," Donnie said. "He's never betrayed my trust."

"Thank you so much for meeting with us," River said. "We really appreciate your time. I can see why Ray thinks so highly of you."

Donnie smiled. "Thank you. I hope I helped you, although I'm afraid I failed at telling you how to locate Michael and Stacy." He stood up and extended his hand again. Tony got to his feet and shook it. "If you find them, will you let me know? I'd really like to know what happened. I hope they're okay." He shook River's hand again. "The foster care system definitely let them down."

After thanking him once more, Tony and River left his office and headed back to the car. Once they were inside, River said,

"Well, we've learned that Sandra Cooper was a foster parent. That gives us our link."

"I agree," Tony said.

"Also, Sheila Jackson had Stacy for a while. And she said the little girl ended up with the Greers."

"But the Greers denied that," Tony said slowly.

"Then they moved to Burlington. And died."

"I think the Snowman followed them here." Tony turned to look at her. "He's here because he needed to kill the Greers. It has nothing to do with my dad."

"That's a relief," River said. "But the Greers said they didn't have Stacy. How does their death link to Michael Wilson? I don't get it."

"Maybe they lied." Tony shook his head. "Again, we're trying to do my dad's job. Let's turn all this over to him. He's the investigator. Not us. Not in this town."

"But how does your dad find Wilson? He has to be using a different name. It would explain how he disappeared."

"Again, that's something my dad will have to deal with." Tony took a deep breath and then let it out. "My head hurts. Let's go back to the house and write all this down. See how it affects our profile."

"Could you please start the car?" River asked. "I'm freezing."

"Sure. Sorry. I guess I was thinking about what Donnie told us."

"Well, I'm thinking about it too, but at least I know when I'm cold."

"Funny." Tony waited until the air turned warm and then put the car in gear, but before he pulled out of the parking lot, he said, "Profiles are written about UNSUBs. I think we both know who the Snowman is, don't we?"

River was silent for a moment before saying, "The Snowman is Michael Wilson. And perhaps his sister."

"I say we finish that profile. Not because my dad isn't looking for an UNSUB any longer, but because we might be able to assist him in locating Michael and Stacy."

River looked over at him. "If we can help in any way, we have to try. The storm will be here tomorrow. We're running out of time."

Tony didn't respond, but he knew she was right. Unless Michael Wilson was found, someone might very well die tomorrow.

FORTY

River was worried. She wasn't certain she and Tony would be able to help Ray stop the Snowman before he took another life. When she and Tony got back to the house, they got something to drink and went straight upstairs. Beth was gone but had left a note saying she had some shopping to do and would be back around four. Probably making sure they had enough supplies before the storm started. River kept checking the radar over Burlington on her phone. Although they were still having flurries, the large storm still wasn't showing up. While it was possible the Snowman would wait another two years to kill, she couldn't rid herself of the feeling in her gut that he was getting ready to take more lives.

"We need to talk to Sandra," she told Tony, who was unusually quiet.

"Why?"

"Because she might know something that could help us," River said. "She's the only victim still alive. She's all we have."

"River . . ."

"I know, I know. Your father's the detective. Not us." She leaned forward and gazed into his eyes. "Look, I realize we're not investigators here in Iowa, but if we were, what would you do now?"

Tony ran his hand through his thick hair. "I'd tell Donnie that he should warn any foster parents in the area to be careful. Especially those who may have had complaints charged against them." He shook his head. "But I can't do that, River. My dad would have to make that call." He was quiet for a moment. Then he said, "I'll phone him and tell him what we found out. He can decide what to do."

"That sounds good. Then we can finally finish this constantly changing profile."

Tony took out his phone and punched in a number. He listened for a while and then said, "Dad, will you call me when you can? We learned something from Donnie that has us concerned. We'd like to talk to you about it." He disconnected the phone and said, "I got his voicemail. Hopefully, we'll hear from him soon."

River sat down at the desk, opened her laptop, and pulled up their profile. She was tired of adjusting it. And now, no matter how objective she wanted to be, she could only see Michael Wilson in her mind's eye.

"Let's go through it again," she said to Tony. "If I read something that's changed, we'll adjust it."

"We can try," Tony said, "but I feel like we're profiling Michael and Stacy Wilson."

River had to laugh. Tony looked at her, his eyebrows raised.

"I swear you're reading my mind," she said. "I was just thinking the very same thing."

"We have to try to get Michael Wilson out of our heads. If we don't, we'll gear this thing toward him. That's not what your dad needs."

"But we both believe it's him," River said.

"I know."

They stared at each other for a moment. "So, what do we do?" River asked.

"We act like the professionals we were trained to be. We can't prove that Michael Wilson is behind these murders. Until we do, we continue to profile this as an UNSUB."

"You're right."

River knew what Tony said was correct. But she was also aware that their training had supplied them with good instincts about unknown subjects. She would have bet every penny she had that the police were looking for Michael and Stacy Wilson. But like Tony said, it wasn't a fact . . . yet. They had to continue as if they didn't suspect who might be behind the killings.

She sighed and began reading through the profile again. She felt as if she could close her eyes and recite it. Antisocial personality, narcissistic, angry, but. . . . She stopped suddenly.

"What?" Tony asked.

"We talked about mixed messages. Fire is an expression of anger, but the crossing of the hands and feet and the insulin overdose show someone who isn't really comfortable with what he's doing. I mean, his anger is there, and he wants to express it, but we wondered if he was carrying out these . . . judgments . . . in the name of someone else."

"Don't go there."

"Look, I know what you're saying, but our *what if* may have been right about Michael Wilson avenging his sister."

Tony got up and walked over to the window. He just stared outside, not saying anything.

"I'm sorry," River said. "I'm just thinking out loud."

"No, don't apologize. It makes sense. Let's just finish and try not to mention his name until we're done."

"Okay."

"River, there's a car outside. Parked down the street. It's been there for a while. I noticed it when we got back from seeing Donnie, but I didn't think much about it."

"You don't think it belongs to one of the neighbors?"

"No. I saw it today for the first time." He turned back to look at her. "I can see someone sitting inside, smoking."

River came over to the window and stood next to Tony. "The dark car halfway down the street?"

"Yeah."

"You think he's watching us?" she asked.

"I don't know, but it bothers me. I think we need to have Dad check it out when he gets home."

"Okay. Hopefully it has nothing to do with us."

"I hope so too." Tony moved away from the window, and River followed him back to the table where they'd been working.

She forced herself to concentrate on their profile, trying to forget the person parked outside. She read through the rest of it. He was a very organized killer. Probably held a job. Could mimic another serial killer, Ted Bundy. Someone who fit into the community. Had friends.

"That makes these kinds of killers harder to find," Tony said, stating something they both knew. "They tend to blend in. I'm afraid this won't help my dad much."

"I know." River leaned back in her chair. "But remember that a profile only narrows down the search parameters. It's not designed to do anything more."

"Well, we know he only kills when it's snowing. We also know that he has a compulsion to leave behind an ornament. A handmade ornament. Your dad said that although the police recognized that the ornament might be important, nothing else was found that told them anything about the killer."

"You mean the two times your dad was able to get someone to look at it?"

"Yes." Tony got up and grabbed the murder book. He shuffled through the pages until he found what he was looking for. "Made of felt, the kind you can buy in any fabric store. Nylon thread.

Stuffing. Button eyes. Of course, there were no fingerprints. One of the snowmen was pretty well burned."

"They were handmade," River said. "So, it had to be something from his childhood."

"We already decided that the ornament and the snow are significant. Something happened to this UNSUB"—he emphasized the word, making it clear to River that he was trying to get them back to working on the profile without thinking about Michael Wilson—"during his childhood. Something that compels him to kill only when it snows." He sighed. "This is the same stuff we already came up with. We're just repeating ourselves."

River reached over and took the file from Tony. She quickly flipped through it, but she couldn't find what she was looking for.

"Please don't get upset with me," she said. "But I need to call Donnie."

"Why would I get upset?" Tony asked.

"Because I don't think you're going to like my question."

Tony took out his phone and read off Donnie's number. River dialed it and waited for Donnie to answer. When he did, he sounded a little stressed.

"Donnie, this is River Ryland. I hope I'm not bothering you."

"It's a busy day, but I'm happy to do anything I can to help."

River looked at Tony. "Is there any way you can tell me when Michael Wilson and his sister were removed from their home?"

"I think so. Can you hold on for a moment?"

"I can see where you're going with this," Tony said, "but no matter what the answer is, it still doesn't prove anything."

"I know, but I have to ask."

Tony didn't respond. River knew him well enough to know that he wanted to hear the answer too. A couple of minutes later, Donnie came back on the line.

"Let's see," he said. He named the year, but it wasn't really what she was waiting for.

"I know this sounds crazy, but can you tell me the month?"

"The month?" Donnie sounded a little confused but told her to wait a moment. "Here it is. It was . . . December. Is that important?"

"We're not sure. But thank you. One other question. I don't suppose there are any pictures or descriptions of what the children had with them, is there?"

"No. Nothing like that. There should be pictures, though, and they're not here. Not sure why."

River thought for a moment. "I don't suppose there is any way to contact the surviving members of Michael's original foster family, is there?"

"I don't have any information about that," he said. "I can give you the couple's names, only because they've passed on. Ray might be able to find someone. I really shouldn't do this. If something comes of it . . ."

"Just blame it on Ray?"

Donnie chuckled. "Yeah, he knows that's how it works. I'd really like to help you. I certainly hope whatever's going on isn't because of a failure on our part."

"It certainly wouldn't be because of you, Donnie. You can only do what you can do. You can't blame yourself for the mistakes of others."

"Easy to say, harder to do." He sighed, and River could hear him shuffling through papers. "Things are a lot easier and faster now with online records." Finally, he said, "Michael's original foster family were the Thompsons. Emily and Austin. They lived in Des Moines. Here's the address of the house where they lived. I think Ray can take it from here." He read off an address, and River wrote it down. "Got it. Thanks, Donnie. You've been a big help."

"You're welcome. I hope you find what you're looking for."

River said goodbye and hung up. She looked at Tony. "You know what I'm going to say, don't you?"

"I'm guessing Michael and Stacy were removed from their home sometime in the winter, right?"

"Yeah, December."

Tony shook his head. "Okay, I give in. Let's finish this profile the best we can, even though it's no longer an actual profile. Then we'll tell my dad that we're pretty sure he's looking for Michael Wilson. And maybe his sister."

River could only nod at him. In her gut, she was certain they no longer had an UNSUB. They had a suspect.

FORTY-ONE

They'd just completed compiling what they'd learned when Tony's cell phone rang. It was his father. Tony quickly recounted their meeting with Donnie and gave him the name of the foster family Michael Wilson had lived with.

"What time will you get home?" he asked after that. Once he heard his father's response, he told him about the car they'd spotted outside. "I'm not saying it has anything to do with us, but it seems strange. Can you check it out when you get here?"

Tony was quiet for a minute and then said goodbye. He disconnected the call and looked at River. "Dad's going to look for any family members connected to the foster family Michael lived with. As soon as he's done, he's coming home. He's going to check out that car parked down the street."

River got up and walked over to the window, carefully drawing back the curtains. "It's still there," she said. The car's exhaust looked like thick smoke in the icy night air.

"Dad will figure out if it's anything to worry about."

"Good." River yawned. "Sorry. I haven't been sleeping well the past couple of nights."

"Me either."

"Do you want to address the elephant in the room?" River asked.

"That we're proving we make pretty good private investigators?"

"But poor behavioral analysts?"

"Not necessarily," he said. "I guess that remains to be seen. The truth is, even though we're convinced Michael Wilson is the Snowman, we still can't prove it. And we don't know how to find him."

"This is where we need to put the brakes on. It's time to turn everything over to your dad. We're done."

"You're right," he said. "Hey, I haven't eaten since breakfast. I don't think supper will be ready until six. I'm going downstairs to see what I can find. Are you hungry?"

"I could eat a couple of your mom's cookies."

"Coffee?"

River nodded. "Unless you want me to fall face first into my plate during dinner, that would be a great idea."

"I really wouldn't want to see you with mashed potatoes and gravy on your face," Tony said, grinning.

"Trust me. No one wants to see that."

"I'll be right back."

Tony walked out of the room, and River went over and sat down in Ray's padded office chair. Her back was sore, but she wasn't sure why. Maybe it was the metal chairs. Not really the most comfortable thing to sit on for hours.

She couldn't help but think about Michael Wilson. He and his sister lost their mother, then their father dumps them into foster care. That would make anyone angry. By the time he left his foster family, he was sixteen. But how does a sixteen-year-old kid just disappear? She knew people did it all the time. Created new identities. It wasn't that hard. Find someone who died, get a fake driver's license, then request a social security card and a birth certificate. They'd seen it often enough while working at the Bureau. But at sixteen? Of course, Michael would have had contact with a lot of kids in the foster care system. Kids who knew the ropes. Maybe it was easier than most people would believe.

River leaned over and rested her head on her arms. She really was tired. She enjoyed being around Beth and Ray, but she was ready to go home. She missed her mother. Which surprised her. Rose's recent change in behavior was beginning to affect her. River had learned a lot about how to react to Rose. At first, when Rose forgot something, River had tried to help her remember. Unfortunately, it only made her mother more confused. Mrs. Weyland had taught her more successful ways to deal with her mom's forgetfulness. The truth was, most of the time, River actually enjoyed being around her mother now.

She couldn't help but think about her brother. He'd asked to bring their father for a visit after the first of the year. The more she'd found out about forgiveness, the more she began to hear a voice inside her urging her to let them come. Well, if it was something God wanted, she knew He'd get her through it. When she went home, she'd ask her mother if she wanted them to visit. If she said yes, she'd call Dan and make the arrangements. It seemed almost impossible that she had changed her mind, but she was finding out that God could do what human beings couldn't. He had the ability to make His people more like Him. Transform hearts and minds. River found it amazing—and it built hope inside of her.

The door opened, and Tony walked in with a tray that contained a coffee carafe, cups, napkins, and a plate of cookies. River laughed.

"Let me guess. Your mom caught you in the kitchen and insisted on putting this together?"

Tony frowned at her. "I think I should be offended that you don't think I can be creative—and classy."

"Oh, I think you can be creative and classy, but not when it comes to assembling food on a tray. The last time we got together to watch football, you put a bag of chips and a container of dip on your coffee table. I had to ask you for a napkin."

It was Tony's turn to laugh. "Okay, you got me."

They drank coffee and munched on cookies, not talking much. River was tired of thinking, and she was pretty sure Tony felt the same way. It was nice to know that neither one of them felt pressured to fill the silence with small talk. River was comfortable around Tony. She couldn't think of anyone else who'd ever made her feel so accepted.

The sound of the front door slamming caused Tony to put down his coffee cup, and then get up and hurry over to open the door to Ray's office. Although River was certain Ray wouldn't mind if she sat in his chair, she got up anyway and moved over to one of the metal chairs. Just seconds later, she heard someone bounding up the stairs.

Ray rushed into the room, his face flushed. River wasn't sure if it was because of the cold or for some other reason.

"That was fast," Tony said.

"I have something I want to share with you, but first of all, the man sitting in the car outside, he was definitely keeping an eye on you."

"What?" River said, trying to ignore the fear that washed over her.

"Relax. It was Bobby. He knew I had to go to the station so he drove down the street so he could keep an eye on the house while I was gone."

"I don't understand," Tony said.

"I told him about the card . . . and the threat from the Strangler's partner," Ray said. "Since he lives so close, I thought it was a good idea to have him as backup if we needed it. He didn't tell me he was going to park outside tonight where you could see him. I told him that from now on, he needs to let us know before he spooks you again. He felt badly about it."

River took a deep breath. "I'm sorry we worried. Please let him know we appreciate it, will you?"

Ray nodded. "I will. Bobby's a great cop. I feel better knowing he realizes what's going on. If you all ever need help, and I'm not home, give him a call, okay?"

"We will, Dad," Tony said.

"Good," he said. "Now, I have something I need to share with you. I found Michael Wilson's aunt. She lives in Des Moines. Hasn't seen him since Edward put the kids in foster care."

"Why didn't the aunt take Michael and Stacy?" River asked.

"Her daughter had been in a pretty bad automobile accident and needed a lot of care. The aunt didn't have a way to take the kids. She felt bad about it. When her daughter recovered, a few years later, she looked for them, but no one could tell her where they were."

Ray walked over to where River sat. "I want to show you something." Tony pulled his chair up next to her. "The aunt had some pictures of Michael and Stacy when they were young. One of them is very revealing. Do you remember when Angie said she saw a man in her house who had a black spot on his face?"

River and Tony nodded. She had an idea as to where this was going, and it made her heart beat faster. This could be proof that they were right.

"Elizabeth . . . that's the aunt's name . . . emailed me these pictures. First of all, here's a picture of Michael when he was six." Ray handed an 8 by 10 glossy picture he'd obviously copied from his laptop. Tony took it and held it so that River could see it too. She couldn't help but gasp. Michael Wilson had a black birthmark on his face.

"That's not all," Ray said. "Here's a picture taken at Christmas. Look at the ornaments on the tree."

River and Tony peered closely at the tree. River gulped when she saw it. It was a felt snowman, exactly like the ones left at the crime scenes.

"Michael Wilson is the Snowman," River said to Tony, who nodded. He looked at his dad.

"We'd come to the same conclusion based on our profile. Everything we came up with fit Michael Wilson. Now we know we were right."

"Remember the school pictures we saw?" River said. "Where Michael's cheek was resting on his hand? Michael and the photographer were trying to hide his birthmark."

"Exactly," Ray said. He plopped down onto his desk chair. "Knowing who the Snowman is *should* help us, but unfortunately it doesn't. We don't have a clue where Michael Wilson is. Or what name he's using."

Ray was right. "Look," River said, "all we can do is give you our profile. Even though we no longer have an UNSUB, maybe it can help you figure out how to find him."

"By tomorrow?" Ray asked. The doubt on his face was reflected in River's mind. Still, she was committed to trying. As she'd said, it was all they could do.

"Let me get something to drink," Ray said. "Then we can go over it. At this point, anything you can add will be helpful."

After Ray left, Tony sighed and shook his head. "I wish we had something that would really send him in the right direction, but I'm not sure we do."

"We can tell him some things that might be beneficial. I mean, we know Wilson probably won't be working a menial job. And we know he's in this area."

Tony sighed again. "Too bad he's not the kind of person who would have a record. That would make it much easier. My dad's also tried looking for similar crimes, but there weren't any exactly like the Snowman's. I mean, except for the Snowman's."

"I know." She smiled at Tony. "Look, we came here to write a profile. We did it. And redid it. And redid it again. At this point, we need to give Ray what we have and put this in God's hands."

Tony stared at her for a moment, and then returned her smile. "Thanks," he said. "I'm glad you reminded me."

"Not a problem," River said. "To be honest, it will take God to stop Wilson from killing anyone else."

Tony pulled his chair up next to River's. Then he took her hands. "Let's pray now, okay?"

As Tony prayed, River could hear the sincerity and urgency in his voice. This was it. Tonight just might determine whether or not they'd done enough to stop Michael Wilson. It really was in God's hands now.

FORTY-TWO

A n hour later, after they'd gone over the profile with Ray, he leaned forward in his chair and picked up the notes he'd written.

"So, Wilson most likely has a good job. His personality wouldn't give anyone a clue to who he really is. You don't think he's got a record. He's probably single, but he might be living with his sister. He may be outgoing at work, but he keeps his personal life very private." He frowned. "You think he's killing because of something that happened to her or to someone else he cares about? But not something that happened to him?"

"Yes," River said. "The way he kills tells us he is angry, but he's not completely comfortable with killing. Giving his victims an overdose of insulin and letting them die before he sets the fire tells us this. We believe he's convinced he's delivering some kind of deserved judgment against people he believes are evil."

Ray frowned. "Well, if he's not comfortable with killing, is it possible he'll stop?"

"We're not sure. Maybe," Tony said. "We think it's possible he waits two years between killings because it's distasteful to him in a way. The two-year gap is self-imposed. Maybe he'll stop once he feels he's delivered all the justice he needs to."

"But you think he may strike again soon?"

Tony nodded. "These kinds of killers are very narcissistic. Their mission is everything. Sandra Cooper thwarted him. My guess is he's been to the hospital in an attempt to get to her, but you've got an officer outside her door. We think that this failure will drive him to kill again."

"We also believe that Sandra's life is in danger once she leaves the hospital," River said.

Ray frowned. "And the only connection you've found is that all of the victims have been involved in some way with foster care."

"Yes, but each case is a little different," Tony said. "Edward Wilson gave his kids up to foster care. The other victims were involved in the system—but a long time ago. Except for Sandra Cooper."

"Who had been accused of child abuse," River said.

"But was cleared," Ray said. He crossed his arms and leaned back in his chair. "So, if Wilson is killing for someone, and not himself, you suspect that person is his sister."

Tony nodded. "We feel that he identifies the most with her."

"But you haven't profiled her?"

"We really can't because we don't have enough information." River cleared her throat. "They may be doing this together, yet Michael Wilson profiles as the kind of person who works alone. But . . . well . . . we were wrong about the Salt River Strangler. We don't want to be wrong again. We have to consider the possibility. If we had to guess about Stacy, that is if she's alive, she would be someone who is overshadowed by her brother. A weaker personality. He probably takes care of her. I doubt that she has much interaction with the outside world. Unfortunately, that's about all we can give you."

River felt good about their profile, but she was still uncertain about Stacy Wilson. Was she really helping her brother? After missing it with the Strangler, she didn't feel confident enough to answer that question.

"The trigger behind this occurred in Wilson's childhood," Tony interjected. "And we know it happened in the winter. Probably in December. And when it was snowing."

"It could be connected to Christmas," River said. "The ornament makes that clear."

"By the way, Dad, did you ever check with the hospitals?" Tony asked. "Look to see if either one of the Wilson kids ever showed up there? It might give you some valuable information. Help us to find out what triggered Wilson's desire to kill."

"No," Ray said slowly. "I guess I figured social services would have that information. They never said anything."

"It wouldn't hurt to look," River said. "If we can find out if someone abused either one of them, it could give us some insight to his motives."

"Good point. Let me see what I can uncover." He picked up his notebook. "Thanks for this, by the way. You know, we've done almost everything we can. We're running out of options. At this point, we've got to believe God will help us."

"River and I were just saying the same thing," Tony said. "We both hope this profile will help you to locate Wilson, Dad. He has to be here somewhere. He was in Des Moines, and now he's in Burlington. When you have a suspect, check to see if he used to live in Des Moines. I realize a lot of people move here from there, but it could certainly help to narrow down the possibilities."

"That birthmark should help you too," River said.

"I'm going to put out a BOLO. He could have changed his appearance in some ways, but that birthmark could be his downfall."

River shook her head. "You might want to hold off on that. If you do, and he sees it, he could run, and you might never catch him. Besides, he might be covering it with makeup. If you have law enforcement concentrating on that birthmark, he could get away."

"But if it stays with the police . . ."

"Wilson has been able to get information he shouldn't have," River said. "I'm not saying you have a leak in your department, but if you do, a 'be on the lookout' could backfire."

"I'll think about what you've just said," Ray said, "but if I feel like a BOLO might save lives, I'll have to issue one."

River and Tony were used to others in law enforcement ignoring their advice based on their own experiences and training. All a behavioral analyst could do was to give an opinion and hope the recipients used it wisely. That didn't always happen, and there wasn't a thing they could do about it.

There was a knock on the door, and Beth walked into the room, a smile on her face. "I know you're all very busy, but can you give me an idea about supper? It's already six."

"You go ahead and eat," Ray said to Tony and River. "I want to follow up this hospital angle."

"You don't have to go to the station to do it, do you, dear?" Beth asked.

Ray hesitated a moment. "I guess I can get it done from here. Let me call Duggan at the station. I'll ask him to check the hospitals in Des Moines."

"Well, good," Beth said, her smile widening. "In that case, supper will be ready in fifteen minutes. My roast and the au gratin potatoes are warming in the oven. As soon as I make the salad, we can eat."

Tony stood up. "Let me help, Mom."

"Well, maybe you could get the drinks. That would be great."

"I'll be there after I talk to Duggan," Ray said.

Although HIPAA laws prevented most people from accessing personal medical records, when someone in law enforcement said that they needed the information to stop or investigate a crime, warrants weren't needed. Still, there were a lot of hospitals in Des Moines. Finding out something from so long ago might not be all that easy.

"Okay, Dad," Tony said. "Don't take too long. You don't want Mom's roast to get cold."

"No, I don't," Ray said, "especially since your mother's roast is the best I've ever tasted."

River and Tony got up and left Ray behind to call the station. As River walked down the stairs toward the kitchen, she wondered if Ray was right. Had they done everything they could? And even more importantly, was it enough to stop the Snowman?

FORTY-THREE

When River woke up the next morning, she got out of bed and hurried to the window. She pulled back the drapes and looked at the sky. Dark clouds were beginning to gather. For someone who loved snow, the sight was ominous and filled her with misgivings for the first time she could ever remember.

She went back and checked the clock on the nightstand. A little after seven thirty. She got back under the covers, turned on her back, and looked up at the ceiling. She'd slept pretty well last night. No nightmares. It seemed that when her mind was filled with other things, like finding the Snowman, the dreams about that night in the river were less frequent. Although that sounded like a positive thing, it really wasn't. The nightmare was worse, but still, her mind was full of thoughts about death. River and Tony had both experienced the loss of friends in law enforcement who took their lives because they couldn't deal with the reality of evil that lurked in the dark, waiting to pounce on the innocent. It was hard to deal with. Of course, if she hadn't initially rejected God, she would have handled what happened with the Strangler better. PTSD certainly wasn't from Him. It was fear, pure and simple, and pretending it didn't exist, like many in law enforcement tried to, wasn't the answer. Sooner or later, the monsters in our minds come out to play.

"Lord," she whispered, "I want to be free of the fear, but I want true healing from You. Real deliverance."

She'd just prayed when she felt words well up inside of her. *Be still and know that I am God.*

She'd had this experience before—hearing the Holy Spirit speak to her—but every time it surprised her. Of course, it shouldn't. Jesus had said that the Holy Spirit would guide us . . . that He would lead us. So why did it still startle her? Her father's church had never taught that God still spoke to people. It was something she was getting used to.

"Thank You," she said quietly. To her, that scripture meant that she should stop trying to figure everything out. That she should just . . . be. And trust that God had the situation well in hand. It made her feel lighter. Happier. She was still concerned about the Snowman, but she decided she was going to do everything she could to relax and believe God had heard their prayers. Slowly but surely, she was learning there really was Someone she could trust entirely. That God wasn't like her parents . . . or anyone else who'd ever let her down. She closed her eyes and worshipped Him for a few minutes. She thanked Him that the reign of the Snowman was coming to an end.

After getting dressed, River went downstairs. The aroma of bacon filled the air. She pulled on the waistband in her jeans. Was it any tighter? If she didn't get out of Burlington before long, she'd have to buy a larger pair.

This morning she was surprised to find that she'd beaten Tony downstairs. Usually, everyone else was eating breakfast by the time she reached the kitchen. Beth was at the stove, and Ray was sitting in his chair. He smiled at her when she came into the room.

"Good morning," she said when she saw him. "Have you heard anything from the hospitals yet?"

He shook his head. "By the time Duggan got someone on the phone, the people he needed to talk to had left for the day. He's checking back this morning."

River took a deep breath. They were still in the dark about how to locate Michael Wilson, and snow was on the way. She breathed out slowly, forcing her body to stay calm. She'd made the decision to be still and trust God, and she wasn't going to allow fear back into her mind.

When working at the BAU, analysts felt the pressure of helping law enforcement find UNSUBs. It was hard not to feel responsible for the lives lost before killers were apprehended. There had been times when the atmosphere in the unit was so tense you could almost cut it with a knife. At the time, it seemed as if worrying about the apprehension of killers was the correct way to respond. But now it looked as if God's way of doing things was the exact opposite of how people handled the same situations.

"River, did you hear me?"

River looked up to see Beth staring at her.

"I . . . I'm sorry. I was thinking about something. What did you say?"

Beth smiled. "Believe me, no apology necessary. When Ray's on a case, I end up repeating things over and over. His mind is usually somewhere else." She patted River on the shoulder. "I just wondered how you want your eggs."

"Oh, thanks," River said, relieved she hadn't offended Beth. "Over hard?"

"You got it. That's how I like mine. Either over hard or scrambled. I hate runny eggs."

"Well, I love them, Mom. Make mine runny."

Tony came strolling into the room. He looked tired.

"Did you have a hard time sleeping?" River asked him.

"Yeah, I did." He sighed. "I keep going over and over everything. Trying to come up with something that will help us find the Snowman before tonight. So far, I'm striking out." He went to one of the cabinets, pulled out a cup, and poured himself some coffee. Then he smiled at River. "I know I said I was putting this in God's hands, but I'm struggling for some reason. Sorry."

"Don't worry about it," River said. "I understand. Still . . ."

"Yeah, I know. I'm working on it." He turned toward his father. "Anything on the hospital angle, Dad?"

"Not yet. Waiting on Duggan. We should hear something before too long."

"Great." Tony sat down next to River. This morning, his gray sweater made his gray-blue eyes appear more gray than blue. He looked at her and smiled again. The gesture made her feel flushed. She looked away, not wanting him to realize how she was reacting to him. She forced her thoughts back to the case.

"So, what do we do now?" she asked Ray.

Ray shrugged. "Nothing we can do. Hopefully, Duggan will give us something to work with."

"Will your chief put out extra patrols tonight?" River asked.

"First of all, he's not convinced that the killer will strike tonight, although he's concerned about it," Ray said. "The problem is that every available officer we have will be dealing with the storm."

River had been thinking of snow in relation to the Snowman but had forgotten that the forecast was for something much more serious than a few snowflakes. Obviously, the town would be dealing with stranded motorists, portions of the city without electricity, along with all the other headaches that come from a major winter storm.

"Churches and homeless shelters will be out looking for anyone living on the streets," Tony said, "but unfortunately, there are people who will escape the searches. The police will also be trying to find anyone who needs help before it's too late."

"I just don't understand people who stay out in terrible weather instead of seeking help," Beth said.

"We've profiled this behavior before," River said. "Some people with mental illness are more afraid of the people looking to help them than they are of being outside, no matter how dangerous it is."

Tony nodded. "Chief Munson is probably hoping that *if* he has a serial killer, the storm will keep him inside tonight. He's got to put the safety of citizens first."

Beth set a plate in front of River with two perfectly cooked over-hard eggs. River was a good cook, but the one thing she'd never been able to master was flipping eggs without breaking the yolk. Not sure why it was hard for her, but she'd finally given up. When she made eggs, they were either scrambled or *take your chances.*

"Thank you," she told Beth. She reached for the bacon and then the toast. After praying silently, she looked at Ray, whose forehead was creased with worry.

"We just need to take what we've done, give it to God, and listen to Him," she told Ray gently. "We don't have any other choice."

"I know you're right," he said, "but I can't stop myself from going over everything again and again. Do you ever feel like you've missed something? Something that's right in front of you, but you just can't bring it into focus?"

"Yeah, I have," River said, frowning. "And almost every single time I was right. Call it intuition or just a gut instinct, I've learned to listen when that happens. I've had the same feeling about this case."

Ray nodded. "It's driving me crazy." He looked at her. "I'm praying we figure it out before it's too late."

FORTY-FOUR

was ready. I'd gone over my mental list twice.

"I really want to go," she said, her bottom lip stuck out in a childish pout.

"I know I promised, but I didn't realize how dangerous it was going to be tonight. This isn't just snow, it's a major storm. I can get around much faster without you. I can't take the car, I have to ride a bus over there, and then get out and walk the rest of the way."

"But how will you get home when you're done?"

"I have a plan."

"Tell me."

I sighed. Why was it always like this? "Will you just trust me? I know what I'm doing."

"But you've never faced a situation like this before. Maybe you should pick another night, when the weather won't be so bad."

"No, I have to do it now. They have to understand that they can't stop what we've decided must be done."

"I'm worried," she said.

"I told you. I've got it all figured out. Trust me, it will be fine."

"I don't know . . ."

I was getting frustrated with her, but I forced myself to stay calm. She was concerned about me because she loves me. How could I get angry with her for that?

"Look, you stay here and keep safe. I'll make it home to you. You have my word."

She stared at me for a moment, but then finally, the tension in her face lessened. "Okay. I'm sorry. And it's not that I don't trust you, but if something bad happened, what would I do? I couldn't go on without you."

"That won't happen."

"When are you leaving?" she asked,

I pulled on my black sweatshirt with the hood, and then my thick black coat. After fastening the coat, I put on my gloves and slung my backpack over my back. "Now," I said, trying to seem completely calm and in control.

The truth was, I wasn't frightened or even worried. I felt excited. Even though I'd had a hard time taking lives after the first two, now there was a sense of satisfaction when it was done. I still didn't enjoy the process, but as long as I could put them to sleep before I started the fire, I could get through it just fine.

"But it's still light outside."

"We've been over this. I told you I need to get inside and hide while the alarm's off. That only happens during the day."

"Okay, okay. Don't get angry with me."

I couldn't help the tears that formed in my eyes. "I'm not angry. I love you."

"I know. I love you too."

I smiled at her. "I'll be back before you know it. You stay safe and warm."

"I will."

As I walked out the door, I was glad we'd ended on a good note. The last thing I wanted was for her to be upset with me. I'd think about it all day, and it would make it harder to concentrate on what I had to do. How the guilty had to die.

THEY'D FINISHED BREAKFAST and were listening to his mother talk about their plans for Christmas.

"You'll come back, right, Smooshy?" Beth asked.

"That was the plan before you called me Smooshy," Tony replied.

"Okay, that's it," River said. She grinned at his mother. "I have to know. Where did he get the name *Smooshy*?"

"Don't you dare," Tony said. "I mean it."

His father burst out laughing.

"Wow, this must be good," River said. "Now you've got to tell me."

Beth shook her head. "I want to, but if Tony says no, I just can't."

"Well, I can," Ray said.

"Dad, no! I mean it!"

Tony saw him wink at River. "I'll tell you later."

"No, you won't."

"Sure, son. Whatever you say."

This time, his mother laughed.

Tony started to warn them again when Ray's phone rang. He picked it up and looked at it. "It's Duggan," he said. He got up and carried the phone into the family room.

Although it was hard to not try and overhear the conversation, Tony stood up and picked up the dirty dishes, carrying them over to the sink.

"You relax, Mom," he said. "River and I will do the dishes."

River stood up too. "Absolutely. You work too hard taking care of us." Before Beth could respond, she held up her hand like a cop stopping traffic. "I know, you enjoy it. But you need to let us in on the fun."

Beth smiled at them. "Okay, I give in. You can do the dishes. Actually, it's not really my favorite part anyway."

River's light laugh made Tony smile. He loved her laugh. And he loved how much his parents clearly liked her. He wished Aimee felt the same way. He was going to have to work on that. Hopefully, something he'd said to her at breakfast had changed her mind. Thinking about Aimee brought up a question.

"So is Aimee coming over here?" he asked his mother.

"Yes, this afternoon. She's going to stay downstairs so River won't have to move."

"Oh, no," River said. "Please don't make her do that. I'll go downstairs."

"I told her that you'd say that," Beth said. "She absolutely won't let you change her mind. It's best to let her have her way."

"Mom's right," Tony said. "My sister is the most stubborn person I've ever known—next to you. If you try to talk her out of something, she'll only dig her heels in harder. I'm sure *you* can relate to that."

"You're very funny," River said. "Okay, but I still feel uncomfortable making her stay in the basement."

"Don't," Tony said. "She'll be fine."

Ray came back into the kitchen, a frown on his face.

"That was fast," Tony said. "Did Duggan find anything?"

"He did. He's going to email me the details, but basically, he discovered visits to the ER several times. Both for Michael and his sister."

"While they were in foster care?" River asked.

"No. The first visits happened while the kids were living with Edward and their mother."

"Their mother abused them too?" Tony asked.

"We don't think so, since she went to the ER herself several times."

"She should have left him," Tony said, frowning. He didn't

understand how mothers could allow their children to be beaten—unless they feared something even worse if they were to do something about it.

"Well, she did leave him," Ray said, his tone solemn. "She died."

"I know you might not be able to answer this," Tony said, "but do you have any idea if he abused his new wife? Or Angie?"

"I had the same question," Ray said. "Asked Duggan to do some checking. No reports at all. Seems like he cleaned himself up."

"But he never made things right with his kids, I guess," River said.

Ray sighed. "So, they decided to settle the score."

"What about while they were in foster care?" River asked.

"I was just getting to that. There were a couple of incidents with Stacy while she was with the Greers. Of course, there were always reasons for what happened. She fell off the slide. Slipped in the bathtub."

"Wait a minute," River said. "The Greers denied having Stacy."

"We suspected they lied," Tony said. "Obviously, they did."

"Were the police contacted?" Tony asked.

Ray shook his head. "Seems the ER doctor who saw her knew Terrance Greer and believed what he said. He shouldn't have. There were other children in their care that had so-called *accidents* too. He should have reported it. By law, he was bound to do so."

"What happened to Stacy?"

Tony's mother had been quiet while Ray shared what Duggan had found, but she was obviously moved by hearing what the little girl had gone through.

His father shrugged. "This is where she disappears. This was during the time that so many kids were lost in the system."

"No hospital records for Michael after being abandoned by his father?" River asked.

Ray shook his head. "No, as we already know, he stayed in

foster care until he was sixteen, then he disappeared too." He took a deep breath and looked at Tony. "Son, I want to thank you and River for all the work you've done. I couldn't have asked for anything better. Not only did you deliver the profile, but you figured out the identity of the UNSUB. You and River made a great decision. You'll be great P.I.s. I have no doubt of it."

His father had always been encouraging, even though he wasn't thrilled when Tony joined the FBI. But he never gave praise that he felt wasn't deserved. Tony knew that what he'd said came from the heart. It meant more than Tony could say. He croaked out a "Thank you," but he was certain his father knew how much his comment had touched him.

"You're welcome. Now, you two relax. I'll take it from here."

Tony nodded, but that would be impossible to do. He glanced at River and saw the same concern in her face that he felt inside. Where was Michael Wilson now and what was he planning?

FORTY-FIVE

River and Tony spent most of the day in the family room. Beth kept them filled with Christmas cookies, fudge, and candied popcorn balls. Although River tried to eat lightly, just sitting on the couch and stuffing her face while they watched Christmas movies or played board games made her sleepy. Finally, around two in the afternoon, she went upstairs for a nap. Beth had asked Tony to help with some of the Christmas lights in the front yard. A few of them had stopped working.

When River got to her room, she took off her shoes and flopped down on top of the bed. Feeling a little cold, she sat up and grabbed the quilt folded up at the foot of the bed. She pulled it over herself and then got the pillow out from underneath the comforter. There were pillow shams that matched the comforter, but River hadn't put them back on. It didn't seem important since she would just take them off again when she got ready for bed.

She could hear Beth and Tony outside, talking and laughing. Images from the movie she'd seen about the crucifixion flashed in front of her.

"Lord," she whispered to God, "when I get home, I want things to be different. Please help me to walk in the kind of love and grace You've shown me. I want to treat my mother in a way that pleases You. I don't know why this terrible disease has happened to her, but I'm asking You to heal her. I know You love her, Lord. But no matter what, let this part of our lives be lived in a way that glorifies You."

She flipped over on her side and was thinking about what Jesus had done for the world when she heard a noise from the backyard. Must be Tony looking for something. She wondered for a moment if she should go out and try to help him, but she knew Beth enjoyed spending time with her son. She probably wouldn't want River to interfere, so she closed her eyes and within a couple of minutes felt herself drifting off to sleep.

I SLIPPED THE KEY INTO THE LOCK. Then I slowly unlocked the deadbolt. People always used the same key for both locks on their doors. Dumb. It only took one key for someone to get inside. I pulled the door open slowly, listening for a warning from the alarm. Nothing. Sure enough, they'd turned it off. A moment of carelessness despite their intent to be cautious.

I slipped inside and tried to close the door behind me. The cold had warped it some, and it took all my strength to pull it shut. It made a louder noise than I'd anticipated. I froze, listening to see if anyone had heard it or would come to investigate. Silence. Good.

I walked slowly through the deserted basement until I found the unfinished storage area I'd seen earlier. Even if someone came downstairs to do laundry, they wouldn't open this door. There wasn't any reason to. Their house was already decorated inside and out for Christmas. I'd seen their tree through the front window. This room would keep me safe until the snow started. I moved some boxes and made a space where I could wait. After I had everything just the way I wanted it, I took the snowman ornament out of my pocket and held it next to my cheek for just a moment. Then I put it back in my pocket. Because of the security system, I'd have to wait until after I completed my mission to hang it up outside. I already had the spot picked out. I smiled to myself. This mission was particularly satisfying. I'd be killing two birds with one stone. I had to cover my mouth with my hand to keep from laughing out loud. Very apropos.

The trap was set. Now to wait for it to spring shut.

WHEN RIVER FINALLY WOKE UP, she looked at the clock. A little after four. She'd slept for a couple of hours. Not sure why she was so tired. Probably because the profile was done. As Ray had said, there wasn't anything else to do, and she'd surrendered it to God. She felt better.

She sat up and wondered what Tony was doing. Suddenly she remembered about the snow. She got up and went to the window, taking a deep breath before opening the drapes. It was getting dark outside already, but not just because it was winter. The sky was full of clouds. As she watched, flakes began to fall from the sky. She quietly prayed they were all wrong. That the Snowman would wait another couple of years. That Ray would have more time to find him.

River went back toward the bed and picked up her cell phone from the nightstand. She quickly checked the weather report. Looking at the radar told her everything she needed to know. The storm was here.

Determined to stay calm, she went over to the mirror and ran a brush through her hair. Then she checked her image closely, making certain she didn't have gunk in the corner of her eyes or drool on her face. After she was satisfied, she put on her shoes and headed for the stairs. She'd only made it halfway down when she heard Aimee's voice. Great. The woman who hated her was here. She paused for a moment to remind herself once again that Jesus loved Aimee too and that River didn't need to feel bad about herself or guilty about what happened to Tony.

Sending up a prayer for patience and peace, she took several more calming breaths and went downstairs.

FORTY-SIX

When River reached the kitchen, she found everyone except Ray gathered around the kitchen table. Aimee looked up at her and smiled as if they were best friends. River didn't like phony people, but she was trying to cut Aimee some slack, not just because she knew God wanted her to, but also for Tony. The last thing she wanted was to be someone who made his life harder.

"Good to see you, River," Aimee said. River noticed that her smile didn't quite reach her eyes. There was nothing to do but make a huge effort to walk in love. Problem was, right now her flesh wasn't in agreement. Not even a little bit.

"I heard your apartment building loses electricity in bad weather," River said, trying not to say something she didn't mean. Or something she did mean. "Coming here was a good idea."

A meow from under the table answered River's next question. She knelt down and came face-to-face with a gorgeous calico cat.

"I take it this is Lulu?" she said.

"Yes," Aimee said. "She doesn't really take to strangers."

Lulu walked out from underneath the table, came straight to River, and began rubbing against her leg, purring loudly.

River wanted to grab Lulu and squeeze the stuffing out of her in gratitude, but she decided to take a gentler approach. If she was skittish, it was better not to make any sudden moves that might frighten her. River purposely didn't look at Aimee, although shooting her a victory smile occurred to her for a fleeting moment.

River picked up the small cat and stood. Lulu cuddled against her as if they'd known each other forever.

"Wow, I've never seen her connect with a stranger so quickly," Tony said. "She must sense that you're a good person."

Was it wrong of River to feel as if there were a smaller River inside of her jumping up and down like a child? Yeah, probably.

"I love cats," she said. She finally risked a glance at Aimee, who didn't look too happy. "My mother has a cat. She can probably tell that I'm comfortable with her."

"Maybe," Aimee said. "Or she's just smelling your mother's cat on your clothes."

Sighing inwardly, River said, "I hope not. I wash my clothes regularly, so I doubt there's any scent of our cat on them."

"Well, I'm just saying that Lulu is very picky. There must be some reason she's taking to you." Aimee stood up. "Here, just give her to me. She doesn't look comfortable. . . ."

"Okay, that's it," Beth said suddenly. She pointed her finger at her daughter. "Sit down, Aimee. Now."

Aimee looked surprised at Beth's outburst. River could understand that. Tony's mother was always so sweet and accommodating. What was happening?

Although Aimee was clearly not thrilled with being ordered around by her mother, she slunk back to her chair and plopped herself down.

"River, put Lulu down and take a seat too, please."

River didn't hesitate. She gently lowered Lulu to the floor and slipped back into her chair. Of course, Lulu immediately jumped up into her lap. She looked at Beth, who rolled her eyes but didn't say anything else to River about the obviously smitten cat.

River glanced at Tony, who looked amused but didn't say anything.

"What's going on, Mom?" Aimee asked.

"Your brother and I both know what you did, dear," Beth said. "Time we all face the truth. You and I both blamed River for what happened to Tony, but I was wrong, and so are you. We need to put this behind us."

"She told you what I said to her?" Aimee asked, trying to look offended.

"No, I told her what happened," Beth said.

"And I shared with Mom what you said to River," Tony said. "So now it's all out in the open."

"You and I were both horrified by Tony's injuries," Beth said to her daughter. Her eyes filled with tears that ran over and dripped down her face. Then she reached over and took Tony's hand. "I never want to see you like that again, son. For a while, we were certain you weren't going to make it. It was the worst time of my life. And when you told us why you were on that riverbank . . ." She wiped her cheeks. "At the time, Aimee and I felt you were there because River told you to go. We believed she should have known it was a trap. We also told ourselves that because of her decision to put herself in danger, you felt you had to put your life on the line to save her." She sighed. "Your father tried to talk some sense into us. Of course, I finally realized he was right. I admitted this to River when she arrived. I apologized, and we've worked it out. Now your sister needs to do the same."

"And what about this guy who worked with the Strangler?" Aimee asked. "Is that protecting Tony? If this psycho wants to kill her, why would she stay around Tony? She's putting him in danger."

"I'm sorry," Beth said, looking at River. "I told her about the card that came for you. I felt badly that she was the only person in the family that didn't know. I don't like to keep secrets. Maybe I was wrong."

"No, you weren't wrong," River said softly. "She's staying here, and she needed to know. Am I allowed to answer her question?"

Beth nodded at her.

"Actually, I agree with you," River said. "I . . . I would have gone back to St. Louis if it wasn't for the storm that's coming." She gathered her strength and met Tony's gaze. "Until this guy is caught, I don't think I should be around you."

She was shocked when Tony stood. The expression on his face was one she'd never seen before. It was as if the color had left his face completely and his eyes burned with . . . something. What was it?

"You listen to me, River Ryland." He looked away from her and addressed his sister and his mother. "This is for both of you too." He turned back and locked his eyes on hers. River felt caught in his intense gaze. "First of all, that won't work. I'll simply follow you wherever you go—which won't be far since you can't leave your mother." He hesitated and swallowed hard, obviously emotional. "What happened that night on the side of the river wasn't your fault. We were behavioral analysts. Not field agents. As far as we knew, there was no way for Joseph Baker to know who we were—or even that we'd worked his case. Our friend and colleague gave him our names for a reason we may never completely understand, but my guess is that her life was at stake. We were told she was in a club not long before she went missing and was bragging about what our team did. Maybe Baker was there. We don't know." He looked briefly at his mother and Aimee. "I don't think I ever told you this, but the FBI looked into what happened to Jacki, but they were never able to find her or figure out why she called us. The only camera in the bar was focused on the bar so the owner could keep tabs on the bartenders. There weren't any cameras on the crowd. Also, when Jacki called us, we had absolutely no reason to suspect anything. River didn't pick up anything in her voice, and I wouldn't have either." He refocused his attention on River. "I know you think you should have known something was wrong, but if that were true, you would have told me, and we wouldn't have gone to meet her."

He leaned forward and stared at his sister. "I hope you hear me, Aimee. I'm not an idiot. I don't need River to look out for me or to tell me what to do. I didn't sense any personal danger that night, and neither did she. The person to blame for what happened was Joseph Baker. He's the only one at fault. I'm sorry I got angry and walked out on you yesterday morning, but I was afraid I was going to say something I'd regret. But I'm telling you now that this is going to stop. It's wrong. You're wrong. Do I make myself clear?"

"I understand what you're saying," Aimee said, her face red with emotion. "But . . . but nothing like this ever happened before. Before you got involved with *her*. And now Baker's got some kind of helper looking for you?"

"No, he's looking for River. Not for me. And for your information, if he comes after her, and I can stop him, I'll do whatever it takes—even if I must put myself in danger to do it."

"Dear, I hear what you're saying," Beth said gently, "and I agree with you that what happened wasn't River's fault, but why . . . I mean, why are you so determined to keep her safe? I know you're a good person, but you could still be working at the BAU. Your injuries weren't bad enough for you to lose your job. Can you just please tell me why you're so committed to River?" She smiled at him. "The truth, please."

Tony looked down at the floor for a moment. When he lifted his head, the color had returned to his face, and he looked like the man River knew.

"I care about River," he said. "She's my partner, and she's my friend. In fact, she's probably my best friend."

"And that's all, son?" Beth asked.

Tony's cheeks flushed pink. "Mom, I love you to the moon and back, but if there's anything else, the first person to hear about it will be River, not you."

It was River's turn to blush. She knew exactly what he was saying, but it only made it clearer that she had to get out of Tony's life before something happened to him. He was too willing to take chances, and she couldn't allow him to put his life on the line for her.

Because the truth was, she was totally and completely in love with him and couldn't stand the thought of losing him. She was convinced that if he was hurt by the Strangler's apprentice, this time it would definitely be her fault.

FORTY-SEVEN

Tony couldn't look at River. What was she thinking? Instead, he met his sister's eyes.

"I'm so disappointed in you, Aimee. River is our guest, and for you to . . ."

Aimee held her hand up as a gesture to stop his next words. "I know, I know. I get it." She began to cry.

Tony got up and went over to her, putting his arms around her.

Between her sobs she was able to get out, "I couldn't . . . if I lost you. I mean . . . I love you so much. I'm . . . I'm so sorry."

Tony already knew why she'd gone after River. They'd seen it time and time again as analysts. People acting out in anger because of fear and love. He'd been so upset with his sister. Maybe he'd gone too far. He didn't say anything, he just held her tight until her sobs lessened. Finally, she gently pulled herself away.

"I'm sorry, River," she said, her words stilted. "I blamed you . . . and I blamed God. It wasn't right. I hope you can forgive me."

River smiled at her. "I've been learning a lot about forgiveness lately. Seems when we realize what Christ went through to forgive us, we really don't have any reason not to forgive others."

She hesitated a moment and then said, "Besides, I understand why you felt the way you did. When someone we love is hurt, it frightens us. Lashing out is perfectly normal. Let's just start over, okay?"

Tony was so proud of River. Her return to God was so real and fresh. He loved seeing her reach out to Him, determined to be who He wanted her to be. It inspired him. He gave Aimee a quick hug and went back to his chair. His mother got up and took a box of tissues from the kitchen counter. She handed one to Aimee and took one for herself.

"I'd really like that, River," Aimee said after wiping her face. "I get the feeling we can be friends if you're willing."

"I'm very willing. So now that we're all friends," River said, an odd twinkle in her eye, "which one of you is going to tell me why Tony's nickname is *Smooshy*?"

It took a couple of seconds for Aimee and Beth to change gears, but they both started to laugh. Although this wasn't a story Tony wanted anyone to tell, he realized that River had found a way to relieve the tension and turn things around. He admired it, even if he had no intention of allowing her to hear the answer to her question.

"Let me just say this," Beth said with a grin. "When your eighteen-month-old child is able to remove his diaper while he's supposed to be taking a nap in his crib . . ."

"Mom, no!" Tony said loudly.

"And his diaper is pretty full," Aimee added, trying to hold back a giggle.

"And you walk into the room," Beth continued.

"I mean it, Mom. Stop!" Tony said, standing up, ready to flee.

"Okay, dear," Beth said in a calming tone. "If you don't want me to finish the story . . ."

"Then I will," Aimee said before he could stop her. "Your mother comes into the room and finds you smearing your . . .

well, you know . . . all over everything. Then you smile at her and say, 'Oooooh, smooshy!'"

Tony was afraid to look at River, but her exuberant laugh made him finally risk a glance. She was wiping tears from her eyes, and the elation he saw on her face made his extreme embarrassment almost bearable.

"I guess our nickname isn't completely kind," Beth said between spurts of laughter, "but we've always kept its meaning between ourselves. Until you."

Even though Tony was somewhat horrified that his mother had shared such an embarrassing story, he wondered if it was because she sensed that River was more than just his friend. He couldn't be certain, but he suspected it was true. Mothers seemed to have some kind of emotional ESP when it came to their children.

"I'm honored," River said with a grin, "but if there are any other stories like this in Tony's past, it might be best to keep them to yourself. As it is, I may never see him in quite the same way."

This caused another round of giggles, and Tony just rolled his eyes. He got a cup of coffee and sat down again, purposely not meeting anyone's eyes. Aimee's sudden snort set them all off again.

"I'll just finish my coffee in my room," he said, standing up again. He felt someone tug at his sleeve.

"Please don't leave," River said. "We're sorry. It's just that . . . well, you've always been this perfect person. You know, in charge of yourself. A protector. A . . . warrior type. Thinking of you as a baby was funny. And touching. I'm sorry if we embarrassed you."

He looked at his sister and mother, who were nodding. But he noticed Aimee's mouth quiver. He frowned at her, and she blurted out, "Yes, we're sorry, Smooshy."

Of course, this brought another round of laughter. He had two choices. Either he could stomp off and then try to figure out how to come back downstairs after tossing away any shred of dignity he had left, or he could tough it out until his family and River moved on to something else. Being honest with himself, he was rather happy that his childhood misfortune had given River a chance to laugh and get the pressure off for a while. He decided his ego was worth the jolt and stayed in his chair. He smiled and shook his head.

"When you ladies are finished, can we change the subject?" he said.

"I guess so," River said. "Although I'll be dealing with some very disturbing images the rest of the day."

"That's okay," Aimee said. "I've had to do that my whole life."

Her dramatic sigh made Beth start to laugh, but she covered her mouth with her hand. After a moment, she said, "Okay. That's it, girls. Let's settle down. I think Tony has suffered enough."

"Moving along," Tony said firmly, drawing the words out, "I assume Dad is on the way home? It's starting to snow pretty hard."

"He told me he needed to check in at the station, and then he'd head back here," Beth said. She got up and pulled the kitchen curtains back. "It's really starting to ramp up out there. Maybe I'll call him and . . ." She stopped and then turned around to smile at them. "He's just pulling in. Nothing like waiting until the last second."

A couple of minutes later, the front door opened. A few moments after that, Ray came into the kitchen, two large bags in his hands.

"What's that, honey?" Beth asked. "I told you I'd stocked the kitchen."

"I know, but I was in the mood for some fun finger food. I don't want you cooking supper tonight, Beth." He frowned and looked around the kitchen. "You haven't started anything yet, have you?"

"No, I haven't. I had something in mind, but I like the way you're thinking." She smiled at him. "What did you buy?"

Ray set the bag down and took out three logs of summer sausage, two trays of sliced cheese, a large bag of chips, and several different kinds of dips. Then he took out two cartons of eggnog, some soft drinks, and some hot chocolate mix.

"Oh, Ray, this looks perfect," Beth said. "I'll slice the sausage."

"You'll do nothing of the sort, Mom," Tony said. "We'll do it. You just sit down in the family room and relax. We'll get everything ready and bring it in."

"How about a Christmas movie tonight?" Aimee said. "I know it's not Christmas yet, but it's the season."

Beth laughed. "We've watched several already, but I'm game to watch another one. You can never have too many Christmas movies."

Everyone voiced their approval, and a vote was taken. Since it was split between *The Bishop's Wife* and *White Christmas*, Ray took a coin out of his pocket.

"Heads, it's *The Bishop's Wife*," he said. "Tails, we'll watch *White Christmas*." After flipping the coin, he called out "Heads! Dudley the angel wins."

"Sounds great," River said. "I've only seen the movie once. Years ago."

Aimee's mouth dropped open. "Seriously? Wow. I've probably watched it at least twenty times."

"My parents didn't really encourage Christmas movies when we were kids," River said. "And after my father left, Christmas wasn't really important to my mom. I only watched it because I stumbled across it once on TV."

"What did you think of it, River?" Beth asked.

River smiled. "I loved it. I'm really looking forward to seeing it again."

Tony had seen it many times, but it was one of his favorites, so he was happy to watch it again. Anything that moved the conversation away from *Smooshy* was okay with him.

His father took his mother's hand and led her to the family room, while he, River, and Aimee sliced the sausage, put it out on a large serving plate, along with some of the cheese, and then dumped the chips into a bowl. After that, they put the different dips into his mother's small crystal snack bowls and stuck spoons in each one.

Aimee took drink orders and got those ready. Once they were finished, they carried everything into the family room and laid it out on the coffee table. Lulu, who was very well trained, didn't go near the food. Instead, she seemed totally in love with River, only wanting to be near her.

"If she gets to be a pain, tell me," Aimee said.

"Actually, I love it," River replied. "If it's okay with you, I'd love to have her sit near me."

"I'm fine with it. It gives me a break," Aimee said with a smile. "But be warned, you may not be able to leave Burlington. I'd hate to break her heart."

River laughed. "I have a feeling this is a very shallow romance. After I go home, I doubt she'll think about me at all."

As the snow fell, they watched the movie about a man who prayed that God would help him build a large church. His answer came in the form of an angel named Dudley, played by Cary Grant. While everyone else seemed glued to the TV, Tony couldn't stop looking at the large windows in the family room that clearly showed the falling snow. Was the Snowman out there right now, planning to kill someone?

"Help us, God," he whispered. "We need You."

FORTY-EIGHT

After the movie and a rousing game of charades, everyone headed to bed. Once again, River tried to talk Aimee into taking her room, but she wouldn't hear of it. River finally gave up and headed upstairs. Although things between her and Aimee seemed to have been resolved, River still felt uncomfortable staying in her room.

No matter what, though, she hadn't changed her mind about keeping Tony away from the Strangler's apprentice. Aimee was right. She was putting him in danger. It was something she would have to deal with, but right now, her mind was on the Snowman. It was late, and everything was quiet. No calls from the police station yet. Maybe they'd been wrong. Perhaps the Snowman wasn't going to make his move this year. Was it possible the two-year gap between killings was such a part of his MO that he felt compelled to stick to it? Organized serial killers were often addicted to patterns. If he didn't strike, they would know they were wrong about thinking he would try to restore his bruised ego. His self-esteem and penchant for delivering justice had led them to believe he would have to reassert his imagined superiority by murdering someone in place of Sandra Cooper. River had never wanted to be wrong more than she did now.

She exchanged her jeans and sweater for sweats and a T-shirt. Then she plopped down on the bed and turned onto her side. She felt tired, but she couldn't sleep. It was like her body was waiting for something terrible to happen even though she'd told herself she was trusting God. She realized that she needed to pray. She started by asking God to keep the people in Burlington safe. She also found herself asking for wisdom and insight. That was the job of the Holy Spirit, right? She remembered a scripture she'd read. She couldn't quote it exactly, but it had something to do with the Holy Spirit leading people to the truth. That's what they needed now.

"Holy Spirit, if there's something we're not seeing, will You please show it to us? If You can use us to stop Michael Wilson, we're willing. Thank You."

She could hear Tony walk past her door and go to his room. Beth and Ray had already gone to bed, but she was pretty sure Ray was still awake, waiting to hear from the station. He was still convinced the Snowman was out there—planning another murder. At least Chief Munson had promised Ray that they would keep his concerns in mind. But how much good would that do during a major snowstorm? Police resources would be stretched thin. She was amazed that Ray was able to be home tonight. Of course, that didn't ensure that he wouldn't be called out as the night went on.

Although River was beginning to feel sleepy, she sat up in bed and reached for the TV remote. If Ray was awake, she felt she should be too. She thought about calling Tony to see if he was just sitting in bed like she was, but she couldn't do it. What if she was wrong and Ray and Beth were trying to sleep? Although their bedroom was way down at the other end of the hall, she was afraid that Tony's phone ringing might disturb them. She certainly wasn't going to his room. That wouldn't look right. She was fairly confident that Ray and Beth weren't worried about them in that way, but still, she felt as if she had to make sure she didn't do anything that might seem inappropriate.

Right before she turned on the TV, she heard an odd noise from somewhere inside the house. Was it from downstairs? The basement? Why did that concern her? If Aimee was still up, it wasn't her business. So why was her stomach suddenly tied in knots?

She changed her mind about TV. She didn't feel as if she could concentrate on it right now. She put the remote back on the nightstand and flipped over onto her back. She found herself going over the profile again. Why? It was done. Yet something bothered her. She remembered what Ray had said. As if there was something they weren't seeing . . . that they should.

The next sound she heard almost sounded like a muffled scream. She realized it had come through the heating vent. River got up and knelt down next to it, but after several seconds of silence, she decided she was imagining things. The alarm was set. No one was in the house who shouldn't be. She stood up and looked around the room, wondering what to do next. She was still on edge. Obviously, it was because of the Snowman. She finally decided to go downstairs and get something to drink. She'd noticed that Beth had chamomile tea. It always helped her to relax. She slid on her slippers and opened the door as quietly as she could. Then she stood in the hallway for several seconds, listening, but the house was still quiet. Finally, she crept down the stairs and walked into an empty kitchen. This wasn't where the sounds had come from. Maybe Aimee was watching TV downstairs. That would make sense. Chiding herself for being so silly, she opened a cabinet where she'd seen the tea. Sure enough, she found the chamomile amid boxes of other flavors. River put a couple of bags in a cup, then she added some water and placed it inside the microwave. A minute and a half later, her tea was ready to drink. She was on her way back upstairs when she heard another noise. This time she could tell it was definitely coming from the basement. Maybe she'd go down and check on Aimee.

River put her cup down on the counter and was headed toward the basement door, when she heard someone coming up the stairs. She started to open the door when she realized that whoever was walking upstairs wasn't Aimee. She'd been wearing soft, slip-on sneakers. Whoever was on the stairs was wearing boots and the footsteps belonged to someone heavier than Aimee.

In that moment, their profile, wondering how the Snowman was getting information, and Michael Wilson's birthmark all popped into her head like someone was trying to pull the threads of a tapestry together for her. She suddenly realized how stupid she'd been. Ray was right. The answer had been staring them right in the face, but they hadn't paid attention. Someone else was in the house. The realization shocked her so much, she put her hand over her mouth to muffle her loud gasp.

River hurried back to the kitchen, turned off the light, and started for the stairs. At the last second, she realized she'd never make it. She ran back to the kitchen and quietly slipped into the pantry, slowly closing the door almost all the way, but keeping it cracked open just enough so she could look out. She waited as she heard the basement door open and shut. The nightlights in the hallway and in the kitchen cast a soft glow. A figure crept past her and toward the stairs, where he stopped for a moment. It was hard to see clearly, but the person at the bottom of the stairs confirmed her suspicions. This wasn't Aimee. Aimee was tall and thin. He was of medium height and build. She didn't need to see his face. It was Michael Wilson. The Snowman. But why? If he was truly angry with foster parents, why was he here? No one here was a foster parent or had ever been one. Wilson was compelled to follow his pattern. Unless he'd decided he had to stop the detective who might put two and two together and prevent him from carrying out his self-imposed mission. If that was true, they were all in danger.

Wilson stood at the bottom of the stairs without moving. He appeared to be listening. Finally, he began heading toward Tony and his parents. River had to do something. They were unaware that he was coming. River crept out of the pantry, slowly opened a drawer, pulled out a large knife, and then quietly made her way to the bottom of the stairs, where she stopped. For a brief moment, she'd wondered if she should pull out some pots and pans and bang them together to alert everyone upstairs that Wilson was coming. But they'd speculated that he could have a gun. They knew he had some way of intimidating his victims. She couldn't take the chance that he'd start shooting.

She was hoping to hear something that would tell her just where he was. Then she heard a door open, but the sound was faint. It had to be Ray and Beth's room. She sent up a quick prayer for help. Taking a deep breath, she climbed the stairs as quickly as she could without making any noise. She hurried to her room and traded the knife for her gun. Then she picked up her phone and dialed 911. The phone rang and rang but no one answered. Calls about the storm were probably clogging the line. She slipped the phone into the back waistband of her sweats and made her way to Tony's room. She couldn't risk knocking on the door, so she opened it as quietly as she could. Tony was lying in bed and his eyes were closed. She walked over to him and quickly placed her hand over his mouth, hoping it would keep him quiet until she could explain. But as soon as her hand touched his mouth, he grabbed it and pulled it away. Thankfully, the lamp on his nightstand was on, and he realized who was standing over him.

"*Shhh*," she whispered. "Don't say anything. Someone's in the house. I think it's Wilson. He may be in your parents' room. I think he came from the basement."

Tony sat up straight in bed, his eyes wide. "Why didn't you stop him?" he whispered.

"Because I was downstairs getting a cup of tea. For some reason, I didn't think to arm myself first."

"Oh. Sorry."

"Get your gun. I've tried calling 911, but I couldn't get through. We need to get to your parents' room right now. I know who the Snowman is."

The overhead light in the room suddenly turned on. River and Tony looked toward the door and found a man standing there, a gun pointed right at them.

FORTY-NINE

Donnie Schweizer," Tony said. "You're the Snowman." For some odd reason he wasn't completely surprised. Why was that? Then it struck him. "Your cheek. The scar. You had a birthmark removed, didn't you? Why didn't I realize . . . ?"

"That was the black mark Angie Mayhew saw," River said. "His job in foster care gave him all the information he needed to hunt people he thought were guilty of abusing children." She looked at Tony. "I'm sorry. I was so busy thinking about Aimee and . . . other things . . . that I didn't see it when I should have."

"At first I hated that nickname," Wilson said with an odd smile. "But now I kind of like it."

"You dyed your hair," Tony said. "I'm guessing you're wearing colored contacts to hide your blue eyes?"

"Brilliant," Wilson said. "But nothing you can say will help you now."

He'd worn glasses when he attacked Sandra Cooper. That's why she'd said his eyes were red. As they'd guessed, it was the fire reflected in his glasses.

They had to stall him. Tony had dropped his phone on the bed when Wilson turned the light on. It was partially hidden by his comforter. Hopefully, Wilson wouldn't see it. Tony had to try to call the station. He had the number on speed dial. Maybe he could bypass 911 since River hadn't been able to get through. If only he could reach it.

Tony realized he needed to get ahold of himself. He was worried about his parents and Aimee, but it was as if the gun Wilson had pointed toward him and River was ten times the size he knew it to be. The pain of the last time he'd been shot made his entire body feel like ice—cold and frozen. He had a hard time catching his breath, but he had to stop this guy. He prayed silently for God's help.

"We . . . we heard about your father . . . Edward," River said. She'd obviously noticed he was in trouble and was trying to give him a chance to gain control of his emotions. "How abusive he was. How horribly he treated you and your sister. If anyone has the right to be angry—to give Edward a taste of his own medicine—it would be you and your sister. I'm not sure why you had to kill his wife, though."

The tightness in Michael's expression softened just a bit. Narcissistic killers like Wilson liked to talk about themselves. About their compulsions. River knew this. She was buying them some time. Tony took a chance and took a step closer to the bed.

"I didn't go there to kill her, but she saw me," Wilson said. "Besides, if she was married to someone like Edward, she had to be just as bad as he was."

"Look," Tony said, working to keep his voice steady. "We get it. We really do. But what we can't figure out is why you killed Sheila Jackson."

"Although we certainly know how messed up the foster care system can be," River said. "Did Sheila do something to hurt Stacy?"

River had used Stacy's name to show that they cared about his sister. That was smart. It was harder to kill people who empathized with you. Tony watched to see if it would have the hoped-for result.

"Yes, she was evil," Michael said. "When she got tired of Stacy, she passed her off on the Greers. They hurt her too, but she got away."

Got away? What happened to her? Maybe she was given to someone who wasn't legally part of the foster care system. Tony hoped she hadn't ended up on the streets.

"How did you ever find her?" River asked. "We couldn't track her, and we really tried."

Wilson's eyes were wide, and although he'd lowered his gun some, his body language showed that he was still dangerous and ready to erupt.

"When I lost my foster family, they tried to put me somewhere else, but I took off and went looking for my sister. A girl who'd lived in my last foster house was at Sheila's when Stacy was there. She told me what Sheila did to both of them." It was as if Michael's eyes were on fire as he talked about the hate he felt toward the woman who had abused his sister.

"And the Greers?" Tony asked, taking one more step closer to his phone. Wilson didn't seem to notice.

"Now that's an interesting story," he said, obviously enjoying his moment to shine. "I changed my name. My whole identity." His laugh was chilling. "You'd be surprised by the kind of people you meet in the system. I ran into a guy who knew how to make people completely disappear and be born all over again. I became Donnie Schweizer, a kid who died when he was young. Got a social security number, even went to college. Earned a degree in sociology. Got a job in Des Moines with a foster care agency and was finally able to locate someone else who was at Sheila's. He told me about the Greers. By then, they'd moved to Burlington."

"So, you followed them here," River said.

This explained the gap between killings. Michael was putting himself in the perfect position to deliver revenge.

Wilson nodded, but then started looking nervous and waving his gun around.

"But what about the Craigs?" Tony asked, taking one more step. He'd reached the bed.

"They killed a kid," Wilson said as if Tony's question was stupid. "I can't allow people like that to take in other children. I had to stop them. Just because everyone else said it was an accident, I never believed that."

Knowing that he'd killed an innocent couple made the anger inside Tony grow, but he had to maintain control. He couldn't risk setting Wilson off.

"And Sandra Cooper?" River said.

Wilson's face twisted in rage. He was clearly furious that Sandra had gotten away from him. "I don't want to talk about her. She's evil, and she's going to die."

"So, you killed your father for deserting you and Stacy," River said. "And then you punished the people who hurt Stacy. The rest of your victims didn't have anything to do with you. You were just trying to protect other children."

"Yes. Someone has to keep the children safe."

Tony suddenly remembered River's dream. *It's about the children.* If only he'd figured it out sooner. Because of what had happened to him and his sister, Michael had decided that he was called to seek vengeance on those who hurt them—and other children. Was River thinking about her dream too?

River moved over just enough so that she hid Tony. She obviously knew what he was trying to do. He slowly reached down to his phone and quickly turned the sound all the way down so that whoever answered would be able to hear them, but Wilson wouldn't realize anyone was on the line. Then he clicked on the number for his father's station and pushed the phone under the bedspread so Wilson couldn't see it, but whoever answered could still pick up their voices.

"Michael, tell me about the snow and the ornament," River said gently. "We wondered what it meant to you."

Tony was surprised to see tears form in Wilson's eyes. "My mother made an ornament just like it for Stacy. When Mama died, Edward took it and destroyed it in front of us. I made Stacy another one with the felt my mother had. Stacy took it with her when she . . . when she left. It was snowing the night Child Protective Services took us away."

"Michael, I'm so sorry," River said. "What happened to you and Stacy was wrong."

"Stacy found me after she got away from the Greers," he said, his voice breaking. "Now I keep her safe."

Tony had to wonder how Stacy was able to find her brother after he'd run away and changed his name. Something seemed . . . off. For now, though, he wasn't going to challenge him. He had a feeling it could set him off. They needed to keep him as calm as possible.

"That's great, Michael," he said. "We're really happy to hear that."

Tony noticed that River had put her hand behind her back. She was pointing to the gun she'd slid into her waistband. He moved closer, hoping to get to it without Wilson noticing.

"That's enough talking," Wilson said. He gestured with his gun toward the bed. "Both of you lie down."

Tony had no intention of following Wilson's instructions. "Michael, what are you doing here? No one in this house has ever been a foster parent."

"And that's exactly why I have to be here," he shouted. "Angie Mayhew went through hell before finding a good family that adopted her. I went through her file." He pointed the gun at Tony.

"Your parents should have helped her. She told her case worker that the police said they were thinking about it. Angie waited and waited for them, but they never came. They deserve to die."

Tony was certain his parents had no idea that anyone had told Angie that they were thinking about fostering her. He suddenly remembered Angie saying that she was angry no one had come for her, but that she'd put that behind her. Had she been talking about his parents?

"That's why you want them to die?" River said.

Wilson's face twisted with rage. "That's only part of it. Your father is trying to stop me. Keep me from delivering justice."

"And my mother?" Tony asked. He was trying his best to stall, but now he was worried that his parents and his sister could be in real trouble. He moved closer to the gun in River's waistband.

"She's guilty too. She didn't help Angie, and she supports your father." He shrugged. "She's not innocent. She has blood on her hands just like he does."

"What have you done with them?" Tony asked. "Did you hurt them?"

Wilson smiled a strange, twisted smile. "They've been taken care of, but this time I'll make certain justice has been delivered. I won't let them get away like Sandra Cooper did. I'm going to make absolutely certain that they die."

"I don't understand," River said.

Wilson sighed, obviously losing patience with them. "I gave them insulin. It should be enough, but I intend to go back and check on them. I wasn't counting on five of you. I only brought enough for four. If it wasn't enough, I'll have to use my gun."

"But you don't shoot people," River said.

"And I don't want to, but I may have to. It's not my fault someone else is here."

He sounded like a petulant child. As if they'd purposely taken away one of his favorite toys.

"Did you . . . deliver justice to the woman downstairs?" River asked, her voice quivering.

"Of course. That's what I'm talking about," Wilson said, his voice tight. "I didn't plan for her."

At that moment, Tony wanted nothing more than to put his hands around Wilson's neck and squeeze the life out of him. He was too angry to speak.

"But she didn't do anything wrong," River said.

Wilson looked at her like she was crazy. "If she wasn't guilty, she wouldn't be here. I have to set the fire soon, and I don't allow anyone to burn alive. It's inhumane."

Michael Wilson was clearly insane. Tony could see that trying to reason with him was impossible. To save himself, River, and his family, Tony had to get his hands on River's gun. It was the only way.

"This is taking too long," Wilson said. He waved his gun at them again. "Lie down on the bed. Now. I'm tired of waiting. If you don't do what I say, I'll shoot one of you." He hesitated a moment and then pointed his gun at River. "Either you get on the bed, or you can watch your girlfriend die. It's up to you."

"Have you used a gun before?" River asked.

Tony could tell that she was frightened. He was too. He had no intention of allowing this man to hurt River. No matter what.

Wilson shook his head. "Most of the time I put the guilty to sleep before they know what's going on. I only use this when I have to. It makes them do what I tell them to do."

"Shooting people isn't easy," River said. "Are you sure you can do it?"

"If I have to. I . . ."

The wail of police sirens began to grow in the distance. As Wilson looked away for just a moment, Tony took the opportunity and grabbed River's gun. He stepped away from her and pointed it at Wilson. But before he could fire, Wilson turned back and aimed his gun at Tony. A second after Tony pulled the trigger, River stepped in front of him. Tony heard another gunshot and River slumped to the floor. Tony cried out the only two words he could find in that moment.

"Jesus, help!"

CHAPTER

FIFTY

I can't believe the chances you took," Beth said. "If something serious had happened to either one of you . . ."

"Mom, we're fine," Tony said. He looked across the table at River. "I can't believe what you did. It was so reckless."

River shrugged and then winced in pain. The bullet had only grazed her arm, but she was still pretty sore. Thankfully, everyone was fine. It seemed that Wilson had purchased diluted insulin from a new source. Besides that, he'd had to adjust to an extra person being in the house. Aimee's presence had helped to save her family's lives. River believed God had arranged things to protect them all. Although it had taken a long time to get Aimee, Ray, and Beth to the hospital that night because of the storm, the amount of insulin in their systems wasn't enough to kill them. If it had been, they might not have made it to the hospital on time. As it was, after an overnight stay, they were all home. River's wound had been treated, and she was released as well. It really was a miracle that all of them had made it through.

Beth got up, picked up the coffeepot, and warmed up everyone's cup. Then she put more cookies on the plate in the middle of the kitchen table before sitting down again.

"I feel bad about Angie," Ray said. "I had no idea she knew we'd thought about fostering her. No one at the station should have told her that. What were they thinking?"

"Everything turned out okay for her, Dad," Tony said. "I think Wilson built up things in his mind because of his anger. I doubt that Angie is upset about that now. She loves her family."

"Still, we intend to visit her," Beth said. "Maybe we weren't there for her back then, but we plan to make up for that now. We may not be her parents, but we can be her friends."

River was certain Angie would welcome people like Ray and Beth in her life. How could she not?

"I realize I keep apologizing to you," Aimee said to River, "but I really am sorry for doubting your commitment to my brother. You took a bullet for him."

"Well, I didn't actually *take a bullet,* I kind of *missed a bullet* for him," River said, smiling.

"You didn't know that," Ray said. "What you did was brave."

"What you did was stupid," Tony said. "Please don't ever do that again. I can take care of myself."

"I know you're worried about this Strangler person's accomplice, River," Beth said. "But please don't leave my son's side. He needs you. You both need each other. I truly believe you're safer together."

"Mom . . ."

"No, son. I'm right about this."

River wasn't certain what to say. She didn't want to lie to Beth, but she'd already decided to leave Tony once they returned home. She felt awful about having to walk away from her mother too, but it couldn't be helped. Until the Strangler's partner was captured, her brother, Dan, would just have to step up. At least Rose had Mrs. Weyland to care for her. The truth was, the last thing she wanted to do was to push Tony away. It was going to break her heart, but she loved him too much to let some crazed psychopath kill him because of her. It was even clearer now that she'd met his family. She couldn't allow them to lose him.

"I hear you, Beth," she said. "He really is kind of needy."

Tony rolled his eyes. "Very funny."

"So how is Wilson doing?" River asked Ray.

"He's going to be okay. After he gets out of the hospital, he'll be arraigned. I'm not sure if he'll end up in prison or in a psychiatric hospital. He's pretty delusional."

"He really believed his sister had found him, didn't he?" Aimee asked.

Tony nodded. "Since he's been in the hospital, he's been having long conversations with Stacy. He believes she's actually there with him. I think he had an emotional breakdown when he couldn't find her when he was younger. His mind brought her back so he could convince himself that she was still alive. Somewhere inside he probably knows she's dead, but unless he gets help, he won't be able to face the truth."

"After listening to River and Tony, I called Chief Watts in Des Moines," Ray said. "On a hunch, I suggested he send crime-scene techs to the Greers' old house. Sure enough, they found Stacy's remains buried in the backyard. She was just a child when she was killed by those monsters."

"I realize that Wilson is delusional," River said, "but besides those who really did abuse children, he killed some innocent people too. Their families deserve justice."

Ray shrugged. "It will be up to the courts to decide what happens. You've done everything you could. Time to let it go."

"I wish you could both stay for Christmas," Beth said, "but I know you can't."

"I told you to stay here," River said to Tony. "I can drive home alone."

Tony frowned at her. "You know I won't let you do that. It's not safe."

"But . . ."

"Just hush," he said. "I don't want to spend our last night here arguing." He looked at his mother. "I know I said I'd try to come back for Christmas, Mom, but I can't. Not this year."

Beth held her hand up. "I know. It was a nice thought, but you need to stay with River. Maybe you can both spend Christmas with us someday. Now, let's have a great meal and share some time together. I want you to both relax and enjoy yourselves. You deserve it."

River smiled at her. She'd grown to love Tony's family. Hopefully, authorities would find the man who was determined to kill her, and she could come back here when it was safe. She prayed God would find a way to make it happen. But for now, she was happy to spend this last night with them. Whatever the future held, she was glad she'd come to Burlington.

HE KEPT WATCHING THEIR OFFICE, awaiting their return. Maybe they'd found his bug, but it didn't make any difference. Neither would their new cameras.

It wouldn't be much longer, and he would finally be able to complete his objective. After that, his new quest would begin.

NOTE FROM THE AUTHOR

Dear Reader,

I hope you've enjoyed this book. I try hard to write stories that will entertain you, but even more importantly, I pray that something I've written will touch your heart. If you find yourself relating to my characters, who struggle with fear, loneliness, and sorrow just like the rest of us, I want to give you some good news. God has the answer to every problem you face, and He loves you with a love that is deep, eternal, and boundless. If you've never asked him into your life, you can take care of that today. John 3:16 says: "For God so loved the world that he gave his one and only Son, that whoever believes in him shall not perish but have eternal life" (NIV). Below is a prayer you can use to change your life forever:

"Lord Jesus, I turn to You in my time of need. I believe that You are the Son of God and that You died on the cross to pay the price for my sins. Lord, I receive You as my Savior, and I want You to be my Lord. Wash me clean with Your blood, and fill me with Your Holy Spirit. Help me to follow You the rest of my life. Amen."

If you've prayed this prayer, will you let me know? You can contact me through my website: www.nancymehl.com. Please find a good local church where you can become part of a family that will help you on your journey. May God bless you abundantly.
Nancy

ACKNOWLEDGMENTS

My thanks, as always, to Raela Schoenherr, who opened the door for me to Bethany House. Although she is no longer my editor, her voice will always be in my head.

Thank you so much to Jessica Sharpe, my new Bethany House editor. Being assigned a new senior editor could be traumatic, but the transition has been so easy, and her wisdom has helped to make my books better. I appreciate you so much!

My continued thanks to Susan Downs who gave me my very first major contract. Here we are, many years later, still working together. You have always been there for me when I needed you. It's definitely a God thing. Thank you for being the person God chose to guide me along my writing path. I love you more than I can say.

Read on
for a sneak peek at

COLD
VENGEANCE

**the thrilling conclusion to
the Ryland & St. Clair series.**

Available Summer 2024.

CHAPTER ONE

Waiting for her to return had pushed his desire for her death to its breaking point. He could have killed her before now, but he had planned her demise to the finest detail and had no intention of altering things in any way. It was perfection. It was vengeance.

River Ryland's time was almost up. And he could hardly wait.

****

It felt good to be back, but Tony St. Clair could tell something was on River's mind. She was distracted and distant. Although she was trying her best to act normally, he knew her too well to accept her behavior at face value. He'd asked her several times if she was all right, but each time she denied there was anything wrong.

It was true that someone was threatening them. A man who claimed he'd worked with the Salt River Strangler, a vicious serial killer now sitting in prison, awaiting execution. But despite his threats, he hadn't actually confronted them directly.

Tony had suspected that beyond trying to frighten them, he didn't have the courage to take it to the next level, but he'd changed his mind after finding out that their office had been bugged. Still, why hadn't the man made his move? Was it because of the steps they'd taken to protect themselves? Tony's apartment and River's mother's house both had top-notch alarm systems. They'd installed cameras in their office, a camera in the hall outside, and the police had been alerted and were watching out for them, making their presence known. Being friends with the St. Louis chief of police had come in handy.

And, of course, he and River were armed, but that wouldn't necessarily keep them safe from a long-range assassin's bullet. However, since he and River had worked for the FBI's prestigious Behavioral Analysis Unit, they were certain the Salt River Strangler's protégé would never resort to anything so impersonal. He wanted to personally finish what his master had started.

River was the only woman to survive the Strangler and his partner—and that couldn't be allowed to stand. The Strangler had murdered several women and then tossed their bodies into old trunks and thrown them into the Salt River in Arizona. The Strangler had kept River alive when he put her in the trunk, wanting her to drown. Tony had no reason to believe the protégé had changed his mind. He not only intended to kill her—he wanted her to die in terror.

Tony would never allow that to happen. Maybe he hadn't been able to stop the last attempt, but this time he would die before he allowed her to be attacked again. He was still recovering from the four bullets he'd taken trying to save her the last time, but regardless of his injuries, he'd vowed that no one would ever hurt River again.

"Why are you staring at me?" River asked, jarring him out of his thoughts. He hadn't realized he was gazing at her. He felt his face grow warm.

"Sorry. Thinking about something, and just happened to be looking your way. It's nothing creepy, I promise."

Even though River had been quiet and clearly tense since

they'd returned from visiting his family in Iowa, she laughed lightly. "I didn't say it was creepy, although I have to admit it made me a little nervous. I was beginning to wonder if I'd forgotten my makeup or something."

"No, but you don't wear that much anyway."

It was true. A little blush and mascara were all she used—and all she needed. River had a natural beauty that some women would kill for. Creamy complexion, eyes inherited from her Vietnamese mother, and the kind of full lips some women got injections to achieve. Of course, she didn't believe she was beautiful, which made her even more appealing.

"Not really the point," she said.

Tony took a deep breath before saying, "River, I know something's wrong. Why won't you talk to me about it? I thought we could discuss anything. I'm starting to worry."

She blushed and looked away, a sure sign she was hiding something. He knew it, and so did she. Their expertise in reading body language meant that it was almost impossible to hide their feelings from each other.

"I guess waiting for our stalker to strike is making me antsy."

Although it was the right thing to say, and it was exactly what he'd been wondering, for some reason her response struck a wrong chord in his gut.

"Surely you're not thinking about what my sister said." When they were in Iowa, Tony's sister, Aimee, had accused River of putting Tony in danger because of the threats she'd received from the Strangler's accomplice. At one point, Aimee had even suggested that River should leave to protect him. But in the end, everyone had agreed, even Aimee, that they were both safer together. That splitting up could make them easier targets. River had concurred—or at least said she did.

"No," she said, shaking her head. "I told you I thought we should stay together. Why would you even bring that up?"

Even though her body seemed to match her words, an alarm went off in Tony's spirit that matched the warning in his gut.

"Listen." He got up from his chair and walked over to her desk. "Promise me you won't even think about leaving me. It's the wrong decision, River. You might think you're protecting me, but you're not. You'd make both of us easy targets. Our friend would be encouraged if he thought he'd only have to take on one of us. Confronting two of us is a lot more intimidating. Your scheme to sacrifice yourself for me could kill us both."

Her eyes widened at his declaration, and he felt sick inside. It confirmed his worst fear. She really had been thinking about taking off.

"Aimee made a good case. . . ." she said, her voice faltering.

"No, she didn't." He spoke more harshly than he meant to. He breathed in and out slowly, trying to control the rapid beating of his heart. "Aimee is my sister, and she loves me, but she doesn't have the training we do. She spoke out of concern for me—not from any kind of knowledge or experience. Please tell me you understand that." He pulled a chair up to her desk and sat down. "We've got to trust the Lord . . . and each other, River. If you leave . . ." His voice broke, and he was horrified to feel tears fill his eyes. What would she think? If she knew how he really felt, would that worry her? Make her rethink their friendship?

Rather than looking repulsed, she reached out for his hand. After a brief hesitation, he put his fingers in hers.

"If I ever did anything that put you in danger again, I couldn't live with myself," she said quietly.

"But if you left and something happened to you, I couldn't live with *that*."

River sighed deeply. "You have a way of making things more complicated than they should be. But in the end, you always seem to be right. Maybe we really are safer together."

He nodded and withdrew his hand. Then he went back to his

desk, trying desperately to contain his emotions. With his head turned, he quickly wiped his eyes with his fingers and then sat down.

He was trying to find some way of explaining his reaction when the door to their office opened, and a young man stepped inside. He was short but athletic-looking with longish blond hair and wide blue eyes. He wore jeans and a Tommy Hilfiger quilted jacket. He seemed nervous and looked at each of them as if unsure which of them he should address.

"Can we help you?" Tony asked, hoping to ease his discomfort.

"Yeah . . . I mean, I hope so," he said. "I . . . I need help finding someone." He blinked several times. "I'm not sure, but I'm afraid she's been kidnapped . . . or murdered."

ABOUT THE AUTHOR

Nancy Mehl is the bestselling author of over fifty books. She's won the Daphne du Maurier Award, as well as an ACFW Mystery Book of the Year Award and a Carol Award. She was also a finalist for the prestigious Christy Award. Her short story, "Chasing Shadows," was in the *USA Today* bestselling Summer of Suspense anthology. Learn more about her at NancyMehl.com and on her blog, the Suspense Sisters: SuspenseSisters.blogspot.com.

Sign Up for
Nancy's Newsletter

Keep up to date with Nancy's latest news
on book releases and events by signing
up for her email list at the link below.

NancyMehl.com

More from Nancy Mehl

Former FBI profiler River Ryland suffers from PTSD from a serial killer case gone wrong and has opened a private investigation firm with Tony, her former colleague. Their first job is a cold case, but when they race to stop the killer before he strikes again, an even more dangerous threat emerges, stirring up the past and plotting to end River's future.

Cold Pursuit
RYLAND & ST. CLAIR #1

Now free of her troubled upbringing, Alex Donovan is able to live out her life-long dream of working for the FBI's Behavioral Analysis Unit. But soon she is forced to confront the past that has haunted her for so long in her first cases as an agent. When serial killers continue to strike, Alex must decide how far she'll go—and what she's willing to risk—to put a stop to the murders before time runs out.

THE QUANTICO FILES: *Night Fall, Dead Fall, Free Fall*